The Living Legend

The Living Legend

By Dan Hendrickson

978-1-7345187-9-5 (Amazon Paperback)
979-8-9854425-0-2 (Amazon Hardcover)
979-8-9854425-1-9 (Ingram Spark Paperback)
979-8-9854425-2-6 (Ingram Spark Hardcover)

Interior design by Booknook.biz

Dedication

This one goes to my good friend Mr. Perry Priester. Perry, I know that first and foremost you are a dedicated minister of the Lord Jesus Christ. But your lifetime service in the United States military and then law enforcement has been an inspiration to me. There are a lot of similarities between you and my character Tommy Williams. Thanks for helping me with this story. I want you to know that I listened to all those stories when you told me about life in the military while we were on patrol in the Safety Van. You are the best!

Acknowledgments

I want to first and foremost thank God Almighty for the joy, peace, and inspiration to write this book. Then I want to thank my wonderful wife Cheryl for all the help she provided in proofreading, editing, and plot suggestions. Next to Teresa Jackson for her beautiful job in her editing. Tom Hyman in his editing, and story counsel, and writer coaching. Hitch and the great team at BOOKNOOK.biz for getting the manuscript into book form and ready to publish. You are all a huge part of this book!

Table of Contents

Chapter 1

The Legend Begins

Saudi Arabia, 1891

Tumaini Aalee, son of Chief Aalee the Noble, ruler of a large Kenyan fishing village on the coast of the Indian Ocean, peers over a crest of rocks at the outlet of a canyon that lies between the ports of Jiddah and Mecca in Saudi Arabia. He and fifty others are hiding behind it, spying on the Muslim raiders that attacked his village two weeks ago and captured his sister and mother to bring to their harems. His father died in that raid trying to defend his people.

Tumaini recruited fifty of the village's young men and pursued the raiders across the ocean and into the Saudi lands. Armed with only spears, bows and arrows, blades, and wits, they plan to attack a party that's outfitted with rifles and modern revolver pistols. That is why they are waiting for nightfall—trusting in the element of surprise, and if everything goes according to Aalee's plans, striking some terror in the enemy when they attack.

Tumaini eases back down behind the rocks and looks over to his father's brother Amire and says, "I count two hundred men with rifles and half of them with the new revolvers on their hips. The sun sets, and though their prophet forbids it, the Muslim raiders are already drinking the wine they stole from my father's storage hut. They will soon ravage our women. Amire, I cannot hold myself back. If they do this, my soul will call for blood, and I will not stay."

Amire grasps Tumaini's shoulder and firmly shakes it. "Peace, my nephew. You are the son of a great chief, and I have known you all your life. He gave you his name, which means *Nobility* and *Wisdom*, and the name Tumaini means *Hope*. I have never known you not to live up to those names. You have led us to our women, and our brothers now have hope to embrace them again. Now we need your wisdom to guide us through this night. Let us show these slavers that they can no longer harvest us like wheat. For more than a thousand years they have raided our lands and stolen our young and our women for their pleasure and service. The white man did that for three centuries until their Christian God showed them their error. Now they aid us. The great queen of England sends her warships to stop the slave ships from taking our people by sea. In America, they fought a great war to stop the enslavement of our people. If we show these great nations that we will fight, they will respect our efforts and help us resist these dogs."

Amire reaches inside his shirt and pulls out the 1872 Colt .45 revolver that belonged to Tumaini's father and hands it to him. "You know this weapon well, my nephew. Since you were ten summers old, you and your father have trained with it. No one in any village has seen a man, white or black, shoot this type of gun better than you. At our camp down below I have the holster, belt, and extra ammo. Tonight, you will free your mother and sisters, and kill the men who took them and your father's life."

As he fights back the tears of rage, Tumaini bows his head and squeezes his eyes shut. Lying against the rocks with Amire, he takes the pistol and clutches it against his chest with both hands. The feel of cold, black steel against his chest calms his racing heart. He opens his eyes and turns toward Amire. "Tonight, we take back our women and teach these dogs that men have no right to own other human beings. We will no longer be harvested like wheat. I swear!"

Six hours later, half the camp of Muslim raiders is passed out from drinking wine and ale and raping the women. Four two-man teams were unfortunate enough to be on lookout duty to guard the perimeter of the camp. But no one will hear a call to arms. Tumaini and his men snuck in earlier and quietly killed all eight men and relieved them of their weapons. All of them were armed with the same Colt .45 that Tumaini now carries.

Tumaini directs the men to fan out in five groups of ten men each and surround the camp. They all crawl in on their bellies with weapons in hand. He has handed out the eight confiscated revolvers to those in the group who had trained with him and his father.

As they make it to the outskirts of the camp, they quietly dispatch those they encounter with blade, arrow, or spear. They are all skilled night hunters, and sneaking up on an animal at night is much harder than sneaking up on a drunken man. They are halfway to the center of the village where the captives are being held when Tumaini lets out an ear-piercing scream and stands with his warriors.

What the raiders see from the campfire's dancing flames sends chills of fear down their spines. Tumaini and his men are dressed like traditional deep-bush African warriors. Tiger, leopard, and panther skin skirts, headdresses, and painted faces, their ebony skin accentuated by the whites of their eyes and teeth as they snarl and attack. The men with the revolvers are cool and methodical in their use of their weapons. Each man also carries a spear that he can fight with if his party is overwhelmed and he is unable to reload.

Surprise engulfs the Muslim raiders, and despite their superior numbers, Tumaini's men rapidly overwhelm them. When three-fourths of the raiders are dead or too wounded to fight, the leader of the group surrenders and begs for mercy. For a moment Tumaini stands poised, controlling the urge to stab the man through the heart with the spear he is carrying in his hand. Wisdom prevails, and he looks down on the slobbering raider. "Take what men you have left and leave us. I will give you no provisions or arms. Whoever of you makes it back to your masters, tell them what you have seen tonight. I am Tumaini Aalee, chief of my village. Know this, slaver—until there is no breath in me, I will fight you and protect my people. When I am gone, others will rise in my stead."

He then raises his spear high in the air and fires his gun. The obsequious posturing and sniveling moans of the Muslim raiders' leader only incite the rest of Tumaini's men. They all scream, and with their weapons drive what's left of the Muslim raiding party deep into the midnight desert.

Later it will be that fearful, bone-chilling image that buries itself deep in all who have the misfortune of being on the other end of Tumaini's wrath. Soon the slavers from the Islamic lands will name him *Shaytan al-Layl,* or "The devil who comes in the night."

The image of a dark-skinned African warrior holding a revolver in one hand and a spear in the other while slaughtering slavers from Asia becomes the inspiration that earns Tumaini his name among his people—*Simulizi,* or *The Legend.*

Chapter 2

Tragedy and Conviction

August 25, 1975, Tokyo, Japan

ENSIGN TOMMY WILLIAMS SITS AT the downtown Tokyo outdoor café impatiently waiting for his father, Ambassador Rodney Williams, to join him. He can't believe that his dad is making him wait so long. Rodney flew in for his graduation from Annapolis last month and barely stayed for half a day before he had to fly back to Japan. He promised his son that when he flew to Tokyo the following month, he would have his undivided attention. Ever since his mother died of heart failure during his senior year in high school, Tommy has felt that every second with his father was a gift, and he always wanted to take full advantage of the time. Tommy is closer to his father than anyone alive. His dad is his best friend and his confidant. Tommy can talk to him about anything; he wants to be just like him in every way.

Rodney Williams is also an Annapolis grad, class of 1950. He graduated in the top one percent of his class and had a stellar career as a navy JAG lawyer. After twenty years of service, he resigned his commission as a commander and accepted a post in the State

Department. For the last three years he has been the United States ambassador to Japan. He is the 187th African American to be appointed as a United States ambassador and is passing on quite a legacy for his only child to inherit.

Tommy imagines no other path for himself than following in his father's footsteps, and he cannot wait to talk about it. He looks up and sees his father step into the ornately decorated patio of the historic downtown garden café. A dark, polished wooden box in his father's hand is the first thing that catches his eye. He stands as his father steps up and throws his arms out to embrace his son.

"For crying out loud, Dad, where have you been?" Tommy mumbles as he returns the hug.

"Sorry, Son. My meeting with the Chinese delegation went longer than I expected." He ruffles Tommy's hair and takes a seat.

Tommy smooths his hair back and looks sheepishly from side to side, then at his father. "Geez, Dad, I'm an officer now. Can you cool it on the public display of parental affection?"

"Ha! You're my son first. That little stripe on your shoulder will never outrank that."

Tommy nods at the box now sitting on the table. "Is that what I think it is?"

His dad smiles mischievously and slides it over to Tommy. "Open it up. You tell me."

Tommy undoes the latching mechanism and slowly lifts the lid. His eyes grow enormous with excitement as he scans the contents and then reads the little bronze plaque at the bottom of the blue velvet lining inside the case.

Model 1889 Colt .45 Certified Original from First 100 Manufactured.

"Holy cow, Dad! Where did you get this? I thought you and Uncle Bill were the last ones able to buy one of these at that special auction."

Rodney sits back. "Well, Son, it turns out that there are many people right here in Japan who like to collect famous weapons from around the world. I caught wind of this one being auctioned off by an associate of mine in the Japanese State Department, and I went to bid on it. When he saw me, he invited me to his office, and he offered it to me for a fair price. So, here's your graduation present. You still remember how to shoot this thing?"

Tommy chuckles as he remembers the countless hours he and his father had practiced with that model of handgun to qualify to enter tournaments and compete in marksmanship. "East Coast Youth Champion in the Revolver Championships '68 and '69. You remember, Pops?"

"Yes, I do, Son. I was there both times."

A balding, middle-aged man comes up holding a tray with a Japanese sake set and places one cup in front of the ambassador and one in front of Tommy.

Tommy eyeballs his dad with an astonished smirk. "So, you're going to drink with me, Dad!? If Mom were alive ..."

Rodney holds the white porcelain cup up to his son. "If your mother were alive, she'd toast with us," he says, holding up the other hand to stave off his son's astonishment. He then swallows against the lump building in his throat. "Here's to the son that has made his father the proudest man alive. May he exceed every expectation and become the man I've always seen him to be." Rodney lifts the cup of sake to his lips and drains the contents into his mouth.

Tommy simultaneously mimics his father's gesture, but has a little more trouble swallowing the sake. As he chokes down the Japanese whiskey, an inferno erupts in his throat and makes its way to his stomach, and he coughs and gags. His eyes flood with tears, and he fears that he is about to lose what is left of his breakfast. Through it all, he can hear his father laughing at his embarrassing efforts.

But as suddenly as the laughter starts, it stops.

Tommy senses that something is wrong. He grabs his napkin and coughs into it as he tries to focus on his father. His father has suddenly fallen backward in his chair. A small round hole is in his forehead. Tommy's military instincts kick in, and he pulls his dad's body to the side and flips the heavy metal table over to take cover. He wraps his arms around his father. Two more shots explode into the iron patio table. Tommy looks over at the box holding the Colt .45. He pulls the handgun out of the box, then reaches for the blue velvet bag next to it and spills out its contents. A handful of bullets clatter onto the floor. He slaps open the cylinder, inserts a bullet into an empty chamber, and slams the cylinder back in place. The 23g Nosler bullet has 360 grains of gunpowder. It's the most powerful round made for that handgun, with a range up to twelve thousand feet.

While still crouching behind the table, he spots a tall building about three blocks away. He maneuvers himself to his knees and places his father in a supine position on the patio floor and peers over the top of the table. As his eyes search the levels of the building, he catches a brief movement in the fifth window from the left. The lack of sun glare at that spot shows that the window is open. He brings the Colt up to the ready position then jumps up, aims, and fires at the window, then dives to the floor again behind the table as one more sniper shot rings out and strikes it.

He looks over at his father's corpse and now notices that a good quarter of his rear skull is blown off, a ghastly sight that will haunt him for the rest of his days. He grabs his father's body and cradles it as he stares off toward where the shot came from. He whispers under his breath, "*I don't know who you are or why you did this, but I am coming for you.*"

The Chameleon is shocked by the obscenest of luck that his quarry's son just had in almost hitting him with a handgun at this distance. It was a one-in-a-million shot that missed his head by less than a foot. He has been at this game long enough to know when to call it quits, so he immediately disassembles his Russian sniper rifle. His superiors do not always tell him why they want targets eliminated, but this time they said that the target had to be dead before he could negotiate an agreement with the Chinese. He always prided himself on taking his shot at the perfect time. When the son had a violent reaction to his drink, he knew it was an ideal time. He must admit that the target's son surprised him. He got control of himself faster than the Chameleon expected. He quickly evaluated the situation and took a retaliatory shot that almost hit its mark.

He has a warrior's instinct, the Chameleon deduces as he peers through his detached sniper scope. The familiar sound of police sirens rushing to the scene catches his ear. He only has a small window of time to clean up his operation and disappear. He begins again to disassemble his rifle and put it away but then takes his scope and focuses one last time on the scene. The son is standing now, helping the emergency medical people with the corpse of his father. Perhaps our paths will cross, Tommy Williams, the Chameleon muses.

One Week Later, Tokyo International Airport

Tommy's eyes dart back and forth nervously as he wrings his sweaty hands together while sitting in the airport terminal, waiting for his flight to Moscow to board. Gazing down at his coach class tickets, he thinks it is serendipitous his father's status as an ambassador for the

United States of America afforded him a passport that allowed him to travel behind the Iron Curtain and right into the heart of that Empire. Thinking things through and counting the cost is something both his parents drilled into him from an early age. His time at Annapolis only strengthened that quality.

But he just saw his dad assassinated a week ago. Since then, he's been in a constant state of rage and passion for revenge. Besides catching a cab and checking into the historic Metropol hotel of Moscow his dad used when visiting that country, he really did not know what he was going to do. All he knew was that the guy from the state department at the embassy told him that the CIA believed the assassin was a Russian known only by the code name *Chameleon*. So, when he got there, he would contact some associates of his father at the embassy and see what he could learn. He had no other plan or strategy but to find the man who killed his dad and make him pay with his life. He realizes he can't take a weapon with him into that country, so he figures he'll just find one when he gets there. Every city in the world has some sort of black market, and he will just have to find Moscow's. He has plenty of money with him because the embassy let him withdraw all of his dad's funds from the local bank he used in Tokyo.

The brown-eyed, short-haired Japanese girl at the terminal desk for his flight calls out for the boarding to begin. Tommy stands and reaches for his carry-on, when two sets of hands grab his shoulders and sit him back down on the bench he just rose from. A large, middle-aged African American man wearing sunglasses and a blue suede business suit, and a bigger white man in navy blue slacks and a white polo shirt keep their hands on him and turn to sit on either side of him on the bench. The man in the suit leans forward and says to the other, "If he tries to run, subdue and cuff him, sergeant."

The man tightens his grip on Tommy's shoulder and replies with teeth clenched and just barely audible enough for the three of them to hear, "Yes sir, General Myres."

General Myres takes off his sunglasses with his free hand, leans back against the wall behind the bench and shakes his head. "What the hell do you think you're doing, Ensign?"

Tommy recognizes the man as the commanding officer of the military detachment for his father's embassy. He sucks air through his teeth. "Just heading out to finish the rest of my stellar graduation leave before I report back to naval command stateside, sir," Tommy replies, not even caring about the arrogance he just showed while addressing a general.

The general's expression is blank, but when Tommy looks at the sergeant, he sees the beginning of a sly smile. He then feels the general push his shoulder back, making him turn in his direction. He sticks his index finger right in Tommy's face. "Look, Williams, we're all torn up about your father. Rodney Williams was the best ambassador I ever served with and a damned good friend. The last thing he would ever want was for his son, who meant more than life to him, to throw his life away on some damned fool vengeance quest that will just get him killed or stuck in some Russian prison for the rest of his life. Hell, kid, you don't even know if that assassin is in Russia, let alone Moscow."

Tommy stares straight ahead at the passengers boarding the flight he's supposed to be on. He briefly considers making a dash for the gate, then looks at the burly sergeant next to him with his meaty big hand holding his shoulder and decides it's a futile notion. He leans back and squeezes his eyes shut. A tear rolls down the right side of his face. "What do you expect, sir? I saw my dad get a piece of his head blown off right as he was toasting my graduation. He's the only family I had left, and now he's gone, and no one knows why."

General Myres releases his grip on Tommy's shoulder and reaches around and gently squeezes the back of Tommy's neck. "Son, no one is asking you to like this, but I can't let you get on that plane. What if by some stroke of crazy luck, you tracked this Russian assassin down, then what?"

"Then I'd kill him the same way he killed my dad. Only I wouldn't do it from three blocks away because I'd want to see that bastard's eyes as the life left them."

"No, you would not, Ensign," Myres replies. "All you'd do is get yourself killed, just like your dad." Myres stands up and holds out his hands, pleading with him.

"Bullshit, sir. I almost got him once, and I won't miss a second time."

Myres then looks over at the sergeant and raises an eyebrow. "You have any input, Sarge?"

The sergeant, who has been mostly quiet till now, turns and looks Tommy straight in the eye. "Ensign, my name is Sergeant Robert Mullins. I'm a Marine Corps Force Recon Specialist anti-terrorist /combat insurgent commander. I'm rated expert in hand-to-hand combat, small weapons fire, sniper, and demolitions. That guy that killed your dad is most likely one of the top assassins in the world and probably has a military resume three times longer than mine. That was one hell of a shot you took last week. I will not lie. I'm impressed by how you handled yourself, but that just means you're good raw material. But if you go up against this Russian, he'll see you a mile off. Before you even know he's around, he'll kill you. You're just not ready for a guy like him, Ensign, and that's a fact."

Tommy sits there for a moment and considers his words. He looks at the general. "So what am I supposed to do, sir? Just forget it happened, go back to the States and go to law school and be a JAG, like my dad?"

Myres smiles and shakes his head. "Well, that would be about the smartest thing you could do, Ensign, but we both know that's probably not going to happen. But I will tell you this. You are going home. The flight I booked you on leaves in thirty minutes, and we already had your luggage transferred over to it before Sergeant Mullins and I met up with you."

He reaches inside his breast pocket and pulls out an airplane ticket to BWI in Baltimore, Maryland, and hands it to Tommy. "You are to report to Annapolis, where you will be temporarily housed until you get your father's affairs in order and arrange for the memorial service. Rodney's remains will fly back with you, along with Sergeant Mullins, who will act as your escort and honor guard commander for the ambassador's remains." General Myres gets up, sighs, and says, "I'm sorry, Tommy, but I could not live with myself if I let my friend's son throw away his life like you were just about to do. The Department of the Navy is going to keep a close eye on you for a while. So, don't get any funny ideas about going after that assassin once you think no one is looking, because we *will* be."

The general turns and walks down the hall to the exit.

Twelve Hours later, Overseas Trans-Pacific flight from Tokyo to Baltimore, Maryland

Tommy and Sergeant Mullins are seated next to each other on the transcontinental 747 plane and, to this point, have hardly said a word. The lights are all dimmed and most of the passengers are sleeping, but Tommy could not close his eyes once. He leans forward and looks at the sergeant. "How do I get special forces training, like you did?"

Without turning or opening his eyes, Mullins replies, "It's different for officers. Apply for and pass a series of pre-opt training and evaluations, after you get a ranking officer to recommend you for your branch."

"You're talking about the SEALs, right."

"For you, Ensign, yes. Not the most popular group in the navy. They're hard to get into and even harder to gain rank in, especially for an officer. Nobody has publicly glorified them yet, like DELTA FORCE, or The Green Beret. But SEALS are as good as any elite special force unit, and their training program is one of the toughest in the world."

"Marines are part of the Department of the Navy, Sergeant. Did you go through that training?"

"Not quite, but I've eaten the same dirt with those guys on several ops, and they pull their weight and get the job done."

"So, I don't have an assignment yet. What do I do about getting a ranking officer to recommend me?"

"I read your record, Ensign. You are quite the enigma. Graduating second in your class, overall GPA 3.96. Three-time academy boxing champion, track and field half-mile record holder with a time of one minute, fifty-two seconds. Now you're heading back there for a while. That means you'd be under the Annapolis command structure. Your old track coach, Lt. Commander Muggins, was an active SEAL until he got injured in 'Nam. I know him; he'll give you that recommend."

Tommy reclines his seat a few inches, folds his hands on his lap, and closes his eyes. "Thanks, Sergeant."

Seven hours later, BWI Airport, Baltimore Maryland

Tommy and Sergeant Mullins get off the plane and proceed toward the luggage claim area of the airport. Once their bags show up on the conveyor belt, Mullins hands Tommy some papers. "This will give you access to go in the back, over there." He points to a door in the back of the luggage claim area. "And see to your father's remains being loaded on the hearse that'll take them to the funeral home you chose. I need to make a phone call, then I'll join you, Ensign."

"Thanks, Sergeant," Tommy replies. He takes the paperwork and his luggage and heads to the door.

Mullins grabs his luggage and heads over to the nearest payphone, dials 0, and gets connected to an overseas operator. He gives her his military codes that allow him to connect to the United States Embassy in Japan, where he is immediately transferred to General Myres's personal line.

"How is our boy doing, Sergeant?"

"Better, but he's still hell bent on finding and killing the Chameleon, sir."

"Yes, him and half the governments of the Western world. Were you able to give him any constructive counsel?"

"Well, yes and no. He asked me about the Navy SEAL program and how to get in." There is silence on the line for about twenty seconds and then Myres replies. "If anyone could get him ready to face the Chameleon, they can. Do you believe he'll get into that program?"

"Sir, with his record from the academy, most outfits in the navy would kill to have him. Getting in will be no problem. It's getting past you-know-who at SQT (*SEAL Qualification Training*), that's the big question."

There is another twenty-second pause.

"You're right. If Ensign Tommy Williams makes it through Fargo's little slice of hell, he deserves a shot at the Chameleon."

Chapter 3

The Path No One Wants Me to Take

April 1st, 1976, Naval Amphibious Base, Little Creek, Virginia

THE BUS COMES TO AN abrupt stop with the slow draw of the air brakes making a loud swoosh, as the navy driver opens the front side doors with his lever. A navy commander steps in and climbs the steps to the space next to the driver. Tommy is on his feet immediately, along with fourteen ensigns. They all come to attention and throw the man a smart salute.

The commander, a large muscular man with big, bushy, red eyebrows, makes eye contact with each man standing at attention. "Welcome to Little Creek, ensigns. My name is Commander Rodney Thorpe, and I am the SQT (SEAL Qualification Training) XO training officer for this base. The commanding officer, Captain Will Fargo, would like to extend his greetings to all you fine young officers and invites you to meet with him in the main courtyard by the flagpole in one minute."

Still at attention, Tommy and the rest of the officers roll their eyes, straining their peripheral vision to spot where the flagpole is. Tommy prides himself on being able to judge distances by eyesight and estimates that the flagpole is about four hundred yards away.

Commander Thorpe steps backward down the steps to the sidewalk and yells, "Captain Fargo is not the kind of man you want to keep waiting! The last man to that flagpole gets to go on a ten-mile running tour of the base with yours truly!"

Each man on the bus grabs his duffel bag and disembarks quickly. Tommy thinks that on his best day he can run the quarter mile in under fifty seconds, but that's in gym shorts and sneakers. Right now, he and the others are all in their khakis and marching boots and carrying duffel bags. Once they are all off the bus Commander Thorpe yells, "What are you ladies waiting for? The clock's been ticking for ten seconds already!"

At that, Tommy bursts out into a full sprint toward the courtyard with everything he has. He does not even look for the others, he just focuses on that flagpole and heads straight for it. He figures that with the duffel bag on his back he is carrying forty-five pounds of extra weight and guesses that he won't make it in the fifty seconds he has left, but that will not stop him from trying.

His vision is obscured as he is wheezing, trying desperately to fill his lungs with oxygen as he takes the last few lunging steps to the flagpole. Through his blurred and watery eyes, he can barely make out the silhouette of the man standing next to it, but he's sure it's Captain Fargo. He reaches out to touch the pole, but before he does, a loud voice booms into his ear. "Ensign, just what the hell do you think you are doing? I just had this pole cleaned and polished. The last thing I want is your greasy, sweaty hands smudging it all up again. Drop and give me fifty push-ups while you ponder the fact that you just tried to insult your new commanding officer."

Being an academy man, Tommy gets it that he is being made an example of and drops to do exactly what he was told. By the time he gets to his third push-up the next man shows up. Having seen what Tommy just went through, he just stops, comes to attention, salutes, and says, "Sir, Ensign William Boder reporting for SQT, sir."

While he's sounding off, Commander Thorpe rides up in a Cushman and looks at Captain Fargo with the snarkiest of grins. Captain Fargo returns the grin and motions him in Tommy's direction. He walks over to Tommy and squats down on his hands and knees, and while Tommy is finishing his push-ups, he sticks his face right down into Tommy's. "Ensign, do you know how long it took you to get to this flagpole?"

Tommy looks sideways as he counts his thirty-ninth push-up. "Sir, no sir. I do not, sir!"

"Well, Ensign, including the wasted ten whole seconds getting off that bus, it took you seventy-seven seconds to get from there to here. That means you disobeyed Captain Fargo's gracious request to meet him here in sixty seconds. It took you seventeen more seconds than he gave you."

Tommy does his fiftieth push-up, stands up, comes to attention, and looks at the other ensigns. The last man in the group scampers to the back, and now they are all at the flagpole, panting and wheezing, but at attention. "Sir, I was the first one here, sir," he replies, but immediately regrets it as the words leave his mouth. Now he is the focus of today's lesson and his new superiors will take full advantage of it.

Captain Fargo steps up to Commander Thorpe and Tommy. "I believe this man has a point. He was first to my flagpole today. And being an officer, he was leading his fellow officers to failure, wasn't he, Commander?"

"I think that is an accurate assessment, Captain," Commander Thorpe says with the same smug face.

Captain Fargo looks at the entire group and sighs. "We are part of a well-oiled interdependent team here at SQT. Each man must take responsibility for his fellows. You are all officers in the United States Navy, and someday you may lead men into battle. How you lead will determine whether some, or all, will live or die." He looks over at Tommy, points at him and continues, "This man led you all to failure today. Commander Thorpe!"

"Yes sir, Captain."

"I believe that it would be unfair to make the last man to the flagpole do the ten-mile running tour of our fine facility. Since Ensign Williams here took the lead, he should take the responsibility for the failure of his peers. He will accompany you on that tour while the rest of these men get settled in."

"That is an excellent idea, Captain Fargo."

"Williams, stow your duffel bag on the back of my Cushman and wait for me behind it. I'll be with you in a moment."

Tommy lets out a sigh, grabs his bag, walks over to the Cushman, puts his duffel bag in the back, and waits for the commander.

Captain Fargo then motions to some of the other officers who have joined the group. Seeing the captain's gesture, they yell at the rest of the men to fall in and follow them. Fargo then steps up to Thorpe. "What did you say his time was, Rodney?"

"Sixty-seven seconds after he got off the bus, and that's with a forty-five-pound duffel bag. The best we ever had was eighty-four seconds, sir."

Captain Fargo stares in Tommy's direction. "Lean on this one, Commander. If he cracks, so be it. If not, we got a diamond in the rough, and we're going to polish the living hell out of it."

"Yes sir, Captain."

Thorpe walks over to the Cushman, sits in the driver's seat, turns the key, and puts it in gear. "Listen up, Ensign. This vehicle will do eighteen miles an hour, but I'll keep it at seven miles an hour for our tour. While you're running, I want you to pay close attention to every detail of this base as I describe it to you. Because tomorrow morning after breakfast you will give the tour to your classmates, and you had better pray you remember everything I say to you, or we will do this tomorrow at eight miles per hour."

As the Cushman begins moving forward, Tommy begins his trek behind it. He looks to the side and notices two other trainees point and laugh at him. He recognizes the one egging others on as the second one to the flagpole. Just as he is trying to remember the guy's name, Commander Thorpe starts talking. "Now, for starters let me properly introduce you to Captain Fargo's flagpole that you almost defiled. They erected it on this base when it was commissioned back in 1945. Since that time, fifteen captains have had the honor of guarding and protecting it for the United States of America. This pole stands twenty-five feet tall, is painted alabaster white, and flies a four-by-six-foot United States flag. Our beloved Captain Fargo has the pole polished and the surrounding area policed twice a day, once before flag raising and again after we lower it. Next, we have the primary office building. It houses base command, mess hall, and our emporium. The hours for the mess hall are … "

One hour and twenty-seven minutes later Tommy and Commander Thorpe are back at the flagpole. Tommy stands at attention while he waits for the commander to release him. "Not bad, Ensign. You kept up and did not empty your stomach once. Now, you have three and a half hours all to yourself before you report for the evening meal. I suggest you get cleaned up and ready by then. Tonight will have its own plethora of exciting and innovative activities. But don't forget about your tour tomorrow. Captain Fargo will want to join us for your stellar tour guide, and your presentation to your peers. Dismissed."

During the run, Commander Thorpe pointed out the barracks that Tommy's unit is assigned to. Tommy quickly makes it to his bunk, stows his gear, and makes his way to the shower. He stands under the scalding hot water, recalling that he has managed to get himself caught in this kind of torture situation before, during his academy "indoctrination training" at Annapolis as a plebe. The way those upperclassmen made his life a living hell for his first three months was something he thought he would never have to experience again. Later, when he was one of the highest ranked senior classmen, he enjoyed extending a little of his own slice of hell to the newest plebes they assigned to him.

He reaches up and rubs a knot out of his shoulder as he finishes rinsing the soap off his body. As he is drying off, he looks over at his bunk and remembers that Commander Thorpe told him he had three and a half hours. Plenty of time for a rest. But then he remembers the tour he must give tomorrow, and he knows there is no way in hell he is getting caught with his pants down on that one. He walks over to his bunk, gets out a fresh pair of khakis and boots, gets dressed, grabs a pad of paper and a pencil, and heads out to go back over each point that Commander Thorpe made and write down as much as he can remember.

Three hours later, Tommy is back at his bunk. He puts his nine pages of notes under his bunk and falls in with the rest of his unit to head to the mess hall for supper.

Commander Thorpe raps on Captain Fargo's door. "Come in." He opens the door and walks in as his captain is behind his desk shuffling papers. "What did our boy do after you dismissed him, Commander?"

Commander Thorpe shakes his head. "He went straight to his barracks, stowed his gear, took a shower, got dressed, and headed back out and revisited every place we went on his run and wrote notes as he did. He barely finished in time to make it back to fall in with his unit for supper, sir."

Captain Fargo stands up, a folder in his outstretched hand. "He's the guy I was worried about. You remember we discussed his case last week? Graduated second in his class, second generation Annapolis man. His dad was a JAG and retired as a commander then went to work for the State Department, and he was appointed United States ambassador to Japan. This kid was a shoo-in for Ivy League graduate school and appointment to the JAG Corps."

"Yes, I remember. A sniper assassinated his dad in front of him last summer, just one month after his graduation. You think he's here on a vengeance quest, Captain?"

"Why else would somebody with his credentials and background come here? The way he was headed, he might have made captain before he was forty. With us he'll be lucky if he makes lieutenant commander by then. The first time his file came across my desk, it stunned me how fast he made it into our program. It usually takes a candidate nine months to a year to qualify for SQT, and he did it in five months—and his scores were off the charts."

Commander Thorpe hands the folder back to him. "So, what do we do, Captain?"

Captain Fargo puts the folder back down on his desk and locks eyes with Thorpe. "If he wants to be a SEAL, then we'll make him prove it. He's smart, and he proved today that he's tough. Now let's see if his motivation for being here will get him through the program.

If he's here for the wrong reasons, his endurance will run out, and no one can blame us for his failure."

"And if he makes it through the program, Captain?"

"Then he'll be one hell of a SEAL. Won't he, Commander?"

Chapter 4

Tommy's Tour

Next Day

A VIVID MEMORY OF HIS dad's bloody head lying in his lap wakes Tommy from a fitful sleep. The sweat is dripping from his forehead and onto the sheets as he sits up and places his feet on the cold concrete floor of his barracks. He rubs the sleep out of his eyes, looks at the clock in the hall, and can barely make out that it is 4:30 a.m. He thinks he has one more hour before reveille. He grabs his khakis and boots, quickly dresses, reaches under his bunk, grabs his notes, and heads to the lighted hallway. There are no chairs in the hallway, so he sits on the floor and leans up against the wall and takes out his notes and studies them. All he can think about is that he will not bear the brunt of another lesson for the crew this day. He studies each line he wrote while visualizing the area it refers to and what Commander Thorpe said about it the previous day.

"What's the matter, Ensign? Don't you like our accommodations here at the wonderful Little Creek Plaza?"

He looks up to see Captain Fargo standing in front of him with those intense brown eyes of his boring into his soul. He jumps up and throws a smart salute, comes to attention and replies, "Sir, I love it here, sir. I was going over my notes for the tour of the base that I will give after breakfast, sir."

Captain Fargo leans in close to Tommy's face and puts his mouth by his ear and bellows, "Reveille is in two minutes, fourteen seconds. You had better be in front of your bunk, with it made and your area policed within five minutes after that! Understood, Ensign?"

"Aye, aye, sir, Captain Fargo!"

Captain Fargo turns and heads down the hall to the end where he can turn on the lights and sound the wake-up bell. Tommy grabs his stuff, heads back to his bunk, makes it, and polices his area as the bell rings and the lights come on.

Five minutes after the bell sounds, Captain Fargo and Commander Thorpe enter the barracks and start inspecting each man and his bunk area. They come to the first man, Ensign Boder. As he is at attention, they briefly look at him, his attire, and his bunk. His bed is not made to spec and his shoes are not properly polished. The next man fares a lot worse. Tommy is third in line.

Fargo walks up to Tommy, inspects every square inch of his uniform, does not say a word, and then moves on to his bunk area. Commander Thorpe just stands back and observes. Fargo pulls his entire area apart and even messes up his bed. When he is done, he steps back and looks sternly at Tommy. "Well, Williams, it looks like your area is up to spec. But maybe the rest of your peers would be interested to know that you got up before reveille and tidied up before they all woke up."

Standing stiff as a board, Tommy uses his peripheral vision to look both ways and tries to gauge his peers' reaction to what Captain

Fargo just said. He swallows nervously as he waits for the captain and commander to move on to the next man.

Fargo looks over at Commander Thorpe, nods his head, and then addresses the entire room. "Since Ensign Williams did such a fantastic job taking care of his own area in his free time, I will forego the rest of this morning's inspection and let *him* inspect the rest of your areas. If he finds anything wrong with you or your area, he will help you fix it. You all have one hour before breakfast. Carry on."

When Captain Fargo and Commander Thorpe leave the room, Ensign Boder laughs hysterically and two others join in. Tommy rolls his eyes and walks over to Boder's bunk and helps him fix what the captain had pointed out, then proceeds to the next guy. Fifty minutes later he finishes with the thirteenth guy, heads back to his bunk and quickly cleans up his area that Fargo messed up, and heads over for breakfast.

Right after Tommy leaves, Commander Thorpe and Captain Fargo walk back into the bunk area and walk around and look at each man's area. "Well, Rodney, he did it. Everything here looks perfect. I have to admit the kid's got hustle."

"Yes, but is he the kind of combat leader we want, or is he just trying to make himself look good? That's the question."

"That remains to be seen. We have our pet project for this group. Now, let's show the rest of these guys what they signed up for. The rest of Ensign Tommy Williams's platoon has experienced their easiest day of SQT."

Tommy falls in at the back and goes through the serving line for his meal. He heads to a table with seven others as they stand at attention and wait for Captain Fargo to begin the meal. When the captain steps in through the door everyone salutes, which is quickly returned. He then looks at the group and bellows, "I have not known a sorrier bunch of lazy-ass piss-ants in my life. Morning reveille and inspection was a disaster, and now I'm told you mamma's babies don't even know how to report to breakfast properly. I can't believe I am standing in a room of fully commissioned naval officers. I was just over at the enlisted men's mess, checking on Chief Mosier and his men. At least they are learning how to follow instructions. Yes, they have been here for a week. But that is because we like to have them ready for you fine gentlemen to practice your leadership skills on. It's hard to believe you guys passed the Mini-Bud Pre-SEAL evaluation process before you got here. The way you're looking now, I am not letting any of you near my enlisted men until I can trust that you won't embarrass me." He looks over at Commander Thorpe. "You and the rest of the trainers teach these boys what we expect, Commander."

"Yes sir, Captain," he says as Captain Fargo walks out of the mess hall. He looks around the room and yells, "Okay, let's begin. Have a seat."

Commander Thorpe walks over to the table next to Tommy's, steps right up to Ensign Boder, and sticks his face two inches from the man's ear as he is about to put a piece of sausage in his mouth with a spoon. "Ensign Boder, why are you using the wrong tool for that maneuver? An officer will always use his fork to pick up and place a piece of meat in his mouth. That is not a bowl of oatmeal in front of you, that is a plate filled with two scrambled eggs, three pieces of sausage, hash browns, and a piece of buttered toast cut diagonally at the corners. Now get down on the floor and give me fifty push-ups, and when you're done, resume eating your breakfast properly."

Boder stands up and pushes his chair backward with the backs of his thighs. "Aye, aye, sir," he replies, then drops and does his push-ups.

Without missing a beat, Thorpe makes his way over to another ensign, asks him why he is slouching at the table, and makes him stand up in front of the table and do one hundred jumping jacks. Commander Thorpe continues this until every ensign except for

Tommy is doing or finishing up a calisthenic. Tommy's eyes are dancing back and forth to different members of his platoon, so nervous about what Commander Thorpe will find wrong with his handling of breakfast that he has not even taken his first bite yet. Commander Thorpe looks over at Tommy and notices that he is sitting straight up with his hands on his knees and eyes forward. He looks around the room, whistles, and yells, "Everyone halt!" He then looks at Tommy. "Ensign Williams, what are you doing?"

Beads of sweat roll down the sides of his cheeks and he swallows against an enormous lump blocking his throat. "Waiting for you to tell me what to do, sir."

Commander Thorpe smiles. "Finally, one of you doing something right. Ensign Williams, you may begin eating."

"Aye, aye, sir." Tommy picks up his knife and fork and smartly cuts off a third of the sausage in front of him, jabs it with his fork and places it in his mouth, sets his utensils down, then chews and swallows it. He's not stupid. Commander Thorpe did not do him any favors by complimenting him in front of his peers. Now they are all going to hate him for making them look bad. But since he has no other course of action open to him at the moment, he continues to finish his meal in the strict fashion they had taught him as a plebe at Annapolis.

Eventually the rest of the platoon finishes the disciplinary exercises. They stand at attention in front of their meals and wait for further instructions from Commander Thorpe. The commander makes his way to each man as they finish and orders them to sit and chow down. Most follow Tommy's example but a couple end up irritating Commander Thorpe and have to go through another round of disciplinary action.

One hour later, Tommy is by the flagpole with Commander Thorpe and Captain Fargo, waiting for the rest of the platoon to fall in for his tour. Tommy is frantically going over his notes as the men are lining up. Captain Fargo looks over at Tommy. "Ensign, you had better not think that I will let you conduct this tour with notes. Commander Thorpe did your tour by memory yesterday and so will you."

"Aye, aye, sir." Tommy folds up his notes and puts them in his pocket. When everyone is at the flagpole, Commander Thorpe addresses the entire group. "Listen up, men. Ensign Williams will take us on a tour of our beloved base. Yesterday, I did this tour at a seven-miles-per-hour pace. Since you all will have plenty of exercise today, Captain Fargo and I will set the pace on our Cushman at four miles per hour. You all will assume parade formation with Ensign Williams in the lead. Fall in."

"Aye, aye, sir," comes the unanimous response. Captain Fargo and Commander Thorpe take their seats in the Cushman. The commander turns the key and the group begins its march.

Tommy begins the tour by saying, "To our right is Captain Fargo's flagpole. They erected it on this base when it was commissioned back in 1945. Since that time, fifteen captains have had the honor of guarding and protecting it for The United States of America. This pole stands twenty-five feet tall, is painted alabaster white, and flies a four-by-six-foot United States flag. Next, we have the primary office building. It houses the base command, mess hall, and our emporium. The hours for the mess hall are ..."

Three hours later the group is back at the flagpole and the fourteen ensigns are standing at attention, waiting for Captain Fargo and Commander Thorpe to finish a private conversation they are having while still in the Cushman. "Rodney, are you sure he got nothing wrong? No one has ever done it perfect the first time."

"Yes, Captain, I'm sure. But remember, we've never had a SEAL candidate that ranked second in his Annapolis graduating class either."

Captain Fargo shakes his head and smirks. "Never thought I would have to use this one, but the kid leaves me no choice." Fargo and Thorpe step up to the group, and the captain bellows, "Ensign Williams!"

"Aye, aye, Captain!"

"Not a bad tour for your first time, but you missed a very important detail."

The sweat seeps out of every pore of his body as he stands at attention, trying to think what he missed. He has to force himself not to reach in his pocket and pull out his notes that his left hand is now feeling beneath the material of his khaki pants. "Sir, what did I miss, sir?"

"The decommissioned bomb shelter under the basement of the headquarters building, Ensign."

Tommy, flabbergasted, looks at Fargo and Thorpe like he has just been sucker-punched by a bully on the playground. "Sir, the commander mentioned nothing about a decommissioned bomb shelter, sir."

"Well, of course not, Ensign. Why should he? It's been decommissioned for over fifteen years, but that should not have stopped you from finding out about it when you revisited your tour yesterday and took all those notes you have in your pocket." Fargo stops for a moment and puts his hand to his chin and then continues. "Commander, I think that we need to do something with that bomb shelter." A devious grin manifests across his face. He points to Tommy. "Once a week for the next few months, I want Ensign Williams to lead a team made up of anyone that is under disciplinary action to clean up that area and make it useful for something. They can do this on any personal time the platoon gets."

"Yes sir, Captain."

Commander Thorpe looks over at Tommy. "Ensign Williams, since you like getting up so early, meet me here at four tomorrow morning, and we'll do your tour training at eight miles per hour."

Tommy ends up doing the tour three more times and finds out that he could do a ten-mile run at ten miles per hour.

Two weeks later Tommy and two others are working in the old decommissioned bomb shelter. While eleven of their peers enjoy some very rare R&R, Tommy, Ensign Boder, and Rogers are busy mucking out the half-flooded shelter under the storage section of the principal building's basement. They found an old irrigation pump, and Commander Thorpe gave them permission to hook up a garden hose to it and run it to the nearest storm water spillway in the street. When they got that all set up, and it started pumping water, Boder pipes up, "That's about all we can do now that the water is flowing. When it drains, the next crew can finish up."

"No way, Boder. If we leave that pump now it will just gum up and overheat and break down. Then Commander Thorpe will have all our asses. We're going back down to clean up all the debris in the water we can find. Once it's as clear as we can get it, I'll report to him, and then we'll wait for him to let us go."

"Who the hell do you think you are, Williams? I'm just here because of some demerits from breakfast this morning. You're here until this project is done. I don't have to take orders from you."

"The hell you don't, Boder. This is Williams's pet project, and whoever I assign to work on it with him is under his command. You got me, Ensign?" Three heads turn in unison, gazing at Commander Thorpe standing in the doorway with the veins of his neck popping out as his intense eyes bore into Boder.

Boder gulps, comes to attention, throws a salute, and says, "Yes sir, Commander Thorpe."

Thorpe ignores Boder and looks over at Tommy. "Good thinking, Williams. Once you have mucked it enough, leave the pump on. It has an automatic shutoff for when it starts sucking air. Then you and your command here can report back to the barracks. The rest of the men's

R&R will be over in three hours. I think the water will be mucked sufficiently in two. That should give you three enough time to clean up and be ready for the next drill."

All three say, "Aye, aye, sir." Thorpe makes like he is leaving but turns back and says, "Oh, and Boder."

"Yes, sir."

"From now on, you will assist Williams every time he works on this project."

Boder gasps, grits his teeth, and throws a stiff salute. "Yes sir, Commander."

Ninety minutes later Tommy excuses Boder and Rogers and goes back into the old bomb shelter to check on the pump to make sure it's not clogged. As he is wading around in the water, he is happy that at least twenty percent has already drained. He is about to leave when there is a gurgling sound from over on the left side, by the old bunks built into the wall.

When he gets closer, he sees that there is water seeping through the wall where some concrete has eroded away. The erosion in the old wall starts just below the water level and goes up about one foot. When he looks closer, he can tell that there used to be something bolted into the concrete. Since it is a bomb shelter, the walls are two feet thick but the bolt holes only go in six inches. He can see that there is a seam right where the bolts were placed. Half of the wall is two feet thick, but the other half is only about four inches thick. He sticks his finger through the hole and digs out some softened concrete above the waterline, bends down and tries to look in to see what's on the other side. It's too dark.

He goes to the room adjacent to the bomb shelter and grabs a flashlight. As he is shining the light into the hole, he sees a smaller room similar to the one he was just in with a set of metal stairs leading up. "Oh, hell no. If I report this, Captain Fargo will make me fix up everything that's wrong out there," he mumbles to himself. He finds a square piece of metal to put in front of the hole to temporarily plug it.

Later that night, after the training is over, Tommy gets permission from Commander Thorpe to check on the bomb shelter project. When he walks into the shelter, he is relieved to see that almost all the water has drained out. They have already figured out that the shelter got flooded a few years back when a water line burst in the basement. That was before Captain Fargo and Commander Thorpe showed up, so no one knew there was a bomb shelter below the basement.

He gets a mop and bucket and cleans up the rest of the water, then sets up some fans to air the place out. He looks over to the area where he had patched the hole and figured out it was once a door. He considers what he should do about it, then goes back up to the basement and grabs some tools and buckets along with a bag of concrete. He picks up a short-handled sledgehammer and knocks the patch out. When it is about half done, he discovers that the patch is only half concrete. Beneath is a heavy metal door that is partially open. This is what allowed him to see into that room earlier. He guesses that perhaps when the flood hit the shelter it somehow jarred the door partway open.

Once he knocks enough of the concrete off, he pushes against the door. It creaks open. The light from the shelter floods into the little stairwell chamber. He takes a quick look around the twelve-by-eight-foot area. When he trains his flashlight on the stairs, he sees that at the top is a hatch that opens by a wheel.

Curiosity gets the best of him and he climbs the stairs and turns the wheel. At first, it won't budge, but he braces his feet against the wall for some leverage and gets it to move a little. After working with it for a while, he gets it to turn and the pressure from the locking screw finally releases. He then presses on the hatch, but when he gets it about two or three inches up, bright white gravel starts to pour in. "Oh, no!"

He quickly wiggles the hatch closed again and tightens the wheel. He looks down on the floor at the painted gravel and realizes there is only one place on the base with gravel like that—Captain Fargo's flagpole!

Frantically he looks from side to side, trying to figure out what to do. There is no way he will tell anyone about this, because he will not be the one to mess with Fargo's precious flagpole. He walks back into the bomb shelter, closes the door, and thinks.

Then it dawns on him. Someone else already covered up this door and closed off the outdoor access to the bomb shelter, so who was he to mess with that executive decision? As the officer in charge of this project, his duty was to put everything back the way it was. He cleans up the excess concrete chunks, mixes some fresh concrete, recovers the door, places the metal slab over the fresh concrete, drills a hole into the wall in all four corners, bolts it in place, pushes shelves in front of the patch, cleans his tools and puts them away.

By the time he is finished cleaning up it is 3:45 in the morning and after a full day of SQT and disciplinary duty he is one tired man. It seems like seconds have passed since his head hit his pillow when the wake-up bell sounds at 5:00 a.m.

Chapter 5

Hell Week

Six months later

TOMMY SPITS A MOUTHFUL OF sand and seawater out as he braces his
portion of the raft on his head and stands on the beach with the rest
of his crew. No one overstated how bad Hell Week is, that is for sure.
Yesterday they were running logs up and down this beach, and the day
before they spent the entire day crawling on their stomachs through
the sand, muddy pipes, and thick brush under wire. He looks around
at the enlisted men he oversees today and feels the determination in
their stares. This is the ninth race today with seven eight-man teams.
First, each team picks up their eight-man inflatable raft and sprints
a quarter mile to the beach and paddles out to the one-mile marker
and back to the beach, then the team picks up their raft and runs two
miles to the finish. Whoever gets there first gets to rest for one race.
So far, Tommy's team has won four and come in second once.

"Okay, guys. You know the drill. We power up that dune and get
past it before anyone else. If we do that, we got this sucker." Tommy
looks over at the dune and spots Boder, who is already there with

his crew. They have been doing well with the rowing, but getting up that dune has been another story altogether. By the time he gets there, Boder is yelling at his men to get up to the top, but they just keep slipping.

Tommy figured out early on that he needed to rotate his men at different sections of the running part. The dune is about twenty feet high and steep, at roughly a forty-five-degree angle. So, he figured he needs powerful pushing and strong pulling. His two shortest guys are about five-six each, so they take the end. Up front is his six-four partner and himself, at six-two. He found that at about halfway up it helped if everyone got out from under the raft and started pulling it up from the sides. Even though he was in front, Tommy forced himself to focus on each man in his group and give them either encouragement or instruction. This is the sixth race they have run, and they are all working well together. As he and his partner make it over the top of the dune and pull the raft, he can feel the men behind pushing, but an "Oh shit!" comes from the rear. One of his pushers lost his footing and slipped.

"Hendricks, Robinson, come up here and pull," he orders the two men on the side as he lets go of his grip and slides down the dune under the middle of the raft. When he gets to the bottom, he stands up and pushes the back end up as high as he can and yells, "Everybody up top, and pull! You too, Rodrigues. We can still win this. Keep moving!" Tommy stretches himself to his limit, using every ounce of strength he has to push the raft forward while the others on top are pulling. The raft slides over the top and he yells, "Pick it up and head for the finish line! I'll catch up."

He looks over a few yards to where the closest team is and sees that they are already up to the top of the dune and getting situated to make their run for home. He scampers up the dune and takes off after his crew. With one less man carrying the raft on Tommy's crew, the other team overtakes his. Tommy rockets toward his men as fast as he can. As he assumes his position in front, there is a gasp from his men when they see the other team pull out ahead of them, but Tommy whistles, catching their attention. "Don't worry, we've got two miles to go, and they're at a full sprint right now. We'll keep on their backs and bide our time."

The first half mile is tough but the other team has slowed to a jog. One of his men yells, "Ensign Williams, do we take them now?"

"No, but tighten the gap between us and keep pushing them."

The last quarter mile is an uphill run to the finish line, and Tommy keeps his crew right on the other crew's heels. At the bottom of the hill he bellows, "*NOW!*"

They all move to the left side of the raft and power up the hill. As the two groups are neck and neck, Tommy looks over and smiles at the other team leader, Ensign Rogers. The man looks exhausted, and his crew, though determined, are losing steam. For a couple of seconds both crews stay neck and neck, but as soon as Tommy can see the crest of the hill and the officers and trainers waiting for them at the finish line, he throws his head back and yells, "*GO!*"

Tommy's crew lets out an enormous cheer and pulls out in front and sprints the last hundred yards to their fifth first place of the day.

As soon as they cross the finish line, Tommy walks over toward Rogers and his crew. "Nice run, Rogers, but you got cocky after the dune and wore your guys out. That's how I took you on the hill."

"You ain't telling me nothing I don't already know, Williams. Congratulations on your fifth win. Looks like you'll sit another one out."

Tommy and Rogers turn to see Ensign Boder's crew coming in seventh for the eighth time. Boder lets go of his hold on the raft with a huff, barks for his men to set it down, and walks off to sulk until they call the next race.

Captain Fargo glares at Boder's reaction and walks up to Commander Thorpe, who is talking to one of the noncommissioned officers about the race. "Commander, I'm concerned about Boder. Our officer attrition rate is already fifty percent. He might be next. If this rate continues, the brass might pull the plug on us. What do you think we should do?"

"Sir, I have an idea."

Fargo and Thorpe turn to see Master Chief Mosier standing behind them. "What do you have in mind, Mosier?"

"Well, Captain, Williams and his crew have won five out of the six races they took part in and Boder's crew have come in last eight times now. He's got some of my best men in his crew, but he ain't leading them right. So why don't we make Boder and Williams switch crews? That way Boder will see that it's his fault because of his command style, and Williams will be challenged to test his leadership on a crew that's demoralized."

Fargo puts his hand to his chin and mulls it over for a few seconds. "I like it. What do you think, Commander?"

"Best idea I've heard all day, Captain. Williams is showing us that he can think outside of the nine dots. This will push that to the edge, and Boder needs to see some success or we'll lose him."

Fargo smiles. "It's settled then." He turns and yells, "Boder, Williams, get over here!"

Tommy and Boder briefly glance at each other from across the finish line area and then simultaneously yell, "Aye, aye, sir!" and run over to the captain.

They come to attention and salute. Fargo looks both men in the eyes. "You know, I don't like what's going on here. Williams, you're winning too much; and Boder, you're losing too much. We'll forego your break, Williams. You and Boder will switch command to each other's crews from here on in. There are five races left. If either of you gets less than fourth place, you'll do more disciplinary duty and have more demerits on your records. Am I understood?"

"Aye, aye, sir," comes the concurrent response.

Tommy walks away feeling sucker-punched as he makes his way over to Boder's old crew. He looks sideways at Boder and can't help but notice the self-righteous smirk on the man's face. One man from his new crew steps up and says, "What gives, sir?"

"Captain Fargo spiced things up a bit, so I'm now your crew leader. Now, tell me exactly how Ensign Boder had you all lined up and what you think could have been done better." Seven flustered sailors start talking at once, so he stays them with a hand in the air. "One at a time. We've got about ten minutes before our next race. We'll set up as we talk."

By the time they're at the starting line, Tommy has heard each man out, albeit briefly, and decides not to change a thing, except for the position his predecessor had taken in the middle. He takes the same position he took with the last crew. "Now listen up, guys. I saw you with the rowing, and you're not bad at all. You have lots of power. Let's get to that beach and row those two miles faster than anyone else. When we're done with that, we'll work on the running part."

They arrive at the beach fourth, and once in the raft they make their way out to the mile marker. One of the enlisted men opted to take the middle right and everyone left that position open to him. Tommy sits next to him on the middle left and rows. The sailor immediately paces everyone as he calls out, "Stroke! Stroke!" and everyone falls into a rhythm.

By the time they reach the mile marker they have passed the three boats ahead of them and are making amazing time on their way back. When they hit the beach, Tommy looks back and spots Boder and his crew two boats behind him, and he takes a second to position the guys for the dune. He then looks over at the stroke-caller.

"When we're at that dune, I want you to call out your strokes like we're rowing, and don't stop until we're at the top."

The sailor smiles and gives an enthusiastic nod as he takes up his position.

At the dune they move up. The trepidation in each man's eyes is palpable as they stare at the dune that has been kicking their asses all day. "Look, guys, you can do this. Just listen to the stroke call and make a step."

Three boat crews make it up the dune past them, but that still means they are farther ahead than they have ever been and as they reach the top, Tommy's crew starts hooting and hollering like they all just won the Olympics. Once he gets them up the dune, they take off for their run. Now in front, he calls back to his stroke caller. "Every time we take a step, call out 'Stroke!' Slow down and speed up on my orders."

By the end of the run, Tommy's team comes in third, just behind Boder's. When his guys cross the finish line, they are jumping up and slapping high fives and acting like they won. Tommy got the kind of morale he can work with and gets the crew set up for the next race. His crew wins the next one, but Boder's crew wins the one after that. The last race is a tie between Tommy's and Boder's crews. By then, both crews are shaking hands with one another and are thanking their crew leaders for the exercise. Tommy and Boder walk up to one another and shake hands and give each other a bro hug.

"You guys are pretty proud of yourselves, aren't you?"

Both men turn around to see Captain Fargo standing behind them, boring into them with his steely eyes. "I don't like ties, gentlemen. Someone should always win, and someone else should lose. You two just broke the natural order of things. You both can think about that as you do KP duty after supper tonight."

Tommy and Boder are in too good of a mood to let the little reprimand affect them as they throw a salute and Fargo dismisses them.

Fargo walks up to Thorpe and winks. "Well, Rodney, I'll call that a win. Boder got a lesson in how to be a better leader, and Williams learned how to think outside of the nine dots while still following orders."

Chapter 6

War Games

TOMMY OPENS HIS EYES AT 4:30 a.m. and curses Captain Fargo for drilling the habit of getting up earlier than everyone else so he could handle all the extra duty he's pulled in the last sixty-nine weeks of SQT under that maniac. He only got to bed by 1:00 a.m. last night. He rubs the soreness out of his shoulder from the four-mile swim Thorpe had them do yesterday, but then he thinks it could be from the two hours of hand-to-hand combat training or the one hour of small weapons practice. The days have become just a blur.

A smile creases his face as he thinks that he is just one week away from getting out of Fargo's *Little Slice of Hell*, as it's called, and moving on to SEAL graduate training. They occupy only six bunks in the officer's section of SQT. Rogers, the last of the eight that dropped, packed his things last week and left. He looks over at Boder's bunk and still finds it hard to believe that he has made it this far, but there he is. Out of the fifty enlisted men they started with, twenty-seven remain. Commander Thorpe told him it was a low attrition rate this time, and he was glad that so many stuck it out.

A flash memory invades his mind and once again the sight of his father's head lying in his lap and bleeding all over his brand-new uniform sends a chill up his spine. He thinks about the sniper that killed him and how no one has ever given him a reason why someone would put a hit on his dad. With his jaw clenched tight and his fist taut with rage in front of his chest, he mutters, "I'm getting ready for you, pal! We'll meet someday. Someday!"

He rolls his feet over the side of his bunk and places them on the cold cement floor as he stands and stretches his tight muscles. Another spasm in his shoulder starts and he thinks, *yeah, definitely the four-mile swim across the bay,* then he reaches down and rubs his ankles. He is amazed at how toughened they've become from the hundreds of hours he's spent doing web-feet swimming and diving. In the last year he's learned to push his body and mind to places he never dreamed possible, and still looks to do more. A sense of pride overwhelms him as he reaches for his khakis that have his brand-new JG (Junior Grade) Lieutenant bars on the lapel.

They just got them a week ago. Captain Fargo played it down, telling the six officers that most navy ensigns automatically received this promotion at a set time after graduation from an academy. But in Fargo's *Little Slice of Hell,* any positive is received like a gift from God. And no matter how hard Fargo and Thorpe tried, they couldn't keep Tommy and the others from being elated at the promotion.

He gets dressed, polices his area, and walks out into the main hall, ready to take his morning stroll around grounds before the wake-up bell sounds.

Captain Fargo and Commander Thorpe sit in the CO's office talking about the last exercise before they pass their current class on. "You know, Captain, it just makes me a little queasy doing this to a group. First, we break them down to nothing and then build them up to super-soldier status, and now we're just going to tear them down again. You ever wonder if this is the right way to send them out of here?"

"Nobody ever said they have to lose War Games, Rodney. They just need to be good enough to beat us, that's all. When we pass them on out of here, they are in the real world, and they'll go up against seasoned soldiers just like you and me. We've been there, and we know how everything can go sideways in a split second. This is an exercise, testing their ability to think under stress and on their feet. We both know it takes combat to bring that out in someone, but War Games come close, and we just might save some of these guys' lives by kicking their asses now."

"So, what's the scenario this year?"

"Defend against a terror attack on a US embassy. Their mission is to protect the ambassador and get him to safety. Their secondary objectives are to defeat the terrorist and capture the leader; or defeat the terrorist and eliminate the leader."

"What kind of weapon will we use for training?"

"I ordered those new paintball training rifles for this one. I know they're no good for accuracy at anything long range. But this is primarily an indoor exercise. I want them to know every shot that hits them."

"Going to be messy. What building are we going to use?"

"This one. It's perfect—three floors, four access points, and—"

"And no good, safe egress from the property except by air. So, they'll have to go for the airlift scenario, and that means getting to the roof and hunkering down until help comes. How long do they have to stay up there till they've won?"

"If they can successfully pull off a maneuver that would adequately cover a helicopter landing up there, I'll give them one hour."

"Who you going to put in command, Captain?"

Fargo gets a mischievous grin on his face. "Lieutenant Tommy Williams!"

Thorpe nods, as if to say *I get it,* then grins. "I thought so. And when they lose, he'll oversee the clean-up project. Just so you know, sir, I like that kid. I'll not let my guys make too big of a mess when we storm this place and take you hostage."

Captain Fargo stares at him for a second then throws back his head, lets out a thunderous laugh, and pats Commander Thorpe on the back. "Oh, no, Rodney. I will not be the ambassador this time. You will. I'll be the terrorist."

Commander Thorpe shakes his head and chuckles. "So, sir, what will you do if Williams figures out how to beat you?"

Captain Fargo steps up to Commander Thorpe and places a hand on his shoulder. "If that kid does that, then the command staff of this base will be the ones cleaning up after the exercise; and I will go find my best bottle of Irish whiskey, and you and I will drink the whole damn thing in his honor."

An hour later breakfast in the mess hall is routine. With only one week left of SQT, no one is breaking any protocols. The officers' dining hall seems a little empty now that there are only six in the trainees' platoon, plus Captain Fargo, Commander Thorpe, and two other training officers. Tommy sits at his place with his utensils placed horizontally on his plate at the top and his hands folded in his lap, waiting for either Captain Fargo or Commander Thorpe to go over the day's routine and dismiss the group.

Captain Fargo stands up from his meal, and the whole room turns in his direction. "Listen up, gentlemen. You are at the last stage of your SQT here at our wonderful Little Creek Base paradise." A slight chuckle reverberates through the room. "This last exercise will allow you officers to put into practice what we have been trying to knock into your thick skulls for the last seventy weeks." He points his hand to the rear of the room at a window that shows the enlisted men's mess hall. "Across the yard are twenty-seven of the finest SEAL candidates I have had the privilege to work with. Some of you haven't been too horrible either." Another round of chuckles. "Now, you're all about ready to head out to SEAL graduate training and then to your first assignments. In those assignments you will lead men like them to defend and protect the United States of America. How you lead those men will determine if they live or die. I never pass an officer to graduate level training unless I am sure that he has the capability and motivation to accomplish his mission and keep his men alive. This last exercise will be your ultimate test. Now, Commander Thorpe will explain the exercise."

Commander Thorpe stands up and nods to Captain Fargo. Fargo leaves the room to give a similar speech to the enlisted men across the yard. "Okay, guys, here's the drill. We will be involved in War Games for the next twenty-four hours. The scenario is that you six officers and the twenty-seven enlisted men will be guarding the United States Embassy in Cairo, Egypt." He pulls down a map of Cairo from a roller hanging on the wall behind him and uses his finger to point out the embassy.

"As you can see, the embassy sits two blocks in from the Nile River and about a half mile from El Tahrir Square, where there is a bridge that crosses the river. NAMRU-3 Air Base is about twenty miles east on the Mediterranean shore, and the British Embassy sits about four miles northeast. In the scenario, they will take the bridge out and terrorists and dissident students will block all roads. Their objective is to infiltrate and capture or kill the US ambassador and as many of you as they can. Your primary objective will be to secure the ambassador, send out a distress call to our air base for helicopter extraction, and set up a defense on the roof to guard the ambassador and allow the helicopter to land safely. The dissidents and terrorists will have no missiles or rocket launchers, only semiautomatic and fully automatic firearms. We will use the new air gun paintball training rifles for this exercise. A little messy, but there will be no question about who has been shot and who hasn't. They will outnumber you, five men to your one; and once you're on the roof, you will have to defend with the ambassador unharmed for sixty minutes."

Tommy raises his hand, and Thorpe acknowledges him. "Sir, are there any other objectives, and what building are we using for the exercise?"

"I'm glad you asked that, Williams, because Captain Fargo chose you to lead your peers here in this exercise."

Tommy gulps and the other five look at him, relieved that they are not in the hot seat.

"The other objective is to capture or kill the terrorist leader, but that has a minimal chance of success, at best. And the building will be this one we are in now."

Tommy, still shocked by the revelation that he will be in command for the exercise asks, "Why a minimal chance, sir?"

"Because Captain Fargo will be the terrorist leader, and he's arguably the best SEAL team commander we have, and he has seen and been in command of more live action than any SEAL officer alive."

Tommy sits back and takes a big gulp of air.

Commander Thorpe continues. "Now, the rest of you officers will have a five-man team under you. Williams will keep two of the enlisted men as his personal aides. That is as much help as I can give you. Williams and you can figure out the rest this morning. The enlisted men will be here in a few moments. Oh, and I left out the best part. I am the ambassador that you all will be protecting." He looks over at Tommy and smartly says, "Don't get any ideas, Williams. I can give you no advice throughout this entire operation, but I'll be watching every move you and your men make."

One hour later Tommy and the other five officers are standing in front of the enlisted men, talking over the war game scenario. Fortunately for everyone, Tommy has every square inch of the base's HQ building memorized. He has a hand-drawn diagram of the building hanging up on the wall, and he is using his finger to point out the four access points to the building that should be covered. "With four teams of six, one would think the obvious strategy would be to assign a group to each access and try to hold out. That might allow me and my aides to get the ambassador to the roof."

Boder steps up and points his finger at the front of the drawing. "But what about the windows on the second floor? They do have bars, but they could still be breached."

"Exactly, Boder. That's why we will only appear as if we are using that strategy. The terrorists number one hundred twenty-five men, and we have thirty-three, so if we try to defend four exits, they'll just hang back and pick us off until we are so weak that we can't repel a direct assault."

One of the enlisted men raises his hand. "What are we going to do then, sir?"

"You guys remember the ensconced defense scenario? Hide in a place that has narrow access and only provides tangible cover on your end. Lure the enemy down the tunnel of death and take them out."

Boder butts in. "Yeah, but that won't hold Fargo off long enough. All he has to do is keep us pinned down until our time runs out, and then we lose. Remember, we need to have the ambassador on the roof, call in that distress call, and wait another hour. We need time ... wait a minute, the ensconced defense is also a ruse?"

Tommy smiles and looks over at Commander Thorpe, who is eyeballing him back very quizzically. He winks and then looks back at Boder. "One of many, my friend. We will come up with many ploys to wear his numbers down. Then we will trap him. Secondary objectives, remember? But don't ask me the endgame just yet." He nods his chin over in Commander Thorpe's direction and continues. "I think it best that we keep the ambassador in the dark until I'm ready to play that card."

Tommy names Boder his XO and has him and his men collect the training rifles and ammo as he and the others set up for the coming game. The principal building of Little Creek Base is not set up exactly like a US embassy, but everybody is acting like it is. So, even though there are windows on the first floor of the base, they are off limits to the terrorists, because the embassy would not have them. Tommy is allowed to have one team stationed on the roof to alert the others when Fargo's attack begins. They allot each team a two-way radio that is on one of the base tach systems. The terrorists are on the other tach. Neither side has the ability to listen to the other side.

They divide the building's floors into four sections of rooms with hallways cutting each section off. There are no entrances to the rooms on the first floor except by the main hallway that runs from the front to the rear entrance. The other hallway goes from one side entrance to the other. The second and third floors do have doorways that enter rooms from those side hallways, except for Captain Fargo's office, which is at the end of a side hallway that is only half as long as all the others. The basement is just one enormous room that has a pool on one side and an exercise section on the other. On the pool side is the door that leads to the storage section and then to the decommissioned bomb shelter. There is only one set of stairways that connect the three floors and the basement, and they are at the center of the building, where all four halls converge.

Tommy stands on the stairway on the main floor and addresses the five officers and twenty-seven enlisted SEAL trainees. "Okay, guys. It's almost go time. In five minutes, the clock strikes noon, and that's when we act like we are on normal security for the embassy.

Fargo and his terrorists will breach our outside gate and perimeter first. That is when you guys on the roof can give us the warning. Commander Thorpe told me that I cannot lay out for you any detailed battle plan based on the limitations of the exercise and foreknowledge of the coming attack. What I have done is worked up a pre-planned evacuation protocol for the ambassador with two scenarios—roof airlift, and ground vehicle escape. When the attack hits, we must look like we are evaluating both scenarios. The terrorists must prove they can breach our interior and have all ground exits blocked before I can commit to an airlift protocol. Remember, if they tag you with a paintball in the head or vital organ area, you're out of the game. Leg and arm shots will make the rest of us treat you as partially disabled. The umpires for the game are the base MPs, and they will be basically on the perimeters but can go anywhere." He looks over at an officer. "Tomlinson, you and your team are on the roof. Keep your eyes open and stay frosty. Those paintballs can easily reach three stories." He then directs his attention to Commander Thorpe. "And what will the ambassador be doing today, sir?"

Thorpe grins. "Whatever the ambassador wants to do. I'll just be strolling around until the shit hits the fan and you have to initiate protective restriction protocols."

Tommy smiles and looks over at Lieutenant Boder. "Boder, your team is on the ambassador. You will act as his aide, and your men will always be within eyeshot of one another. "If … anything was to happen today, the first protocol is to take him safely back to his office, which is designated the most impenetrable area in the embassy."

Boder steps up to Commander Thorpe. "So, your office is our ensconced defense location?"

Tommy cuts in. "No, Boder. For this exercise, Captain Fargo's office is the ambassador's. That is where we will initiate the ensconced defense scenario."

"Ha! You like to live dangerously, don't you, Williams?" Thorpe says as he shakes his head and laughs. "I'd pay good money to see Fargo's face when he realizes he has to have a paintball fight in his own office!"

One of the enlisted men steps up to Tommy and hands him some uniforms and hats that have a commander's rank on them. "I could only find two, Lieutenant. You said to leave his dress uniforms alone."

"That's fine, sailor. We'll make it work." Tommy grabs the uniforms and smiles as he looks back at Thorpe's astonished expression.

The commander points at the uniforms but bores into Tommy's eyes with a barely controlled rage. "What do you think you're doing with my extra uniforms, Williams?"

"Sir, our job is to protect the ambassador at all costs. If that means one of us catching enemy fire while pretending to be him, then it's our duty to do so."

Thorpe stands there for a moment, red-faced and tight-jawed as he thinks. He then sighs, lowers his hand to his side, relaxes his shoulders, and shakes his head as he laughs. "You got guts, Williams. I'll give you that. Go ahead and use them. But if those uniforms are all messed up with paintball gel, you'll be spending the rest of your time at SQT cleaning them and running obstacle courses." He moves in real close to Tommy, sticks his finger in his chest, and continues, "That's because you did not ask to borrow them first."

A foghorn sounds from outside and Tommy steps back and looks at everyone. "Okay, people, that's it. Game time." He looks back at Commander Thorpe and then over at Boder. "The ambassador is your responsibility, Boder. Carry on and keep in touch on your two-way." Commander Thorpe turns around and walks off toward the mess hall and Boder hand-signals his men to assume positions in proximity as he follows. Tommy gets on his radio and checks in with the other team leaders as he heads for the basement.

Captain Fargo looks through his binoculars at the principal building of Little Creek Base. He is surrounded by a lieutenant and sixty-five enlisted men as they stand just outside the gate where Tommy and the other officers were dropped off sixty-nine weeks ago. He has spotted the roof lookout that Williams has stationed, and after thoroughly scanning the front perimeter and checking in with his other forces behind the base on the beach, he is confident that Lieutenant Williams isn't pulling any shenanigans by being unfairly combat-ready for his raid.

"When do we attack, Captain?"

Fargo puts his binoculars down. "Just have all the men ready on this side, Lieutenant, but stay out of their line of sight until I give the order. You have four hundred yards to cross when you move out, and because of these damn paintball guns' range, you must wait until you're within thirty yards before you can hit anything. Williams has men three stories up and that could add another fifteen yards to their range. Some well-placed lucky shots and he'll start picking you off before you can retaliate. We'll give him an hour to sweat it out. Then, on my order, you move across that courtyard like a bunch of rampaging Vikings. That will keep his eyes on you while the forces I'm leading from the beach sneak in through the base from the rear. Carry on, Lieutenant. I'm heading around back now."

An hour passes. Tommy's radio chirps. "Lieutenant Williams, Tomlinson here. I have about sixty hostiles mustering at the gate by the access road."

"Tomlinson, stage two men on the roof facing rear and look for a second group. When the frontal assault gets within fifty yards, rain fire, but pay attention for friendlies."

"Copy that, Lieutenant. Tomlinson out."

Tommy looks at his two aides. "Briggs, you go to Boder and tell him we're starting the ground escape protocol with our first decoy. Grab one of Thorpe's uniforms and put it on and meet me with four others at the jeep on the west side of the building. Each man is to have extra ammo and one paintball grenade each."

Three minutes later the enlisted man finds Boder heading up the stairs toward Fargo's office with Commander Thorpe and relays Tommy's message. "Okay, sailor." Boder points to a man at the bottom of the stairs. "Bixby, you go with him and meet Lieutenant Williams at the jeep," he says and hands Thorpe's uniform to the man.

"What are you guys up to? You know the rules of the War Games are that there is no road access available for that scenario. Captain Fargo and his men will not take you seriously. Once you leave the courtyard, they'll count those men dead and you'll be down that many in personnel."

Boder shakes his head. "Sir, Williams didn't share all of his strategy with us, but I got a feeling he is counting on Captain Fargo not taking him seriously."

Five minutes later, Tommy's aide joins him at the jeep dressed in Commander Thorpe's uniform. Tommy smiles and hands him a paintball gun with ammo and one grenade. "Okay, guys, here's the deal. We all know that ground escape is impossible. But we are supposed to be acting like we know nothing yet. So, being head of security and knowing how close the British Embassy is supposed to be, and that it is a viable haven destination in a genuine terrorist attack, I'll let Fargo think I'm using that assessment to justify this op. But I also know he ain't going to buy it and will expect us to be pulling a bluff, which we are. We will make him think it's a defensive bluff, but we're going on the offense."

Fargo's Frontal Assault Team

Lieutenant Bates leads his men across the courtyard for the attack on the embassy. Endeavoring to act the part of a bunch of crazed terrorists, they are screaming and yelling curses at the men on the roof. As they approach the flagpole, which is about four hundred yards away from the main entrance of the base, a jeep pulls out from the west side of the building, turns left, and heads for the east side. Through his binoculars Bates counts six men in the jeep. Five are in tactical assault gear, but his eyes get big as saucers as he recognizes the uniform of one of the men. He immediately gets on his radio. "Captain, there is a jeep pulling out of the building and heading east with six men in it and I think one of them is Commander Thorpe."

The jeep travels to the east end of the building and then turns left.

"Sir, he went around the east side of the building."

Captain Fargo pulls out his radio from its holster and puts it to his ear. "What do you mean, a jeep? Williams was briefed that a ground escape scenario is impossible. Why are they going east?" Fargo squints and crunches his teeth together. "If that guy thinks he can take off to somewhere on the base and hide Thorpe until we're all tangled up in a firefight and then sneak him to the roof, he must think I'm as stupid as he is. Chase them down! We'll cut them off from this angle."

"Yes, sir!" Bates puts the radio back in the holster and yells, "Okay, guys, we're going after that jeep. First guy that takes the ambassador out gets a beer on me!"

As the jeep reaches the north end of the building, Tommy has the driver take another hard left and head for the west end, where they started out. He pulls out his radio, holds the mic to his mouth, and yells, "Boder, let them have everything you got!" He hops out of the jeep, grabs a spray bottle of laundry bleach and soaks down the tires, hops back in, and yells, "Go!"

At fifty yards into the building, Bates starts to hear splatting sounds around him. He looks up to see that he was so caught up in carrying out Fargo's orders to go after the jeep that he forgot about the men on the roof. Before he can call a hold, twenty of his men are hit and taken out of the competition. He raises his gun and calls out the return-fire order when the same jeep screeches around the corner and heads right for them. He tries to look for a spot to retreat to but there is no place close enough that will give him adequate cover, so he directs half of his remaining men to fire at the roof and the other half to fire at the oncoming jeep.

With the forces coming from the front now in a crossfire, Tommy yells "Now!" at the driver. The jeep pulls sideways, screeching to a full stop twenty-five yards in front of Bates's men, and everyone jumps out and gets behind it for cover.

The effect of the screeching stop is startling. Black smoke pours up from the bleach-soaked tires as they scrape across the concrete. With the smell of burned rubber penetrating their nostrils and the smoke obscuring their sight, Bates's forces stumble in confusion. Tommy then hurls paintball grenades at them. That, combined with the friendly fire coming from the roof, obliterates the rest of Bates's forces. Tommy gives the order to spray Bates's men one more time just to be sure they all admit that they got hit and then calmly walks over to Bates, who is lying prostrate on the ground with a very pissed-off look on his face.

"Williams, that is about the stupidest, most ridiculous fiasco I have ever seen. How you pulled this off is one in a million," Bates says, shaking the anger from his core. "What do you think you've gained?"

"For starters, sir, we've just cut the terrorist threat in half and now we can tap into their communications." He steps up to Bates, reaches down and grabs Bates's radio from his belt. "I'll relieve you of this, sir."

As Bates's men are getting back up on their feet, a jeep with a couple of navy MPs serving as umpires for the war game pulls up. The driver steps out and walks up to Tommy and Bates, shakes his head and smiles. "Lieutenant Bates, looks like you and your men are out of the competition. You need to head over to the staff housing section and wait until the war games are officially over."

Bates shrugs his shoulders and looks over at his men. "You heard him, we're out of it. Let's go, guys." He then looks over at Tommy. "Sorry about losing my temper, Williams. You just really surprised me. Fargo will have a cow when he finds out." He then looks over at the man who is wearing Thorpe's uniform and notices for the first time that it's not Thorpe. He throws back his head and laughs hysterically. "Damn, Williams, you like to push your luck to the limit, don't you?" He strolls off with the rest of his men.

"*Bates!* Where the hell are you? Have you caught that damn jeep yet? We're about halfway there and see nothing coming this way," Captain Fargo's voice booms out from the radio Tommy is holding.

Tommy looks down at the radio. For a split second, he is tempted to try to fool Fargo by answering and pretending to be Bates, but then he thinks Fargo probably won't fall for it. He reaches over and pushes the mute button on Bates's radio and looks back at his men. "We'll monitor their communications until Fargo figures out that we have one of his radios. Okay, let's head back to the embassy."

Captain Fargo stares incredulously at his radio for a second, clicks the mic, and says, "Okay, all team leaders, the enemy is monitoring our communications. We will go to sight-to-sight communications." He grabs the radio and shouts, "*Williams*, I know you can hear me. Pick up!"

"Yes, sir, Captain Fargo."

"I don't know what shenanigans you just pulled, but don't let it go to your adolescent head. When I am done with you, you'll be spending your last week here cleaning this place up with a toothbrush, because I am going to personally kick your ass so bad you won't be able to sit down for a month."

Tommy smiles and winks at the men in the jeep. "Sir, they never made it clear to us what happens if we win."

"Humph! On that frosty day in hell, son, the command staff here at the base will clean up the mess."

"Sounds like a deal to me, sir. Williams out."

Captain Fargo holds the radio out in front of his face and does his damnedest to crush it in his grasp. He throws it on the ground and looks over at his lieutenants and yells, "Come on, let's go teach this little bastard a lesson in humility!"

The line goes silent and Tommy hands the radio to one of his men. He taps the driver on the shoulder. "Take it right up to the front doors. We'll jump out and open them, then you drive it in as far as you can."

Tommy and five others hop out and open the front doors as he directs his man with the jeep in. Once he's pulled into the building as far as he can, he pulls the parking brake lever taut and hops out. "Okay, everybody back here. We're going to lift this baby up and turn it over."

Once it's about two-thirds off the ground, he tells them to hold it there as he skootches around to the front and grabs the tow hook cable connected to the electric pulley motor on the front bumper, pulls it out and loops it around the roll bar, then fastens it to the top of the inner stair rail. The entrance hall inside the front doors contains three more steps before entering the main hallway. He makes the line tight. "Okay, guys, that should hold. Get up here."

The five men let the jeep down. The line holds. When they are all up and inside, Tommy runs down and switches the electric pulley motor on. The jeep tips forward and falls on the rail as it slides upward, where it finally gets stuck against the inner door well. Once he decides they have wedged it in far enough, he turns off the electric pulley motor and looks back at his men. "Rodrigues, Wilson—you two cover this exit. No one is breaching this anytime soon, and if they try, the two of you can keep twenty men tied up here in a firefight." Both men salute and take defensive positions in front of the blocked door. Tommy reaches down and grabs the radio mic. "Boder, do you have Commander Thorpe in Fargo's office yet?"

"Yes, I do. He's making himself quite at home, sitting at the captain's desk."

"Tell him not to get too comfortable. I'm coming up with a decoy who is wearing a nice, clean uniform. Is the other one on the roof yet?"

"Yes, he's up there, and Commander Thorpe said he will be the judge of whether his uniform is clean or not."

"Tell him we'll be there in a minute. Are the other three exits covered? I'm sure Fargo will split his men up to test each one. We need to take out as many of them on the outside as possible before they breach."

"Yes, three four-man teams, plus cover from the roof."

"Okay, I'm on my way up."

Tommy walks into Captain Fargo's office for the first time since he has been at the base, and he is taken aback by how nicely it is decorated. None of the trainees are ever allowed in the base commander's office. The entire atmosphere is turn-of-the-century British. Commander Thorpe has his feet propped up on a highly polished, dark oak desktop with a glass frame. He has a glass of bourbon in one hand and an expensive Italian cigar in the other. The polished bronze of the oak in the desk accentuates the deep auburn curtains that cover the slightly shaded window panes behind it. The shelves and cabinets are also made from black oak. He remembers hearing that Captain Fargo served in World War II, Korea, and Vietnam. The office is decorated with items from each of those conflicts, along with pictures and other memorabilia.

"You sure you want to have a paintball firefight in here, Williams?" Thorpe asks as he slams down the last of his drink.

Tommy looks from left to right, then at Thorpe, with an enormous smile on his face. "Yes, sir. I think I do." The man wearing Thorpe's uniform steps into the office behind Tommy and says, "Everything is ready, Lieutenant."

"Okay, then. Commander, you will come with me, and this man is taking your place at that desk."

Commander Thorpe stands up and walks over to the man wearing his uniform and reaches out and grabs the collar and pulls it to his nose. "You're getting it all sweaty, sailor. I expect it laundered, pressed, and the belt spit-shined and polished when it comes back to me."

The enlisted man comes to attention, throws a stiff salute, and says, "Aye, aye, sir, Commander Thorpe!"

Thorpe does not return the salute but looks back at Tommy and grunts. "Okay, Williams, let's go see what kind of party you got going on."

Tommy leads the way to the stairwell into the basement.

"He's here, Williams," comes Boder's voice over the speaker.

Tommy reaches over and grabs his radio. "Boder, send up the signal flare that we've called to have the ambassador airlifted out of here."

"So, you got one hour to hold that roof and keep me safe from Captain Fargo. You really think you can win, kid?"

"Holding the roof isn't the only way we can win, sir. There were other options," Tommy says while leading Thorpe to the basement.

"Capture or kill the enemy leader. Are you serious? Williams, on my best day I don't know if I could hold that roof from Fargo for an hour, and I sure as hell would never try to capture or kill him. That's like trying to wrestle a grizzly bear with your bare hands." He looks back and forth and then continues. "Why are we going to the basement? The objective is to have me on the roof so the chopper can transport me out of here."

"You'll see, sir."

They come to the main floor and an officer on Tommy's team reports. "Okay, Williams, everyone is in place. I still don't see how this will work, but it's your ball game, not mine."

Tommy nods. "Look, they have roughly sixty men coming to attack. I want to cut that number in half by the time they breach our perimeter. We can't afford to lose over five of our own down here, so once they're in, you take your guys to Fargo's office and send the rest to the roof. I'm taking five with me and Commander Thorpe. Try to take out as many as you can at the office and tell the guys on the roof when Fargo heads that way. You'll know when I make my move."

Fargo's Staging Area for Breach

The flare goes up, and from his position inside the equipment building on the east side of the base HQ, Fargo looks down at his watch. "It's 1800 hours. We have one hour to be on that roof and put a paintball in Thorpe's chest. Are all four teams ready, Chief?"

"Yes, sir."

"Okay, send the signal. I want to be in that building in the next ten minutes. Keep an eye on that roof and cover our attack as we make it to the entrances."

Fargo has ten of his men lined up to cover the assault by firing at the roof from the east and north sides while the rest run to their assigned entrance. Twelve men make it around to the front entrance. Two of them are taken out by Tommy's men on the roof before Fargo's men retaliate and cover. As the remaining men make it to the front entrance, they all stop and do a double-take at the sight before them.

One of them puts his hand to his mouth and yells, "Captain Fargo, there's a jeep stuck in the doorway—"

SPLAT!

The man reaches up and touches the slimy residue of paintball gel on his forehead. Following the rules of the game, he walks away from the exchange, sits down, and folds his hands on his lap, showing that he is not in the game anymore.

"What do you mean there's a jeep in the doorway?" He listens, but no response comes. The rest of Fargo's frontal assault force moves inside the door and to the upended jeep wedged into the stairwell. One man gets up close and peers around the side. "Chief, the towing cable is fastened to the—"

SPLAT!

Before he can finish, Tommy's two men stationed just inside the door unleash a barrage of paintballs. The ambush is deadly. The paintballed victims each turn around and go outside to sit down and wait for the umpires to come and release them from the war game.

Thirty seconds later one of Fargo's men covering the roof comes running up. "Captain, the whole team that we sent around front has been taken out. One of them yelled that there's a jeep wedged in the stairwell of the front entrance, and they're being ambushed!"

Fargo grinds his teeth and stares back at the man. "You mean to tell me that that maniac Williams rammed a jeep into the front door of my building and used it as cover to wipe out one of my units?"

"Uh, that pretty much sums it up, sir!"

Captain Fargo throws his head back and laughs. He then pats the man on the back, grabs his rifle, and says, "I guess we can train them pretty damn good around here, huh? Let's go see what this lunatic Williams has up his sleeve next."

Tommy, Thorpe, and the five men with them enter the basement by the workout area and make their way over to the pool. Tommy takes his men down the stairs and opens the door that leads to the storage area next to the old bomb shelter. He walks over to a shelf, grabs a sledgehammer and a pickax, goes to the entrance of the bomb shelter, takes the sledgehammer and smashes the padlock on the door several times until it gives some, then uses the pointed end of the pickax to pry the lock from the wall.

"You know, I have a set of master keys in my pocket. One of them fits that lock, Williams."

Tommy eyeballs Thorpe. "Huh, I guess hindsight is twenty-twenty, sir! Follow me."

Tommy grabs his radio and clicks the button. "Boder, tell me as soon as Fargo leaves the office area for the roof."

"You got it, Williams."

"Boder?"

"Yeah, Williams."

"When he does, let me know how many of Fargo's men are out front anywhere near the flagpole. And be ready to give me cover when I yell for it."

"Okay, Williams. Hope this works. Boder out."

"I think you'll be pleasantly surprised. Just make sure that Fargo does a lot of fighting before he spots our decoy man on the roof. Williams out."

He puts the radio back on his hip and then tells one guy to pick up the tools and go into the bomb shelter. "I need one more thing." He steps over to the tool shelf and finds what he is looking for. It's a heavy duty, electrically powered grinding wheel. He grabs it, along with an extension cord and walks into the bomb shelter, sets it down, closes the door, and locks it from the inside. He looks over at Commander Thorpe and can tell that curiosity is about to eat him alive.

"Got something you would like to ask me, sir?"

Thorpe shakes his head. "Okay, Williams. You got me baffled. I know you don't plan on hiding down here because in less than an hour the whistle will blow and if I'm not up on the roof, you lose." He looks at the tools and back at Tommy. "So, what's your plan? Dig a tunnel to the surface and ambush Fargo from behind? Not a terrible idea. But it would take you guys about a week to dig your way out of here."

Tommy smiles and walks over and grabs the pickax and uses it to pry the shelves away from the concrete wall. He then pries off the metal sheet he had fastened to hold the concrete patch he placed there over a year ago and looks at Commander Thorpe. "I don't have to dig something that's already been dug."

He then uses the pickax to knock the wall down. One of the other men grabs the sledgehammer and helps him. Five minutes later the hole is big enough to serve as a door. He stops, wipes the sweat from his head, and looks at Thorpe. "Care to take a look, Commander?"

Thorpe steps into the little stairwell chamber that Tommy had discovered, lets out a whistle and says, "Williams, you are in some hot water for not reporting the existence of this to Fargo."

"You know, I thought about that, Commander, and so I went to the base records room that you gave me permission to use when I was preparing for my tour and looked up the history on this bomb shelter. Turns out it was originally built separate from the old principal building here in 1952. It had two access points from the surface, one east and one west. When they expanded the building out twenty-five yards, they buried the south access under the flagpole and joined the north access to the principal building in the basement. So, since it is a documented fact that this access well is here, and you just wanted me to restore the bomb shelter from the recent flooding, I fixed the corroded doorway to this wall and refastened the shelves to it."

"Well, I guess that means if Captain Fargo and I had done our homework properly when we got assigned here, we would have known about it. Funny, it shocked me to learn that the bomb shelter was even down here when you got disciplinary duty. We all just chalked it up to Fargo's meticulous attention to detail that he is so famous for. Looks like you got one up on him in that department, Williams. What's your next move?"

"Well, sir, as soon as Boder calls …"

The radio chirps and Boder says, "Williams, Captain Fargo just breached the west exit. We're heading to the roof."

"Damn, that didn't take long!" Tommy exclaims, then reaches for his radio. "Boder, how many did you take out before they breached?"

"Twenty-five tops, maybe less."

"Did we lose any?"

"Three casualties. One arm injury."

Tommy does some quick calculations. "That makes our numbers even. Maybe our guys in Fargo's office can take out a few more before they make it to the roof. Okay, make sure someone from Fargo's group hears that you're going to his office."

"Already did. Boder out."

Captain Fargo steps through the west door after counting how many men he lost in the breach. He counted twenty-six casualties and three wounded. He looks at the man in front of him and yells, "Chief, how many of Williams's men got taken out?"

"Three to four, tops, sir."

"Damn, now they outnumber us. Take everybody up to the roof as fast as possible. Look out for ambushes on the second and third floors."

"Sir, some of them are heading to your office to retrieve the commander and take him to the roof. Should we follow them in?"

"My *OFFICE!* What the hell? Uh, yes, but I'll have any man's ass in a sling that gets any paintball gel on anything in there. Do a sweep of each floor and look for anyone that's hiding." He looks from side to side, then looks down and grumbles, "Rodney, you son of a bitch. You probably think it's funny as hell that he used my office instead of yours."

Lieutenant Mike Preston and the seven men in his unit make their way to the third floor, meeting no resistance. Fargo's office is down the right hall that leads straight to the door that enters the outer office, where his secretary sits at her desk. To the right of that desk is the door with Captain Fargo's name over it. Lieutenant Preston and his men ease their way down the hall, hugging the sides with their paintball rifles pointing at the outer door. Preston gets to it first and reaches down and twists the knob and eases the door open. There are no lights on, but Fargo's door is partially open and sitting at the desk is a man in a commander's uniform. Preston can't make out his face, but he says, "Looks like they didn't have time to make it to the roof. All I got to do is put one paintball shot on his chest, and we've won. Cover me."

Preston crouches down low and scoots in closer and takes aim and mutters under his breath. "Sorry about the office, captain. If I win this for you, I think you'll understand."

He takes aim but suddenly a drape drops over the doorway from the top and five men stand up from the dark corners of the outer office and barrage Preston's men in the other doorway. Preston's men return fire and the firefight lasts about forty-five seconds before everyone can see that everyone is completely covered with paintball gel. They all look at one another and decide that they have no other choice, so they sit on the floor and put their hands in their laps. The drape covering Captain Fargo's office lifts and the man wearing Commander Thorpe's uniform steps through.

Suddenly Captain Fargo himself steps up to the doorway, points his rifle at the man and pulls the trigger. One paintball splats against his chest. Fargo steps in and looks at him closer. "You're not Commander Thorpe! Where the hell is he, and what are you doing wearing his uniform?" The man remains silent as per the rule of the game—dead men cannot talk.

Fargo looks closer at the mess in the outer office in exasperation. "Geez, Maggie will have a fit Monday morning when she comes to work."

With trepidation, he steps up to the paintball-drenched sheet hanging over his doorway and pulls it to the side to look in his office. He scans it from top to bottom and side to side, then gives out an enormous sigh of relief. He shakes his head and walks to the door to the hallway and looks down at the men. "You guys go report to the umpires." Then he checks the time. "Twenty more minutes. It's time to show Williams how this game will finish." He yells out into hallway, "Everyone on me, we're heading to the roof!"

The flagpole tips and leans to the side as the white gravel disappears, forming a hole right beside it. As the hole gets bigger, the flagpole continues to dip sideways until the flag is barely a foot off the ground. Tommy is the first to make his way through the old rusty hatch from the bomb shelter entrance. First, he scans the area for hostiles and when he's confident there are none he starts to climb out. Once out, he lays his rifle down and hurries over to the flag and takes it off the flagpole line and yells for one of his men to come over and help him. The next man out runs over, and he and Tommy fold up the flag in proper military fashion. Tommy hands the flag to the man and grabs his radio. "Williams here. Are you guys sure there's no one down here?"

"This is Boder. No. The roof reported. Everyone went in when Fargo breached the west door."

"Okay, Boder. Are they done at Captain Fargo's office yet?"

"I think so. The guys at the roof entrance think they saw some men quietly gathering at the bottom of the stairs."

Tommy looks around the area, assuring himself that none of Fargo's men are there. Then he glimpses the umpires over by the gate staring incredulously, stunned, at him and his men. He waves and looks over at the man holding the electric grinder wheel and says, "Follow me."

One of the other guys blurts out, "Lieutenant Williams, if all of Captain Fargo's men are inside and heading for the roof, shouldn't we just take another entrance?"

"We've come too far to be sloppy now, sailor. If it was me, I would leave at least one man at each accessible exit just in case."

At the front entrance Tommy grabs the electric grinding wheel, tells the man with the extension cord to plug it into the outdoor outlet that the gardeners use, and then walks in to where they left the jeep. "Okay, guys, when I cut the cable, the jeep will fall back. That will make enough noise to get the attention of anyone still on the first floor. So, you three head to the three different exits and stay out of sight until you hear something, then come in and support us."

The three take off around the building to station themselves at the exits. Tommy then lies down beside the wedged-in jeep and starts the grinder, places it on the cable, and cuts through it in a matter of seconds, then jumps back and out of the way. The jeep does not fall right away. Just as he is about to tell the guys to tug on it from the sides, there is a huge groan and then scraping of metal against the steel doorframe and the jeep falls back and down. It bounces twice before it settles.

Before Tommy can say anything, a paintball misses his head by inches, and he looks up and yells "Fire!" as he dives for cover. When he looks up again, three of Fargo's men are taking cover around the stairwell in the middle of the building, firing at him and his men.

They exchange about five rounds each back and forth when they hear someone say, "Oh, shit!" Tommy cautiously stands up to look and to his amusement and satisfaction, Fargo's three men are now seated on the floor with their hands in their laps.

In the stairwell that leads to the roof, Fargo checks the time. He's only got fifteen more minutes to take the roof and put a paintball on Thorpe's chest. He holds up two fingers with his right hand, then points to each side of the doorway entrance to the roof. Four men form in front of him and cautiously make their way to the top. Once there, the front two kick the door open and fire straight in front of them. As they plow the field, the two behind step stealthily beside them, burst out of the doorway, and take out Williams's men, who are hiding to ambush them as they emerge from the stairwell. Tommy's men have done well so far, but Fargo's men are all seasoned vets and the roof does not provide much cover, and these guys know how to take a roof.

Williams's men do their best, but Fargo and his men are out on the roof and fanning out in a V formation that allows for no viable strategy for Tommy's men except to stand and fight. Within forty-five seconds, only three men are standing in front of Fargo's target. They are holding their rifles at the ready and are desperately looking from side to side as Fargo's men close in on them. One throws down his rifle and puts up his hands and says, "I am out of paintballs." The other two follow his example and do the same.

Fargo steps forward and holds his rifle at the ready, smiles, and shakes his head. "Williams and you boys gave me a run for my money. I believe you've learned something here at our beloved base. Okay, boys, step aside. Sorry, Rodney, but it all washes out, right?"

The three men step aside, and Fargo shoots the man in the commander's uniform in the chest. When he focuses on the man's face, he stares in slack-jawed astonishment and confusion. "You're not Commander Thorpe! Where the hell is he, and where's Williams?"

"Right here, sir!"

As he and his men turn toward the direction of the voice, a barrage of paintballs hit Fargo's men before they can return fire. The only one who is not hit is Captain Fargo. Tommy walks up to him, points his gun at his chest and says, "This embassy is sovereign United States territory. You are under arrest for attacking it and killing United States citizens and soldiers." Just as he finishes speaking, the horn sounds that marks the end of the game.

Fargo looks behind Tommy and sees Commander Thorpe standing there, grinning from ear to ear. Thorpe chuckles and says, "You know, Captain, this kid had more tricks up his sleeve than Bugs Bunny does with Elmer Fudd. But don't worry, I think we can fix the flagpole."

Fargo stares at Thorpe for a moment while the words sink in. Then he runs over to the side of the roof that faces the flagpole and looks down, seeing it for the first time tilted over to the side. He looks straight up in the air and screams, *"WILLIAMS!!!"*

Five days later, Tommy is doing his best to maintain his cool as he endures the humiliation of having to do the swimming pool obstacle course six times in less than an hour, and then do a ten-mile run, and then go to Captain Fargo's office and polish his desk and furniture, all for the fifth day in a row.

True to his word, Captain Fargo had his command staff clean up the HQ building at Little Creek, but he included his highest-ranking noncommissioned officers in the command staff for that operation. Fargo also oversaw the restoration of his beloved flagpole, but he made Tommy and the other five SQT officers restore the stairwell area of the bomb shelter that he was previously unaware of. After checking with his superiors in naval command, he had the flagpole area moved over five yards and left the hatch to the bomb shelter exposed. Tommy and the others sanded that down and refinished it and installed a heavy-duty padlock on it to keep it secure.

Last Day of SQT, September 15th, 1978

Captain Fargo and Commander Thorpe sit up on the stage behind Rear Admiral Toby Winston as he gives his congratulatory speech to the SQT graduates. Fargo looks over at Thorpe and can tell that the man can barely sit up straight, and he has to admit that he is having trouble in that category himself. Last night they finished cleaning up from War Games, and he had brought out his best bottle of Teeling Irish Whiskey from Dublin. When Thorpe asked him how much it was worth, the man almost had a fit when he told him that it cost nine hundred dollars two years ago. They spent the better part of the evening and into the morning drinking it in honor of Lieutenant Tommy Williams, the only SQT officer trainee in history to beat the command staff at Little Creek in War Games.

The graduation ceremony is being held at the parade grounds of Little Creek Base. The admiral's last remarks are regarding the importance of the navy having their own unit of special forces specifically trained to handle land, air, and sea operations. "I know that the path you have chosen is not the most glamorous one our beloved navy has to offer. Nor is it the easiest path to attain a higher rank. But be assured that your country appreciates the hard work and sacrifice you will do for her. Godspeed to all of you!"

Everyone in the area stands and hoots and hollers with applause. The admiral turns and acknowledges Captain Fargo and Commander Thorpe and steps off to his seat on the side of the stage.

Captain Fargo steps up to the podium. He takes a deep breath and tries to calm the volcano of pain going off in his head from the monstrous hangover he is dealing with. He looks out and the first person he spots is Tommy. "You men have all passed your SQT to my and Commander Thorpe's satisfaction. A feat for which you should be proud. As you go on to your next level of training, do not forget what it took to get you there." He looks straight at Tommy and continues. "Never underestimate what it takes to do our job and do it right. Tricks and fancy maneuvers may squeak you by"—a laugh goes through the graduating class because they know that comment was directed at Tommy—"but your adherence to the fundamentals that you learned here will determine your success, and, yes, your life and the lives of those you serve with. Congratulations. Dismissed."

The men do their ceremonial cheer and disperse. Fargo takes another deep breath and turns around to face Commander Thorpe. Thorpe looks at him quizzically. "Aren't you ever going to let that kid know how highly you think of him?"

"That diamond still needs some polishing," Fargo replies. "But he'll know when he needs to know. Come on, let's go meet our next group."

The other five officers and twenty-seven enlisted men in the graduating class make their way to family and friends in the audience. Everyone has someone there, except for Tommy. He stands there for a moment deciding where to go when someone taps his shoulder from behind. He turns and immediately comes to attention and throws a salute. "Admiral, Lieutenant Tommy Williams, sir."

"At ease, Lieutenant," Admiral Winston says with a sparkle in his eyes. "So, you are Ambassador Rodney Williams's boy. I heard you opted out of the JAG program and came here. The craziest thing I ever heard. I knew your dad. We graduated from Annapolis together."

"It's great to meet you, sir. That was a very inspirational speech," Tommy says and relaxes a little.

"Thanks, Tommy. This program doesn't get much press. Not like the Green Berets or Delta Force. The secretary of the navy asked me to come down here and speak at your graduation because he wants more attention on you boys and how well we're training you."

Tommy raises an eyebrow. "Secretary Thompson sent you, sir?"

Admiral Winston puts a hand on Tommy's shoulder. "He told me to tell you he is sorry he could not come, but our new president has him busy these days, and he could not make it away from Washington."

"That's all right, Admiral. Please tell him I understand. I'm sure he's still peeved about my turning down law school to become a SEAL."

Winston pats his back. "I heard he blew a couple of head gaskets over it, but that was last year. I'm sure he's over it. Well, I have to go, Tommy. Take care and go get 'em at graduate training!"

Tommy shakes Admiral Winston's extended hand then salutes. "Thank you, sir. I will."

Chapter 7

When I Am Gone Others Will Rise in My Stead

Small Fishing Village South of Gazi, Kenya, July 13, 1979

MAKENA DRIVES HER DAUGHTERS, ADIMU and Chineye, to her late husband's mother's home on the coast. They have been in a heated debate since leaving their home several hours ago. "Mama, I don't want to stay at Grandmother's house all summer. What about my friends?"

"Chineye, we have talked about this. It is safer here than in Gazi. The abductions of girls are getting more frequent than ever. President Amoi himself invited me to speak at Parliament! How can I focus on that when I am worried about you and Adimu?"

"She is right, Chineye. Grandmother's is much safer, and we can spend every day on the beach. Stop worrying about someone stealing your boyfriend. Besides, since Papa died, we are all Grandmother has left in the world. We should spend time with her."

Chineye glares at her sister for mentioning her fear about her boyfriend. "I'm not worried about Jaali. He told me he'd be faithful."

Makena smiles sadly. "Chineye, you're too young to have a boyfriend."

"Mama, you were only two years older than me when you married Papa and then had us."

"I know, Chineye, but though we learned to love one another, ours was an arranged marriage, and I have come to believe that I do not want that for you … Oh!"

Chineye smugly smiles, knowing that she has caught her mother with her own words. "Well, Mama, that is interesting because you have not even met Jaali's parents yet, and we've been together for an entire month."

Makena rolls her eyes and sighs. "Very well, Chineye, we will continue this discussion at another time. We are almost to your grandmother's home. If you want to have peace in that house, I suggest you do not talk about your friend Jaali around her. She is the one that my parents negotiated my marriage to your father with, and the subject of a boyfriend may cause her to have a heart attack."

Makena pulls into the driveway of a nice little, two-story beach house just outside her ancestral village and parks her 1957 Volkswagen Beetle. She is instantly greeted with a very stern look from a woman in her middle sixties who has the same piercing eyes as her late husband.

Brigid steps off the porch, looks at Makena and solemnly nods, then turns to the girls and throws her arms open wide and brightly smiles. "Adimu, Chineye, my treasures! Come bring your things inside. I have your father's old room set up for you. Go settle in while your mother and I talk."

They look to their mother, who nods, and then they grab their things and head into the house.

Makena steps up to her mother-in-law and takes both of her hands. "Brigid, you can't talk me out of it. I am determined to follow this path."

Brigid bores into Makena's eyes for a moment, then sighs. "Makena, you are not him! His cause cannot be taken up by a woman. Especially someone like you. You are not a warrior. All you have ever been is my son's wife and your daughters' mother. How can you even think that those people in Nairobi will take you seriously? You, Adimu, and Chineye are all I have left in this world. What will I do if I lose any more of my family?"

Makena wipes the tears from her eyes and embraces her mother-in-law. "I must try, Brigid. The evil men from the East still believe they can harvest our people like wheat and herd us like cattle into their cursed service."

"Have you at least done what I asked and changed your name back to that of your ancestors?"

"Yes, Brigid, I have. I will never associate the name Azeem with what I will do in Nairobi at Parliament. No one there will even know that I have daughters, let alone where they are. To them I will be Makena Aalee, the great-granddaughter of Tumaini Aalee, 'The Legend.'"

Nairobi, Kenya, Capitol Building, July 15, 1979

Makena makes her way into the capitol building of Kenya in the city of Nairobi. As the presidential guards open the doors to allow her access to the building, a cold sweat forms on her eyebrow as she considers what it took to finally gain this audience with President Daniel Arap Amoi and Parliament. She spent years petitioning former President Kenyatta to allow her to set her case before him but was denied at every turn. Since his death some eight months ago, and the special general election confirming his successor's presidency, things changed for her and her cause is finally getting a hearing. She understands it will still be an uphill battle to gain enough support to make a difference, but like her ancestor, she will fight for this just cause until her dying breath.

A tall, thin man with a shiny, bald head, wearing black-rimmed glasses and dressed in a traditional European three-piece business suit, comes through a door in the hall that she was directed to and introduces himself. "Madam Aalee, I am Undersecretary Bosher Arachar. I will serve as your guide today as you prepare to address Parliament."

"It is a pleasure to meet you, Undersecretary Arachar. When will I be addressing Parliament today?"

The administrator takes his clipboard and flips through the pages and puts his pen at a certain spot, then looks up. "Here it is. Madam Aalee to address Parliament and President Amoi about concerns for sporadic cases of human trafficking from Kenya to Arab and Muslim-controlled states, 4:45 this afternoon."

"Four-forty-five in the afternoon. Undersecretary, there must be some mistake. Parliament adjourns at 5:00 p.m. Fifteen minutes is not enough time for me to adequately present this problem to the government. Why is the wording 'sporadic' and 'human trafficking' in there? I specifically petitioned President Amoi to address the continuous abduction of our people for slavery in Arab and Muslim-controlled lands. There is nothing sporadic about it. The shanghaiing and kidnapping of young people, especially on our coast, is practically a daily occurrence, which I might add, is completely ignored by our local law enforcement and military."

The man stares sternly at Makena for a few moments, huffs, looks back down at his clipboard, jots a note, then looks up and smiles. "Madam Aalee, I have changed the word 'sporadic' to 'continuous,' and the words 'human trafficking' to 'slave trade.' As for the timing of your address, it is beyond my power to change. I suggest you prepare to give a presentation that will catch what is left of Parliament's attention."

Makena moves in closer to the administrator and points her right index finger at his face. "What do you mean, what is left of Parliament, Undersecretary?"

His eyes jolt from side to side, making sure no one is within earshot of their conversation. He then steps in closer and continues in a much quieter tone. "I am sorry, Madam Aalee, but by that time more than half of Parliament will have left and the president rarely stays past noon."

Makena can hardly control her breathing as the rage of betrayal threatens to overpower her. She is readying to give this administrator a piece of her mind, but he holds up a staying hand while looking at the day's schedule. "My God! This is preposterous." He lowers the clipboard. "It says here that General Amri Tumba was scheduled to speak to Parliament for one hour at 10:00 a.m., but he has some urgent state business to attend to and has cancelled his address. Because he cancelled, Parliament is now scheduled to adjourn at 4:00 p.m., and it does not include your address in the new schedule. I just received this new schedule before I walked out here. After taking care of you I was on my way to make copies and have them distributed to everyone."

Exasperated, she looks over to the wall in the hallway and finds a bench to sit on. Once there, she clenches her fists to her chest and weeps.

Undersecretary Arachar again looks back and forth, scanning the hallway to see if anyone is looking, then sits down next to Makena. He sits there for a moment, torn between what he wants to do and what others are trying to force to happen. He sighs and puts a hand on Makena's shoulder. "Madam Aalee, my family is from the same village as yours. My great-grandfather followed yours on his crusades against the Arabian slavers of that time. We have old photographs of them standing together after freeing dozens of our people in one of his raids against those vile men." He reaches up and takes his glasses off and wipes the beginning of a tear from his eye.

Makena turns to him in astonishment. "If this is true, why were you so cold to me? We are of the same tribe and share a common ancestral cause."

The undersecretary sits up straight and puts his glasses back on. "Madam Aalee, I was not forthright with you when I said that the scheduling of parliamentary proceeding was beyond my power. In fact, that is my power as undersecretary." An enormous smile crosses his face as he looks directly into Makena's soft, brown eyes and continues. "Today, you will replace General Tumba's time slot to address Parliament, and you will have his hour to present your cause!" He opens his clipboard and jots down a few notes. "It will take me a few moments to redo this day's agenda and then make copies to be passed out. Please let me escort you to the waiting area where you may refresh yourself and prepare for your presentation." He looks down at his watch then back at Makena. "Parliament will convene at 9:00 a.m. and you will be the second speaker, at 10:00 a.m."

Office of General Amri Tumba, Head of Kenya Internal Security, 10:00 a.m.

Pasto Niazai of Afghanistan sits in the ornately decorated office of General Tumba, head of security for the country of Kenya. The man reminds him of his own superior, General Uriah Turakine, of The People's Liberation Army of Afghanistan. Both men love to live lavishly and flaunt their self-importance to the masses, whom they feel destined to rule. Tumba is a medium-sized man with bushy, graying hair, bloodshot brown eyes, and the reddish cheeks of a man who has spent many a year enjoying the taste of hard liquor. Pasto has always been a soldier and maintains the disciplines of a man who more often than not must be ready for combat at a moment's notice. He takes another sip of ice water from the glass in his hand and inquires, "Were you able to sabotage Madam Aalee's address to Parliament today, General?"

"My dear friend, not only was she scheduled to speak last when hardly anyone would still be there, but I cancelled my own address at the last minute. That got her completely removed from the roster. President Amoi never stays past noon unless there's pressing business to attend to. I'm afraid that Madam Aalee's cause will not touch his ears today."

Tumba's intercom buzzes. He reaches down and presses the switch. "Yes, what is it? I'm in a private meeting and told you not to disturb me!"

"I am sorry, General, but Madam Aalee is addressing Parliament right now and President Amoi is seated directly in front of her, hearing the entire thing!"

"*What*! That is impossible! I made sure that the schedule change was sent to Undersecretary Arachar this morning. Besides, it's only ten now, and she wasn't scheduled until late this afternoon. Unless ..." Tumba's face goes ashen. He leans back in his chair and looks up at the ceiling. "Bosher gave her my spot this morning."

Pasto gets up and walks over to Tumba's side of the desk and leans in close. "We have paid you an enormous amount of money to help us expand our business in your country, Tumba. If Madam Aalee gains support to obstruct our efforts to buy new slaves for our Arab and Muslim clients, we will take our business to a more accommodating country, and you will not have our support in your upcoming coup attempt."

Makena Aalee steps up to the podium after being introduced by the chairman. She looks out nervously across the room at all the different representatives from the provinces of Kenya. She can't help but feel that some of them will want her killed for what she is about to say. The room is enormous, and full of very important men. The icy steel of panic seizes her heart, but then a memory of her great-grandfather Tumaini Aalee comes to her. It was the first and last time she would ever see him. She was only nine years old when her mother and father journeyed to his home in the country to pay their last respects to the dying man. When she was allowed to approach his bed, she could see his intense, gray eyes staring into her soul and feel his strong, bony hand clasp hers, holding it to his chest. He uttered the only words he ever spoke to her: "Someone must rise and continue the fight. Make the legend live on!"

At first, she did not understand why he said that to her. Her mother and father told her that it was just the ramblings of an old and dying man. But as she grew up on the coast of Kenya, she saw for herself that Tumaini Aalee's work was far from done.

Emboldened by the memory, she takes a deep, calming breath and begins. "President Amoi and esteemed members of Parliament, greetings. My name is Makena Aalee and I come from a coastal village near Gazi. Many of you may remember the stories of my great-grandfather, Tumaini Aalee, The Legend. For over forty years he was chief of my ancestral village and, along with his proud warriors, protected and rescued our people from the Islamic slave traders that raided our coasts for over a millennium. He alone stood up and prevented them from taking our people to the sheikhs and rulers of the Arabian lands and beyond to become slaves in their accursed harems.

"I am here today to tell you that this vile business is still a reality within our borders. Although today they do not sail into our villages like pirates and take our people captive, let me assure you that the business of slavery is still just as alive and vital as it was in Tumaini's day. They have changed their methods. Now they lure our young children to sign up for work abroad, or they use drugs and alcohol to lure people away from their families and then abduct them. Some stalk our nightclubs and festivals where they wait for people to stray away from the crowds and then shanghai them.

"Today we call it human trafficking and talk about it as something other than what it has always been—*slave trading*. Our own police and military stand by and watch as this happens all over our country. When a distraught mother or father reports a child missing, they are told to forget about it and move on. When they press for answers, they are threatened, then jailed and/or end up disappearing themselves.

"My great-grandfather told our people to stand together and show these vile people that we will no longer be wheat for their harvest or sheep they can herd. Tumaini Aalee is with us no longer. His brave warriors no longer patrol our coasts against Islamic slavers. But his legacy taught us that we *can* stand up against them and stop them from stealing our lives. President Amoi, members of Parliament, I beg you to pass legislation that will force our police and military to protect our citizens from this accursed practice. Our people are our most precious resource, and they deserve your protection. Please give your attention to your monitors as I play a film presentation of interviews and footage of actual modern-day slave trading of our citizens."

A forty-five-minute-long, documentary-style video—a presentation to President Amoi and the full House of Parliament of Kenya—begins to play. Several news agencies in the country pick it up as well.

Makena steps back up to the podium when the film ends. "Now you have the truth. It is up to you as the government of Kenya to cut out this cancer that has plagued our lands for far too long. Thank you!"

The entire hall is silent for a few seconds. Then President Amoi stands and raises his hands and claps. He turns and looks at the others seated in the room, meeting many stares of astonishment with a raised eyebrow and an unspoken demand for them to join him. Slowly, others in the room comply and follow the president's example and stand to clap as well. He then steps up to the podium next to Makena Aalee and shakes her hand and gives her a nod as she exits the speaker's platform.

He looks around the room and says, "Madam Aalee has reminded us this day that we have long been slack in taking up the responsibility her ancestor freely took upon his shoulders for us. I will see that our police and military take a much more aggressive approach to this horrible phenomenon that plagues our society. But it is up to you in our Parliament to pass legislation that will permanently stop these atrocities once and for all. I will wait eagerly to see what you, with your combined talents and wisdom, can come up with."

President Amoi then steps off the floor and exits the hall. He makes his way to his office in the other half of the capitol building, tells his secretary to hold all his calls, and sits at his desk. He picks up his phone and dials the number to the head of internal security. A nervous General Tumba answers. "President Amoi, I was just about to call you. I—"

"You think you can play games and manipulate my government behind my back, Tumba?"

"No, sir, I just have not—"

"Tumba, if you value your position here in Nairobi you will shut your mouth and pay heed to everything I say. For starters, if it comes to my attention that any aggressive action is taken against Undersecretary Arachar for altering the changes you made in today's parliamentary proceedings, I will have you removed from your position, charged with treason, and shot! You may think that the money you have filtered into our treasury from your Islamic friends and their business practices here in Kenya will protect you from my wrath, but it will not. Now your dirty little secret is in danger of being exposed to the rest of the world. You promised me that these dealings would appear sporadic. But what I saw today puts our country in danger of condemnations from world powers—the United States, Russia, and China—and more than likely trade embargoes and sanctions from the United Nations. Madam Aalee's ancestor is a national hero, and with her leading this crusade, who can tell how far it could go. I swear, Tumba, if this comes to heads being taken, it will be yours and not mine that will roll."

"President Amoi, I hear you. And trust me, I am quite in favor of keeping my head right where it is. But no matter how upset you are with my slight downplaying of how many are being taken by our very generous Islamic friends, Madam Aalee is the one who poses the genuine threat here. We need to deal with her, or all of our heads will roll."

President Amoi sits back and closes his eyes as he ponders Tumba's words. "You have a point, Tumba. We must act, but not here, and not now. They televised her presentation all over the country, and I am sure it will soon be on major networks around the world. Let her have her little fifteen minutes of fame. I'll do as I have promised and have you make a grand show of stopping the human trafficking. Work out a deal with your friends that will allow me to save face and appear that we are taking aggressive action. Then, when the public is lulled to sleep, we will move on her."

Makena steps out of the parliamentary chamber and into the hall where she first entered. She can hardly believe the response President Amoi gave her. She closes her eyes and thanks God for the blessing and heads toward the exit. When she turns to grab the handle of the door, an arm wraps around her shoulder in a protective embrace. She looks up to see Undersecretary Arachar. He pushes the door open and walks outside with her. He looks from side to side as he moves her briskly across the courtyard to a waiting government car. "Madam Aalee, I don't know if you are in danger, but I am not taking any chances. I do not think that General Tumba is stupid enough to move against you or me here, but we have now made an enemy of him—and perhaps President Amoi as well."

Arachar opens the door to the black sedan as Makena looks up at his kind eyes in astonishment. "Undersecretary, I don't understand. President Amoi just gave me his public support, and I have never met General Tumba."

Arachar puts his hands on Makena's shoulders and shakes his head. "Oh, Madam Aalee, if you are to manage in this world of presidents, generals, and parliaments, you need to understand that money and power rule. You have passion and love for your people and those too are powerful, but only if you gain allies who have much of the former."

Makena lowers her head and slips into the back seat of the car. "So, today was for nothing, then?"

Arachar kneels down and grabs her hands and looks gently into her eyes. "No, Madam Aalee. Today was not in vain. For you have gained an ally in me. I do have a little of both money and power, and I will use what I have to help you."

One Hour Later, Office of President Amoi

"Never forget, Daniel, that if it were not for me, you would not be sitting in that chair. All the coastal provinces are loyal to me, and their representatives will vote the way I tell them to," Undersecretary Bosher Arachar says as he meets President Amoi's nervous gaze.

"Bosher, please, I publicly defended her on the parliamentary floor and called for immediate action by Parliament while promising action of my own. What else do you expect of me, my old friend?"

Undersecretary Arachar takes off his glasses and leans into President Amoi's face. "I expect you to keep that dog Tumba on a short leash, and I expect you to see that Makena Aalee lives a long and productive life."

President Amoi holds up a hand to stave off Arachar's invasion of his personal space, then stands and walks around his desk and shakes his finger at the man. "Remember who you are addressing, Undersecretary. If you must know, I have already warned Tumba that he will be shot if he takes any action against you. As for this youthful woman from the coast"—he smiles mischievously—"what is it, Bosher? She seems a little too young for you. What would your wife say, hey?"

Bosher rolls his eyes and huffs. "You are such a fool, Daniel. She is the great-granddaughter of Tumaini Aalee. It is his very cause that she spoke to you and the others about today. If our predecessors had backed him in his bid for your office sixty years ago, who could tell where our nation would be today. His name still commands respect. She could ignite a fire in our people that neither you nor I could stand against. I for one will stand with her and maybe finish the work her ancestor started. I suggest you decide on which side of this historical event you wish to land!" He steps back and raises an eyebrow. "As for my wife, I insist that you stop bringing her up, even in private."

President Amoi slinks back to his chair. A look of desperation crosses his face as he contemplates the undersecretary's words. "Bosher, we needed money. Our treasury is being drained by the demands our poor country puts on it. General Tumba offered a temporary solution. He promised me it would be sporadic and go hardly noticed. I know now that he has allowed it to go further than he promised me it would, but now I will make a bold and public effort for all our people to see. Surely that will appease Madam Aalee's pleas for help."

Undersecretary Arachar stares at President Amoi for a moment, then shakes his head and walks toward the door. Without looking back, he says, "Daniel, you are a pathetic puppet of a man. Our country needs a leader, not a politician. Mind my words—if anything happens to Madam Aalee, I will use all my resources to expose and depose you." He opens the door and walks out.

President Amoi turns his chair toward the window and stares off into the sky. "What do you propose we do now, Tumba? He can hurt us … a lot."

Next to the fireplace that sits to the right of his desk, a hidden door opens and General Tumba steps through it from the president's private lounge. "I believe that Undersecretary Arachar and Madam Aalee must meet their end together. My associate from Afghanistan has many resources at his disposal. Let me confer with him, and we'll develop a plan to quietly rid us of them both."

"Do what you must, Tumba."

September 17, 1979, Mombasa, Kenya

Makena sits at her desk on the second floor in the little office they gave her at the police headquarters in Mombasa. Her life has truly been a whirlwind of activity since leaving the capital. Though she is no warrior in the conventional sense of the word, like her ancestor she has his spirit and drive. For countless weeks she has spent herself meeting with local officials in government, law enforcement, and the military. Her passion has inspired many to join her cause and the news outlets are starting to recognize Makena Aalee as the descendant of her famed ancestor.

Undersecretary Arachar has been her truest of allies, and true to his word, he has opened many doors for her to work with the police and military to aid her in the campaign to stamp out the slave trading of Kenya's citizens. As she is going over the most recent results of a police raid on the docks earlier that week, that resulted in rescuing thirty children from being shipped out in cargo containers that were being loaded onto an ocean liner, the phone on her desk rings.

"Madam Aalee, it's Bosher. How are things going there in Mombasa?"

"Very well, Undersecretary. As you know, we just completed our fifth and largest rescue. The local police are coming around and are complying with the directives you sent, and we have even exposed a few of the corrupt ones who are part of the slave trade. The fall festival downtown is tonight, and we're getting ready for our sting operation to catch some slavers that will target that event."

"That's why I'm calling. I do not agree with your actively taking part in the operation. You're not trained police or military personnel. The danger is too great. If anything were to happen to you at this stage in your campaign, all our efforts would come to naught."

"Undersecretary, please, how can I ask others to back this cause if I don't commit to it fully? These vermin we are after tonight are the worst of the lot. They lie in wait in dark alleys and isolated areas around the city and target young girls and boys who stray from the crowd. They're like the old-style pirates that raided our coasts in my great-grandfather's day. Capturing a gang of these devils will go a long way in bolstering support for you and me."

There is a lengthy silence on the other end of the phone. She can feel that the undersecretary has grown very protective of her. Being twenty years younger, she has begun to hold him in her heart like a dear uncle.

Finally Bosher sighs. "Very well, if you insist, Madam Aalee. I've dispatched a military unit from the capital. They'll serve as your bodyguards. They'll answer only to me and will be at your complete disposal. I left specific instructions with their commander to never leave you alone. She and her unit should be at your office very soon. Her name is Colonel Adessa Eloi. She and her unit have served as governmental executive protection specialists throughout Kenya for some time. She's accomplished. I trust her."

"Thank you, Undersecretary. I'll comply with your wishes and humbly accept the help. Our people are leaving to patrol the northern part of Mombasa soon. Will she be here before then?"

"She should be there at any moment ..."

Makena hears a knock at the door. She hangs up the phone, peers through the stained-glass window and sees the silhouette of a military officer. She opens the door and invites her in.

A tall, stern, beautiful woman in a Kenya Security Force colonel's uniform steps into Makena's office. "Madam Aalee, I am Colonel Adessa Eloi. Undersecretary Arachar dispatched my unit to be your personal bodyguard."

Makena smiles up at the colonel and holds out her hand. "Colonel Eloi, it's a pleasure to meet you. It's quite a shock for me to think that such a professional as you will protect me. The undersecretary just spoke very highly of you."

Colonel Eloi shakes Makena's hand. "Bosher Arachar and I have known each other for a long time, Madam Aalee. He's a brilliant statesman and a truly kind man."

"Please have a seat, Colonel, and please call me Makena. I cannot persuade the undersecretary to call me by my first name, but I'd feel much more comfortable if you would."

Colonel Eloi takes the seat in front of the desk and flashes a generous smile. "It would honor me to use your first name, Makena, in private, but I'll insist that I and my unit address you as Madam Aalee at all other times. I had a lengthy conversation with Bosher about how important what you are doing here is. Because of your great-grandfather's legacy, we need to build your reputation upon his to win the support of the people."

Makena grabs the glass of water on her desk to mask the blush the colonel's words have caused. "It'll take a little getting used to, but I've had a similar conversation with the undersecretary, and he thinks the same. You see, I grew up in the village of my ancestors. We have always owned land because our family was the ancestral ruler of our tiny village. But that position died with my great-grandfather, and we became simple farmers, like those around us. By the time I was born, his legacy still burned strong in our villagers' hearts, but he was old and feeble, and he rarely came out of his home. I only met him once before he died. He asked me to carry on in his stead.

"Later, my parents told me that he asked all his close relatives the same thing. His son, my grandfather, tried and was killed a few years after my father was born. Since that time, my family has thought of his goals as unattainable."

She stops for a moment and takes a deep breath to calm her heart.

"I am not a warrior like Tumaini Aalee was, Colonel. But as I grew up in our village, I saw for myself that his words to me were based on reality and not some old-fashioned notion or desire to regain lost greatness. He was right. People still go missing and slave traders from Islamic lands still deal in the buying and selling of our people. I chose to do what I can in his stead."

Colonel Eloi's hard stare softens, and her eyes become moist. "My grandmother would sit all her grandchildren around the fire on late summer nights when we visited her here on the coast and tell us how when she was only eight years old, Tumaini Aalee and his brave warriors saved her and her sisters from being taken as slaves. I can still see her eyes sparkle with mystical glee as she told us how he and his warriors appeared out of the night shadows dressed in jungle warrior fashion, armed with spears and pistols as they stormed the camp, screaming their battle cries and annihilating the slavers." She rubs the tears out of her eyes and continues. "Tumaini Aalee is the reason I joined the security force. I too want to continue his legacy and protect our people from the vile institution of slavery."

Colonel Eloi stands and straightens her uniform. "So, Mad … uh … Makena, when do we leave for this next operation of yours?"

Makena looks down at the clock on her desk then stands and takes up some things. "Right now. The transport will be waiting for us outside. Uh, I do not think that there will be enough room for your entire unit, but I think we can fit you in with us. Will that suffice?"

"That is acceptable, Makena. As long as I can remain with you my unit will follow behind and provide cover."

One hour later, an unmarked police car sits on the southern perimeter of the festival. Colonel Eloi's unit is standing around near the car, all wearing civilian clothes. The police assigned to the stakeout are near them in police cars, patrolling within a two-block radius. Makena's contact with the local police told her that if any of the shanghai gangs were out tonight, this is the most likely place for them to strike, because it's closest to the docks where they would want to bring their captives.

Makena reaches down and grabs her bottle of water and Colonel Eloi places her hand on her arm and shakes it. She looks up as a group of young people are walking by them, headed away from the festival. There are two boys and four girls, and they are laughing and acting silly until they see Makena and Eloi in the car, and then they warily eye Makena and quickly shuffle down the street.

Before she can say a word, Colonel Eloi picks up her radio. "Wait until they're a block away, then follow them. Keep them within eyeshot, but don't let them see you." A man standing nearby wearing an earpiece connected to a handheld radio under his jacket turns to the side and nods his head, then subtly motions for the rest to follow him.

Colonel Eloi looks at Makena. "Inform your police to take two patrol cars—one goes two blocks right and the other goes two blocks left of the street that those young people just headed down. Slowly move up until we call them."

Makena uses her radio to contact the police assigned to her and gives them the instructions. Colonel Eloi, who is in the driver's seat, waits a few moments for the young people and her men following them to be far enough down the street for her to follow. She puts the car in drive and without turning on her headlights lets the vehicle creep forward. They are within two blocks when Colonel Eloi's radio chirps. "Colonel, two vans just cut in front of the group and men are getting out now with guns. What are your orders?"

"If they hurt any of them, intercede. Otherwise, let them take them."

Astonished, Makena grabs her arm. "What are you doing? We have to stop them now!"

Colonel Eloi reaches up and grabs her hand while still driving slowly and keeping her eyes forward. "Makena, we need to find out where they're taking them. There are others that are being taken tonight. We must follow these back to where they are going, and then we can save many more."

Understanding dawns in Makena's eyes. She flashes Eloi a devious smile, then uses her radio to contact the police. "Two vans have just intercepted the group three blocks ahead. Do not stop them. We will follow and see where they are going. Please call in all the units we have tonight to follow them."

There is a moment of silence, then a frantic voice comes back over the speaker. "Madam Aalee, we can't let them go. We must apprehend them now. I'm proceeding to their location."

Colonel Eloi grabs the radio out of Makena's hand. "Officer, this is Colonel Eloi of the Kenyan National Security Force. You are to comply with Madam Aalee's request. I have complete command of this operation by the authority of Undersecretary Arachar."

A few moments go by with no response from the patrol car, and Eloi presses the button on the mic and continues. "Be warned, my people are monitoring all of your communications, so do not contact anyone on another frequency, or we will know about it. If you do not comply, I will have you arrested along with your superiors and replace you with my people. Is that understood?"

The police car that Makena and Eloi are talking to is now stopped, and the two officers inside are yelling at each other. "Why should we listen to her? We set this whole operation up by way of General Tumba, and he outranks this Colonel Eloi. He'll back up our proceeding as planned."

"This is why I outrank you, idiot! General Tumba told us not to let anyone know that it involves him. If we use his name, he'll have both of us shot. Besides, this Colonel Eloi answers directly to Undersecretary Arachar, and even President Amoi will not openly come out against him. We have no choice but to follow her orders."

The other man sighs and shakes his head. "If we follow them back to where they are taking the cargo, the entire operation in Mombasa will be ruined. This Madam Aalee—there'll be no stopping her after this."

His partner stares at him for a moment. "Do not underestimate General Tumba, my friend. He has many resources." He then grabs his radio. "You are in command, Colonel. We will do as you say."

"A wise decision, officer. Now, have all your people stay behind and out of sight as we proceed. I will have my entire security force meet me at the Shanghai gang's destination. We will perform the arrest. The police are to take care of perimeter security only."

Makena listens in confusion.

Eloi puts a hand on her shoulder. "I know you think that you have friends here in the police force now. But the truth is they've been conspiring with the slave traders and only throwing you scraps here and there to keep you pacified, thinking that you're making progress in your campaign. But what you've caught so far are simply pawns."

"But we rescued thirty children just this week! Surely that was a huge dent in their efforts!" Makena exclaims.

"Makena, do not misinterpret my meaning. You are on the verge of accomplishing something truly great here. But tonight, we will ignore the pawns and take a couple of knights off the board!"

Thirty minutes later, the two vans that abducted the young people at the festival pull into a large storage facility next to the dock. Once inside, they pull over to an area with thirty similar vans parked in rows of ten. Forty armed men are escorting dozens of young girls with their hands tied behind their backs and sacks pulled over their heads to large storage containers that are transported by cargo ships. Screaming and crying can be heard throughout the facility and people are pushed, shoved, and sometimes beaten. One girl breaks away and runs. But being blindfolded and bound, she trips after only a few paces and two of the armed guards kick her in her stomach twice and pick her up and put her back in line.

A voice booms over the loudspeaker. "Do not damage the merchandise. Whatever we lose from this shipment will come out of your cut."

As the men are stepping out of the vans that have just pulled in and getting ready to unload their prisoners, the man who was just speaking on the intercom looks over in their direction in astonishment. He throws the microphone down and runs over to the driver of the first van. "Keanjaho, what are you doing here?"

The man gets out of the van and stares at him. He throws up both hands. "What do you mean, what am I doing here? I'm bringing back our cargo!" His eyes then lower to the ground and he mumbles, "You put us closest. We were lucky and captured six tonight."

The man's eyes dart nervously back and forth and then focus on the driver. "That is my main issue with you, Keanjaho. You have two vans and yet your team always comes back with the lowest numbers. The last two vans that pulled in before you brought us twenty people. That's why we were going to let them have—"

"You were going to let who have what, boss?"

A loud noise makes both men turn their heads to the entrance of the warehouse. Two military assault vehicles armed with grenade launchers and fifty-caliber machine guns and several army transport trucks with dozens of armed, uniformed Kenyan Security Forces pull into the facility.

As the soldiers unload and form a perimeter covering all exits to the streets, a voice from a handheld speaker booms. "This is Colonel Adessa Eloi of the Kenyan Security Force. I order you to put down your weapons and surrender yourselves to my custody. We will meet any resistance with lethal force!"

Keanjaho and his boss are so shocked and scared that they throw their hands up and fall to their knees. But from an upper level of the building, shots ring out at Colonel Eloi's men. She jumps behind the nearest assault vehicle and then looks back to the car where she left Makena and yells, "Get down!" She turns toward her men who were with them at the start of the night and yells, "Protect Madam Aalee!" Then she takes her handheld PA device and directs it at the assault vehicles. "Return fire at those offices!"

Two men manning the fifty-caliber guns point them at the offices and open fire while the rest move at ground level. The noise from the machine gun fire is earsplitting and Colonel Eloi has to turn her handheld PA up when she yells, "Protect the prisoners! Watch where you are shooting!" She looks up at the damage her fifty-caliber guns are doing to the offices on the upper level, and a big smile creases her face as she watches the windows and walls dissolve before her eyes. Once they finish, she yells, "Cease fire!"

Cautiously, Eloi surveys the area for any active combatants. Some of her men start searching the parked vans; others head toward the cargo containers where men with guns are now on their knees with their hands on their heads. There are dozens of young women in lines in front of the cargo containers with their hands tied behind their backs and hoods over their heads. They have thrown themselves to the ground and are screaming and crying in fear. Her men are still making their way to that group when a couple of men with assault rifles peer around the storage containers. It looks like they are trying to make their way toward the prisoners to use them as human shields.

Colonel Eloi reaches over and grabs a rifle with a scope on it from the assault vehicle she is standing behind, puts it to her shoulder and aims at the closest of the two men. As he is reaching out to grab a young girl in front of him, she squeezes the trigger and the man drops to the ground with a hole in the center of his forehead. She then aims at the other one who is trying to flee and shoots him in his hip. He also falls to the ground. She yells, "Take the one still alive back to a medical unit! Tell them to make sure he's conscious. I want to talk to him."

She makes sure that the combatants are all subdued, then walks over to the car she and Makena arrived in. "Madam Aalee, I believe it is safe for you to come out now. Please join me as we inspect what these vile men were doing here."

Makena jumps out of the car and runs in front of Colonel Eloi to the closest group of prisoners and starts undoing their bindings and taking their hoods off. She looks back at Eloi. "Please order your men to help me. Then have someone bring these kids some water and anything else they need!"

"Of course, Madam Aalee." She looks back at one of her sergeants.

"You heard her. This is her operation, so do as she says. And sergeant …"

"Yes, Colonel Eloi?"

"Have our friends join us and tell them they are free to set up anywhere they want to."

The soldier salutes, makes a call on his radio and then steps over to Makena to help her. They make it to a girl whose head is still covered. Makena takes the hood off and is shocked. She looks no older than twelve or thirteen. The teenager's eyes are wild with astonishment. "You were the one sitting in that car watching us when we left the festival! We thought you were with those men who captured us."

Makena puts both hands on her shoulders and gently shakes her and stares into her frightened eyes. "Oh, no. We had to follow your captors back here so we could rescue the rest of these kids. I promise you that I will do everything in my power to see that men like these can never hurt someone like you again."

The teenage girl meets Makena's compassionate gaze with uncertainty for a few moments, but then her shoulders sag and tears well in her eyes. She clutches onto Makena and sobs in her arms. Makena holds her gently and strokes her hair, then kisses the top of her head. A flash of light bursts behind them, and they both turn to see a TV news crew with several cameras pointing at them and the other freed prisoners.

A reporter stands next to Colonel Eloi and endeavors to interview her. "Colonel Eloi, how did your team know where to find the abductors in this facility? The police in Mombasa could never track them."

Eloi looks straight at the camera and points at Makena. "For that answer and more, I suggest that you ask the great-granddaughter of Tumaini Aalee. Her name is Makena, and she is in charge of this entire operation." The reporter immediately rushes over to Makena and starts barraging her with questions.

Four hours later, Makena and Colonel Eloi are helping her men load the last of the prisoners on a bus to take them back to their homes.

Makena asks, "What was the last count, Colonel Eloi?"

"We rescued five hundred and thirty people tonight, most under the age of sixteen and most female. Also, we arrested eighty-two abductors and killed ten. We think the two that tried to use one prisoner as a human shield are major bosses. We have one man in custody who was overseeing the truck traffic on the floor here. He says he will testify to that, for a deal. This little operation of yours has severely crippled this organization's efforts in Mombasa. Now we can look forward to greater attention from the entire country." She puts both hands on Makena's shoulders. "Tumaini Aalee's legend lives again, and we have you to thank for that, Madam Aalee!"

One Week Later, Office of General Amri Tumba

General Tumba sits at his desk reading the reports coming in from up and down the coast describing how shanghai gangs are being shut down by local volunteer militia and police sympathetic to Makena's cause. Something has to be done and done quickly or all his dreams of taking over the country and deposing President Amoi will come to naught. The intercom on his desk buzzes.

"Yes, what is it?"

"Sir, President Amoi is walking into the office right now!"

Tumba jumps up from his desk and rushes over to the door and opens it just as the president is reaching for the knob.

"General Tumba, we need to talk!" Amoi storms over to Tumba's bar, pours himself a glass of rum, and sits in the chair in front of the desk.

Tumba walks around the desk and takes a seat. "What can I do for you, Mr. President?"

"Don't be coy, Tumba! You know exactly why I'm here. Since the raid on the facility in Mombasa last week, the news has spread. The press has plastered the picture of Makena Aalee holding that teenage girl they rescued on every television screen and newspaper in the country for the last six days. I've heard that *Time Magazine* is interested in doing a story on her and using the picture as the cover in an upcoming issue. That dog of yours from Afghanistan called me on the phone today and threatened to leak information to the news media, proving our involvement with the human trafficking in Kenya. How does he have my private number, anyway?"

"Mr. President, you know that we are not calling it human trafficking anymore," Tumba replies sarcastically as he lights his cigar. "Madam Aalee has exposed it for what it truly is and has always been—slave trading!" The president is seething and in no mood for jokes, so Tumba continues. "Colonel Niazai has repeatedly called me over the past few days and has threatened my life at least half a dozen times. As for your private number, you know that his boss is now completely owned by the Russians. And the KGB does have ways of getting any information it wants."

"Tumba, we have an election coming up in October. All the seats in Parliament are at stake. With the reputation that this Makena Aalee is gaining, whoever even appears to oppose her crusade will be demolished in the polls. All the coastal provinces have already pledged their support, and far too many of the others are wavering.

If I do anything publicly that looks like I'm not fully behind her and Undersecretary Arachar, they will pull away from me and I will have no power in that body at all."

"Yes, Mr. President, and you will be up for reelection in another year yourself. So, Madam Aalee would seem to be marching into a position as a person who could oppose you and win."

President Amoi springs out of his seat. The glass of rum drops from his hand and spills on the floor. His face turns red and contorted as he shakes a finger at Tumba. "You watch your mouth, Tumba. I see what game you're playing here. Some backwater village girl whose only claim to notoriety is a genetic connection to an age-old folk hero will not depose me. Nor will I stand idly by and watch you manipulate things behind the scenes, so that it all turns to your favor. I will declare martial law and have you both executed before that day ever presents itself!"

Extending both hands in a gesture of peace, Tumba stands and meekly replies, "President Amoi, please calm yourself. We have the same problem and face the same enemies. Makena Aalee is not your only foe here. Undersecretary Arachar is the genuine power we both need to be concerned with. Now that his attack dog Colonel Eloi is guarding Makena Aalee, she is almost untouchable. We need to come up with a strategy that rids us of the three of them while still keeping you in favor with the people."

"What do you propose, Tumba?"

"Patience for now. We must make it through these next elections first. I propose that we both publicly give our adamant support to all that Undersecretary Arachar and Madam Aalee are doing on the coast. Then we encourage our friends in Parliament to do the same. When we have secured your power in Parliament after the elections, then we can take care of the problem."

President Amoi takes a fresh glass and pours himself another helping of Tumba's rum. "What about your Afghanistan friends?

Won't they be upset with us about Madam Aalee running roughshod over their organization for the next month and a half?"

"Pasto Niazai has already pulled his primary people from Kenya and is targeting other countries until we can get this setback under control. All that's left are the local gangs that freelance for him and his associates. He doesn't care how many of them are eliminated. He and I have discussed this at length, and he believes the best way for us to get rid of our problem is to lure Undersecretary Arachar, Madam Aalee, and Colonel Eloi out of the country to a place where he can take them out."

October 20, 1979, Office of Makena Aalee, Mombasa Police HQ

Makena, Colonel Eloi, and Undersecretary Arachar sit in front of the TV in her office watching the coverage of the latest parliamentary elections. The last of the polls closed over two hours ago and the announcer is reading the results.

"In a landslide victory for President Amoi's administration, all incumbent members of Parliament have been reelected for another four years of service. Since Madam Aalee's impassioned speech on the parliamentary floor five months ago and his staunch show of support for her, President Amoi has substantially gained in popularity throughout the country. All the incumbents subsequently pledged their support to the cause of stamping out the rising human trafficking activity in Kenya. With Madam Aalee's determined attitude and the full support of the government, an estimated three thousand people have been rescued from human trafficking gangs up and down the coast. President Amoi's popularity is such that there have been no announcements of anyone declaring that they will run against him in next year's presidential election."

Undersecretary Arachar turns the TV off, then holds up his hand in a cautioning gesture. "This is excellent news in that we will not see that support for us diminish in the foreseeable future. But don't forget, half the people who are publicly supporting our efforts have also lost millions because of it. That includes President Amoi. These people do not forget or forgive this kind of offense against them. When they think it's safe, they will retaliate, and we must be ready."

Colonel Eloi steps over to him and places both hands on his shoulders. "Bosher, you must run against President Amoi. The coastal provinces are already behind you. With Makena's support you could win, and for once we would have a leader who is not a corrupt puppet."

He removes his glasses and rubs his weary eyes. "I know you're right, Adessa. It's just that I thought I could do better by working behind the scenes and controlling what Parliament voted on. I have had the position of undersecretary through three different administrations. You know how the game of politics is played in our country. Once a man leaves the office of president, he usually has to live the rest of his life abroad, or be constantly on guard against old rivals."

Colonel Eloi laughs. "If any one of them tries, they will have to go through me and my people first, Bosher. And that's not an easy thing to do, is it?"

"No, Adessa. It is not." He then looks over to Makena, sitting behind her desk. "But now we have Madam Aalee to protect as well."

Makena jumps up out of her chair. "Don't you use me as an excuse to not do what you know you must. This is about the people of Kenya and not just one person. We have proven that we are a force for good as we stand together and support one another. As you have stood with me and taken risks, I will do no less for you."

Chapter 8

Unexpected Career Curves

November 4, 1979, Pentagon, Washington, DC

LIEUTENANT TOMMY WILLIAMS WALKS THROUGH the naval section of the Pentagon on his way to the office of the secretary of the navy. Though it's a personal visit, he is still in his dress blues and sporting his brand new Naval Special Warfare (SEAL) Officer's pin on his lapel. Having put in his seventy-one weeks of SQT (SEAL Qualification Training) and a year and a half of SEAL graduate training, he is as ready as anyone can be to be deployed and serve his country.

As his hand grips the handle of the door into the outer office of his late father's Annapolis Academy roommate, he can't help but think about how he has been a little nervous concerning this meeting. Secretary Thompson, like his father, graduated from Annapolis in the early 1950s, and like his father pursued a career as a lawyer in the navy JAG Corps. Tommy's dad, Rodney Williams, made it to commander before he left the navy to join the State Department. Within a few years they appointed him as ambassador to Japan.

Tommy will never let anyone in authority know that he joined the SEALs to be trained to take down the agent that killed his father. But it is still the fire in his soul that   drove him through and made him excel beyond all his peers during the two and a half years of SEAL training that he has just finished.

He takes a calming breath and walks into the reception area of Secretary Thompson's office. He puts on his best smile and steps up to the receptionist's desk. It is manned by a beautiful young African American woman in her middle twenties. She is just finishing a phone call and is writing something on a pad when he steps up and says, "Hi. Excuse me, uh ..." He looks down at the Pentagon clearance badge on her lapel and continues. "Alysha, Lieutenant Tommy Williams to see Secretary Thompson. I have an appointment."

She looks up briefly to check the Pentagon pass on his lapel then reaches for the phone and punches a number. "Mr. Secretary, Lieutenant Williams is here. Yes, sir, I will." She turns and points to a hall to her left. "You can go right in, Lieutenant Williams. It's the only door in that hall."

Tommy stands there for a moment, trying to think of something clever to say to this beautiful woman. She looks up at him. "You'd better hurry up, Lieutenant. He's been waiting for over an hour for you. The secretary has a very full day today."

"Uh, okay. Thank you, Alysha."

He hurries down the hall. Just as he is about to go in the door, Alysha turns and looks at him, then turns to look at another girl across the floor of the reception area and fans her hand in front of her face. *What a hunk!* The other girl giggles and nods her head.

Tommy knocks on the door and is greeted by a familiar voice. "Come in." He walks into Secretary William Thompson's office. The secretary and the ambassador were best friends, and Tommy's dad always made him call the man Uncle Bill. But seeing how he is visiting him at work, he's determined to call him by his official title. Like his dad, the secretary is a middle-aged African American. At the funeral for his dad, he told Tommy to look him up after he finished his law degree and started working as a JAG lawyer for the navy. When he changed his plans and went into SEAL training, he thought that Thompson might not approve and so he never reached out to him. Then he got his orders to report to DC, Naval Intelligence Division, for some more training, and in his orders was a note from the secretary saying, *Once you are in town, make an appointment and come see me.*

Tommy steps in, comes to attention, and salutes. "Mr. Secretary, Lieutenant Williams reporting, sir." The secretary is on his feet and holds out his hand. "At ease, Tommy. This meeting is informal."

Tommy relaxes a little and takes the chair in front of the secretary's desk. "Thanks for the invitation to come and see you, Mr. Secretary. How long has it been, sir? Since Dad's funeral, I believe."

Secretary Thompson leans back in his chair and lets out a vast sigh and then smiles. "You know, Tommy, I don't have any children of my own, and when your dad was killed three years ago, I was all ready to step in and be there for you like he was. Then you signed up for the SEALs. Damn, I was so mad I wanted to spit nails. You were half a percentage point from graduating number one in your class at Annapolis. You could have gone to Harvard or Yale law school on the navy's dime, no questions asked." He shakes his head and picks up a letter and reads it out loud.

"*Lt. Tommy Williams is one of the most impressive candidates we have ever had to go through SGT training. He has showed an unusually high aptitude in combining original maverick-style thinking with cohesive team leadership, and stellar cooperation and communication with his superiors. Lt. Williams can follow and lead to the highest standard and can also be trusted to think on his feet and outside the nine dots when the need arises.*

I recommend him for classified stealth intelligence operations. Captain William Fargo, Senior SGT Instructor/Base Commander."

Tommy sits in the chair and stares at the secretary for a few moments, shakes his head, and looks at the floor while awkwardly squirming in his chair. He finally says, "Geez, Uncle Bill, I thought that guy hated my guts. The entire time I was there, all he did was yell at me and embarrass me in front of everyone." He then looks up and is greeted by the smirk on the secretary's face and realizes what he just called him. "I'm sorry, Mr. Secretary. That letter just stunned me."

"It's okay. I said this was an informal meeting. Oh, and since you did not try to get my niece's phone number in the outer office when you came in, I'll go easy on you from here on."

He chuckles and puts the letter down. Aware that Tommy is even more off balance, he raises his hand to stave off Tommy's embarrassment. "Alysha is my sister's daughter. She's here for an internship before she starts graduate school at Georgetown next year. Most of the young officers who don't know she's my niece try to hit on her, but she's good at taking care of herself. The way she handled you was fun to watch."

He points to a monitor behind his chair that shows Alysha's reception desk and the area surrounding it. "I can even listen in, if I want." He pushes a button and office sounds come in over a little speaker.

Before he can push the button again, Alysha looks up and says, "Mr. Secretary, I have a call from the White House coming through right now. Apparently, there's another crisis in Iran."

Tommy gets up, but the secretary motions for him to stay. "We upped your security clearance when you reported to Washington. You can stay. This could prove educational."

Tommy sits back down as the secretary picks up his phone and punches a flashing red button on the end labeled *Chief.* "Mr. President, Secretary Thompson, sir. How may I be of assistance?" He listens for a few moments. "I understand, Mr. President. I will confer with the Joint Chiefs. We'll give you our recommendations ASAP. Thank you, sir. Goodbye."

All the training and discipline that Tommy's been through fails to contain his curiosity. He coughs and mumbles, "So, what did the president want, sir?"

The secretary shakes his head. "Apparently the embassy in Iran has been overrun by dissident students. They're demanding we release the former Shah of Iran immediately."

"Sounds like a job for the navy SEALs, Mr. Secretary," Tommy replies a little too quickly.

Secretary Thompson smiles. "Well, I don't disagree, Tommy. But knowing the president, this one will go straight to Delta Force if they sanction military action. But the secretary of state will insist on diplomacy at all costs; and with the election year coming up, the president will do whatever he thinks gives him the most advantage with the American people."

Tommy squirms in his seat. "You know, all these politicians are making us look like a bunch of wusses all over the world. We need to stop messing around with these folks and show them they can't push us around, sir!"

"From your mouth to God's ears, Tommy. I agree. But we have to follow the commander in chief. Now, before I head to my meeting with the other chiefs, let me tell you what I wanted to see you about. You're reporting to Naval Intelligence later for what your orders say is further training. Well, that's only partly true." Secretary Thompson leans back in his chair and smiles. "It's quite serendipitous that your father and I were so close. His having been an ambassador and my being the secretary of the navy makes it easy for me to set you up as the perfect African American golden boy of the navy."

Tommy sits up and stares at the secretary for a moment, then jumps to his feet. "Hold on, Uncle Bill! I didn't just go through two and a half years of hell to come out and be someone's poster child. I'm a SEAL officer, and that's how I want to serve!"

The secretary shakes his head and laughs. "You have Rodney's temper, that's for damn sure. Tommy, sit down. I don't have as much time to talk as I wanted."

Tommy straightens his uniform and sits back down.

"Appearances can deceive, Tommy. The golden boy image will be your cover. When you report to Naval Intelligence's CO, Captain Terry Smithers, he'll explain all this to you. Your SEAL trainer said you'd be best for classified intelligence stealth operations, and that's what you'll be doing."

Secretary Thompson stands up, stuffs some papers in a satchel, and heads toward the door. Tommy leans back in his chair, resting his chin in his palm. "So, am I still a SEAL, or am I something else?"

"Oh, you'll always be a SEAL, Tommy. But even more so than the regulars in your outfit. You'll have to get used to no one ever knowing what it is you really do."

Secretary Thompson leaves the office with Tommy still sitting in the chair. He looks around the room and recognizes some pictures of the secretary and his father on a fishing trip. He remembers his dad telling him that of all the people in the world, he can always count on his old Annapolis roommate to have his back. Tommy walks over to the picture and picks it up. He smiles at the image of his dad, standing arm in arm with Thompson, holding a two-and-a-half-foot halibut they had just pulled out of the bay near Baltimore thirty years ago. He sighs. "Okay, Pops, you trusted this guy. I guess I will too." He puts the picture back on the shelf and heads down the hall to the reception area.

He finds Alysha staring at him from her desk. She smiles and rolls her eyes. "I thought I recognized your name. You're Ambassador Williams's son. He and Uncle Bill were best friends."

Tommy walks over to her and holds out his hand. "And you are Secretary Thompson's niece."

She lightly touches his hand and twirls back to her desk. "Guilty as charged, Lieutenant." She reaches down and grabs an envelope and hands it to him. "These are orders to be at the Naval PR Department office next Tuesday for a photo op. Uncle Bill asked me to make sure you show up on time, so I'll pick you up that morning from your housing. Captain Smithers of Naval Intelligence is already aware of this, so he'll make sure your schedule is cleared."

Tommy picks up the orders. "Okay, my address is—"

"We know where you're staying, Lieutenant. I'll be there at 8:00 a.m., sharp. I have to be at work here by 10:00 that morning, so don't be late or the secretary will eat you alive, and so will I."

Tommy nods and heads to the exit.

The woman that Alysha talked to earlier leans across her desk. "The secretary said to send a car with a marine driver to pick him up for that photo shoot. What are you up to, girl?"

Alysha offers a mischievous smile. "Let's just say that this girl wants to know Lieutenant Tommy Williams a little better."

They both giggle and go back to work.

Outside in the main hallway, Tommy spots a marine guard stationed at the door. "Corporal, can you tell me how to find Captain Smithers's office at Naval Intel?"

The corporal points to his left. "Five sections down that way. Just check in with the receptionist at Naval Intel when you get there, sir."

"Thanks, corporal. I'll do that." He turns in that direction and walks to his next appointment.

Office of Captain Terry Smithers, Commanding Officer of Naval Intelligence

Captain Terry Smithers is a 1955 Annapolis grad. His aptitude for analytical thinking and grasp of world politics earned him several posts in naval intelligence before being assigned to the big chair. He's short and wears round-rimmed glasses that always look like they are about to fall off his face. And since he's naturally blond, it's sometimes hard to notice the mustache and goatee he meticulously trims and shapes. One of the first things the current president did when he took office was to fire the top eight hundred CIA operatives. Since that time, Captain Smithers's organization has been more heavily relied on to fill in the void those firings caused.

He sits at his desk with Lt. Commander Larry Higgins, one of his black ops unit commanders, going over several portfolios of recently graduated SEAL officers. He's had his doubts about some of Secretary Thompson's recommendations for the new unit he's developing but also has to admit that every one of the SEALs he has looked at is a superior officer. His misgivings lie more in the candidate's ability to lead a double life. SEALs are a no-nonsense outfit, and every one of them has gone through some of the harshest military training in the world. But now he will ask some of them to make their family, friends, and comrades think that they have opted out of that and taken cushier, high-profile assignments.

He pulls out the portfolio of the next candidate they are to brief. "This one worries me, Larry. He is the son of Ambassador Rodney Williams, who was assassinated three years ago in Japan. This kid could have done anything he wanted to in the navy. Graduated number two in his class at Annapolis. A month after graduation his dad was taken out by sniper fire right in front of him while they were eating lunch at an outdoor café in downtown Tokyo. After that, he abandoned his plans to enter law school and be a JAG like his dad and instead applied to the SEALs. He went through the program with a vengeance. His chief trainer said he's the best he's ever seen. Said in the report that the more grief he gave the kid, the harder he pushed." He puts the portfolio down and looks at the commander. "I think this kid is out for vengeance and is looking for anyone who'll give him a chance to get it."

Higgins picks up Lt. Williams's portfolio and looks at it for a moment, laughs, and puts it down. "Shit, Captain, I thought Will Fargo thought I was the best to go through the program. This kid must be something else. I'll tell you this—if he got Will to vouch for him, then this Williams can keep himself locked in and on scope no matter what's eating him, and I can work with a guy like that. Besides, didn't we decide that the hit on Ambassador Williams was KGB related?"

Captain Smithers raises an eyebrow. "That was our best guess, but nothing conclusive ever came out of the investigation. Why?"

"Well, Captain, it just seems to me that this kid might be exactly what we're looking for. He's a SEAL all right, but he's also pissed off about what happened to his dad. These days ninety percent of what we do is to play cat and mouse with Russian intelligence, which includes dancing with the KGB. Let's just be upfront with him and say if he'll play ball with us and take on this African American golden boy image, we'll keep him in the loop about the investigation of his father's assassination, which is still ongoing, last I heard."

"That's a potentially career-ending game. You want to play with the son of the secretary of the navy's dead best friend? Commander, are you sure—"

The beep of the intercom interrupts his words. "Captain Smithers, Lt. Williams is here for his appointment, sir."

"Send him in, Barbara. Hold all calls until we are done."

"Yes, sir."

An hour later, Tommy leans forward and glares at Lt. Commander Higgins. "So, what you're saying is that if I go along with this charade and be the navy's token golden boy as a cover, and then assist you in black ops stealth missions, you'll help me figure out who killed my dad?"

Before Commander Higgins can respond, Captain Smithers interjects. "Lieutenant, you've already received your orders from the secretary himself. We're here to evaluate whether you're qualified mentally and emotionally to do this kind of work. Lt. Commander Higgins is just offering you some incentive to play ball with us. But I promise you, if you pass this interview and I assign you to Larry's unit, we'll keep you posted on every detail of the investigation."

A chill of excitement buzzes through Tommy's whole body, but he feels he's got to play this one cool. He does not want these guys to have too much leverage over him. He sits straight up and smiles innocently. "You know, I bet if we work this thing right, we can make the navy look like the best place in the world for a young African American man or woman to get ahead in life. Meanwhile, the lieutenant commander and I can get in there and kick some commie ass and win the Cold War while we're doing it."

Captain Smithers glances over to Lieutenant Commander Higgins, who gives him a slight nod. He then turns back to Tommy. "Well, Lieutenant, I think we all understand each other. You're in our program. Higgins here will be your CO from here on out. Get settled in quick. Then you report to him for training and assignments. Oh, I almost forgot. On Tuesday next week we'll send a car to pick you up and take you to the Naval Public Relations studio for a photo op to begin your recruitment campaign persona. They want you in your full-dress blues, Lieutenant. Be ready at 8:00 a.m. sharp."

Tommy stands and salutes. "Sir, is there anything you can tell me about my dad?"

"We'll prepare a file for you, Tommy, which you'll get when Higgins here feels you're keeping your end of the bargain. But I'll tell you that we're about ninety percent sure it was a KGB hit. And seeing how the shot was taken from over a quarter mile away, it was done by one of the best snipers in the world. Your father was deep in negotiating some trade agreement involving the United States, China, and Japan. We know the biggest opponents to that deal were the Russians. That's all I'll tell you for now."

Tommy nods. "Thank you, sir."

"You're dismissed, Lieutenant."

Tommy turns and walks out the office door. Once on the other side he mumbles, "Yeah, tell me something I don't know about Dad, Captain."

Washington, DC, Tuesday, November 6, 1979, 8:00 a.m.

Tommy stands out on the curb of his new apartment complex in his dress blue uniform, waiting for Alysha to pick him up. A brand new, sleek, black Pontiac Firebird Trans Am pulls into the parking lot and right up to his curb. He can't help but admire the gold bird on the hood, made famous by the film *Smokey and the Bandit*. Mesmerized, he walks around the whole car admiring every square inch. As he kneels to get a better look at the front grille, the horn sounds off in his face. He looks up as Alysha opens the door and gets out of the driver's seat to yell, "Let's go, Lieutenant! I told you I'm on a tight schedule today and the clock's ticking."

Unlike the previous time he saw her, Alysha is not wearing a simple office blouse, jacket, and skirt with her Pentagon ID tag on her lapel. The ID is now strapped to a bracelet, and she is wearing a form-fitting, low-cut, tan jumpsuit with bell bottoms. And instead of being pulled back into a bun, her hair is loose and full, falling down to her shoulders, and she's sporting a couple of big gold earrings that he can't help but notice go very well with the trim of the Trans Am she is driving.

"Damn, girl, I don't know what looks better—you or this fine automobile you are driving," Tommy says as he walks around the car, opens up the passenger door, and climbs in.

Alysha puts the car in reverse and spins the tires as she backs up before he can buckle up. She then stops and puts it in first gear. "Save the cheesy lines for the bimbos, Lieutenant. I'm not trying to impress anybody but myself." She then stomps on the accelerator and peels out of the parking lot.

Tommy reaches across his shoulder and grabs the seatbelt strap and clips into the buckle. "So, what's with the tough girl act? If you're into me, all you got to do is say so ... *whoa!*"

Alysha gears down and steps on the accelerator again, and Tommy's seat flies back into the reclining position. His eyes get as big as saucers. He looks up at Alysha, who has a subtle smirk on her beautiful face.

"Damn, Lieutenant, I'm sorry. I keep meaning to get that fixed. I just got the notification for the recall about that seat latch in the mail last week. Hang on. You can lift it up at the next stoplight, and I'll show you how to secure it."

The next stoplight is about five minutes away, and Alysha is driving like a NASCAR driver, so Tommy opts to stay down until she stops. When she stops, he pulls the lever, and the seat pops back up. "You have to hold your hand on the lever and keep it in position the rest of the way."

When they get to the Naval PR office parking lot, Alysha pulls in, stops the car, and looks over at Tommy. "This is it, Lieutenant

Williams. They're all set up and ready for you. There will be a marine driver over to pick you up when they're done."

Tommy lets out a gasp and rolls his eyes. "Thanks for the thrill ride, Alysha. Next time I drive."

Alysha reaches in her purse and pulls out a little white card and hands it to him. "It's a date. Pick me up at 8:00 tonight, and don't be late."

Dumbfounded, Tommy grabs the card and looks at it. It says: Alysha Billows, 4454 East Hampton Street, Apt. B2, Georgetown, Washington, DC, 555-8721. Tommy gets out of the car while staring at the card and mumbles, "Uh, okay, Alysha. See you then."

She looks at Tommy, now standing beside the car. "One more thing, Tommy. If you tell my uncle about this, you'll regret the day you were born." She then pops the gear shift into first and peels out of the parking lot.

Tommy stands there for a moment, watching her tear down the street, then smiles. He looks at the card one more time before shoving it in his pocket and says, "Damn, she called me by my first name."

Twenty minutes later, Tommy is sitting in a chair while a twenty-something redheaded girl vigorously dabs makeup on his face and then powders it. She has a thick New York accent, and after fifteen minutes in her chair, Tommy is convinced that she does not know how to stop talking. At one point she gets so caught up in a story about what her Siamese cat did to her favorite pillow this morning that she accidentally jabs Tommy in the eye with an eyebrow brush. "Oh, geez, Lieutenant, I am so sorry! Are you okay?"

He reaches for the towel on the bench next to him and holds it to his eye, rubs it for a moment, and then a wicked smile crosses his face. "I guess that's it for the photo shoot. My eye will be all bloodshot. You don't want that in any pictures."

The girl sighs and nervously looks from side to side, then gets an idea and swiftly darts over to a cart and picks up a large bottle of saline solution and brings it back over to Tommy. She gets a large towel and wraps it around his shoulders and tucks it into his collar. "Just lean your head back, Lieutenant, and look straight up at the ceiling." She then pours some of the solution in the eye that she jabbed and follows by gently dabbing it with another towel, repeating the process several times. The treatment eventually works.

Tommy gets up and scrutinizes his eye in the mirror and grudgingly admits that there is no redness or visible damage. But, having used so much saline solution, his makeup girl has removed all of her previous work, and the top part of his shirt is soaked through. The studio manager finds another shirt that will go with his uniform before they start the photo shoot.

For the next eight hours, there is one setback after another. They do, however, take a myriad of photos in the studio and then around DC, during the latter of which Tommy meets up with some VIP admirals and politicians from around the capital. He has pictures taken with them in front of landmarks like Arlington National Cemetery, the Washington Monument, and the Lincoln Memorial. As a group comprised of one admiral, a couple of representatives, and a two-term senator from Massachusetts leave the Lincoln Memorial, the senator grabs Tommy's shoulder and holds out his hand while still in front of the camera and says, "Lieutenant, I just wanted to say that I think your father was a great patriot and an example to us all. If he were alive today, I'm sure he'd be so proud of all you have accomplished so far." He then wraps his arm around Tommy and smiles at the camera as he not-so-subtly motions for the man to take another picture of just the two of them. Tommy surmises that this is probably the first time this clown ever became aware of Ambassador Rodney Williams and his assassination in Tokyo.

At 4:30 p.m., Tommy gets out of the Naval PR car and heads back into the studio to debrief with the officer in charge. The studio manager, a Lt. Commander Garrington, grudgingly admits that he barely got one quarter of the work done that he wanted to for the day and tells Tommy they will have to schedule another day.

At 5:00 p.m., a very frustrated and exhausted Lt. Tommy Williams is waiting in the front office of the Naval PR building for his Marine Corps driver. He muses that his worst day of SGT training could not even come close to the kind of torture he had to endure today.

The front door opens and a marine looks around the room, spots Tommy and immediately salutes. "Lt. Williams. Staff Sergeant Robert Tsosie, sir."

Tommy stands up and returns the salute. "Thanks for being on time, Sergeant. This has been a long day and I got a hot date tonight, so let's head straight for my place."

The man smiles. "Sir, Lt. Commander Higgins from Naval Intel ordered me to bring you straight to him. We have a mission debrief in forty-five minutes, and the Lt. Commander don't like it when we're late."

He looks the man in the eye. "*We*, Sergeant?"

"Yes sir, Lt. Williams. I'm on the same team as you are. They canceled your original driver about fifteen minutes ago. I was just leaving my apartment, which is about five minutes from here, when they contacted me to come get you."

Tommy rolls his eyes and heads toward the door. "Well, at least now I get to go somewhere and talk about something they trained me for. Let's go, Sergeant."

Both men leave the facility and walk out to the parking lot. Staff Sergeant Tsosie points to a light gray Ford Fairlane in the parking lot. He and Tommy get in, and they head toward the Pentagon.

Tommy enters the Naval Intelligence office with Staff Sergeant Tsosie to be greeted by Lt. Commander Larry Higgins and five other navy enlisted men. Higgins motions him to the front of the room. He steps forward and gives a salute. "Lt. Williams reporting as ordered, sir."

Higgins returns the salute, looks around the room, acknowledges Tsosie, and waves his hand. "Everyone, take a seat." Tommy heads for a chair, but Higgins stops him. "Hold on, Lieutenant. Let me tell everyone who you are. Men, this is Lt. Tommy Williams. He did his SGT training under none other than our good friend, Captain Will Fargo." A couple of *whews* and sighs come from the men. Higgins continues. "Not only that, boys, but Fargo recommended him for classified intelligence ops. He said, and I quote, 'Lieutenant Williams is one of the best officers I've graduated from this program. He is a maverick that can think outside the nine dots and still maintain a disciplined adherence to the chain of command.' End of quote."

The entire room is stone-cold silent. Tommy wonders what they are thinking. He nervously wipes away the cold sweat that breaks out across his brow. "Look, Lt. Commander, guys. I thought that guy hated my guts. The entire time I was there, a day did not go by that he didn't find ten things I did wrong. I promise you, I kissed no one's ass to get that kind of recommendation. The first time I heard what he wrote I was shocked."

For about five seconds, the room remains silent, then everyone, including Higgins, bursts into laughter. Tommy's eyes bulge as he looks over to Higgins for clarification. After the laughter dies down Higgins walks over to Tommy and pats him on the back. "Lieutenant, everyone in here except for Tsosie is a SEAL, and we all went through Captain Fargo's 'little slice of hell.' If you were an ass-kisser, you wouldn't have lasted ten minutes with him."

Another man walks over to Tommy. "Lieutenant Williams, Chief Charley Swanson, sir. We all know Captain Fargo painfully well. The fact that he gave you that recommendation means you must be part Superman. Because someone would have to be about three quarters steel to take all the punishment he'd dole out to any man he would say that about." He offers his hand to Tommy. "Welcome to the team, sir." Tommy grabs his hand and shakes it.

"Okay, everyone, take a seat," Higgins says. "We got business to talk about." He pulls out some papers and glances at them for a moment, then looks back at Tommy. "For starters, Lt. Williams here is now my XO. He will go through a probation, training, and evaluation period, but he is the second highest ranking officer here, and you all just heard what Fargo thinks of him. Anyway, you all know that a couple of days ago some students stormed the embassy in Iran and took our people hostage."

Tommy interrupts. "Sir, does that mean that the SEALs will mount the rescue?"

Higgins rolls his eyes and continues. "No, Lieutenant, it does not. The president wants to exhaust every diplomatic effort before involving special forces in a rescue attempt. When and if that order comes, you can bet your shoe straps that it will be Delta Force and not us that gets it. But the Joint Chiefs have asked Naval Intelligence to do some snooping around over there to find out anything we can. There is a group of senators leaving for Cairo, Egypt, tomorrow at 10:00 a.m. They are going there to start diplomatic talks with Iranian officials. We will be on that plane with them. Our cover is that we are escorting Lt. Williams and Staff Sergeant Tsosie there to do some PR for the Navy and Marine Corps."

Tommy turns in his chair and looks back at Tsosie, raises his eyebrows and grins. "You too, huh! What's your deal?"

Tsosie starts to answer but Higgins interjects. "Staff Sergeant Tsosie's father was one of the World War II Navajo code talkers. Tsosie is also quite a linguist himself and is fluent in twelve languages and can understand to one degree or another ten more. Plus he was stationed in that part of the world for three years. When Captain

Smithers discovered Tsosie here, he was part of a Marine Corps special ops recon unit. He had him transferred to this unit, and his cover is to do PR, promoting enlistments with Native American citizens."

Tommy smiles at the commander and shrugs. "So, basically, Tsosie and I are your ticket to go anywhere and do anything because we're all just pretending to show how grand life is in Uncle Sam's little slice of heaven called the Navy and Marines. Nice gig, Commander."

"No one is pretending, Lieutenant. All the PR stuff is real. After a couple missions you two are going to be the Department of the Navy's poster children. Before you know it, everywhere we go they'll roll out the red carpet for us. That way we can do our A-job and no one's the wiser. Tomorrow we accompany all those VIPs to Egypt, suck up to them, let them take a bunch of pictures with you two, and then when all the fanfare dies down, we do some reconnaissance and find out what's really going on in Iran with the hostage crisis. The plane leaves at 10:00 a.m. from Dulles. You all need to be there at 9:00 a.m. for prep."

After Higgins goes over specific jobs and tactics with the crew, Tommy walks out of the building at 7:30 p.m. and spots Tsosie heading for his car. "Sergeant, I need a favor! Can you give me a ride to Georgetown? I need to be there before 8:00, or I'm toast."

"Sure, I guess. What's up, Lieutenant?"

"Remember that hot date I told you about when you picked me up? I've got thirty minutes to get to her, and she's not the type that will take kindly to my being late."

"Okay, but if you're late tomorrow morning, Higgins will have your ass in a sling."

Twenty-nine and a half minutes later, Tommy gets out of Tsosie's car and runs across the Georgetown cobblestone side street to a house that has a four-car garage at the first level of its four stories. Alysha's Trans Am is in front of one of the garage doors and it is running, but no one is in it. He scans the area and spots a little ornately styled, vintage wrought-iron-gated entrance to his left that opens to a red brick walkway. Beyond the gate on both sides of the walkway are thick, green bushes accentuated with large white and pink flowers. The bushes are over six feet tall, and because of that and all the trees in the yard, he can only see down the path and can barely make out the fourth floor of the house through the top branches. He holds his hands to his mouth and yells, "Alysha!"

"Just keep following the path. I'm right around the corner."

He makes his way around the next bend and comes to a pathway that opens up on both sides to expose a large stone porch with several iron chairs and tables on either side of the mahogany double front doors. As beautiful as the front entrance to the house is, it does not compare to the beauty of the woman standing in the doorway waiting for him.

Tommy takes a deep, calming breath as his eyes devour Alysha standing there in her full-length silver evening dress, accentuated with intricately woven black designs. He especially likes the sensual, sleeveless style and the slit up the right side. Caught up in the feast for his eyes that she is providing for him, he forgets to say anything as he walks up the steps to greet her.

"Fifteen more seconds and you would have been late, Lieutenant. Do you like playing it this close to the vest?" She lets out a small sigh, walks up to him and straightens his uniform, and uses her hand to smooth his hair back. "Well, at least you dressed appropriately. Come on, we'll take my car to the state dinner."

"Huh?" Tommy says as he remembers that he had no time to get out of his dress blues from the photo op. "What state dinner?"

"At the White House, silly. The president is sending a delegation of senators to Cairo, Egypt, tomorrow to meet with Iranian officials about the hostage crisis. We're invited to the dinner, and Uncle Bill is meeting us there."

Tommy stops for a second and rolls his eyes. "You mean this isn't an actual date, but just some more PR stuff? What was all that about not letting your uncle find out?"

Alysha walks up to Tommy and gently rests her hand on his chest as she presses in and lightly kisses him on the cheek. "Just making sure you know how to follow orders, Tommy. Besides, if you play your cards right, we can make this a very nice first date." She then turns and grabs his arm and pulls him to the parking area. "You're driving, Tommy. After all, I can't be seen driving the navy's new golden boy around. Someone might think I work for you or something. We couldn't have that, now could we?" She smiles demurely. "What they will see is the son of the late Ambassador Rodney Williams escorting the niece of the secretary of the navy to a prestigious state dinner at the White House, and that, Lt. Tommy Williams, is exactly what we want them to see."

Tommy walks her around to the passenger side, and as he opens the door, he remembers the malfunctioning seat from the ride this morning and objects as she gets in. "Oh, don't worry about the seat. I put the bolt back in as soon as I got home this morning. It works perfectly." She looks up and giggles at Tommy's confused look. "It's a little trick my grandmother taught me to keep male passengers from getting too grabby while I'm driving," She flashes him an innocent smile.

Tommy rolls his eyes as he closes the door and walks around the back of the car to the driver's side. "Man, this girl likes to play games," he mumbles as he gets in and drives off.

One Hour Later, White House State Dining Room

After going through the security checkpoint, Tommy parks Alysha's Trans Am and they proceed to the State Dining Room, where the small but prestigious gathering is being hosted by the president and the first lady. Their turn to shake hands with the president and first lady is next, and Tommy releases Alysha's hand from his arm, then steps up and throws the president a smart salute. "Mr. President, Lt. Tommy Williams, sir. May I present Miss Alysha Billows."

The president takes Alysha's hand and lightly kisses it. "You're Secretary Thompson's niece, aren't you?"

"Yes, Mr. President. It is such an honor to meet you and your lovely wife ..."

Before she can say any more, the first lady steps up and takes Alysha's hand from the president and says, "That is a lovely evening gown, my dear. Wherever did you get it?"

Tommy remains at attention as the president looks over at him, steps closer and quietly says, "At ease, Lieutenant." Tommy relaxes a little and the president continues. "I knew your father. A more dedicated statesman there was not. We all miss Ambassador Williams. You surprised us all when you decided not to follow in his footsteps. I know it disappointed Secretary Thompson. He wanted to recruit you to his personal staff after you graduated from law school. That tells me how smart he thinks you are." The president leans in closer and quietly continues, "So, tell me then, which do you think will be more effective? This diplomatic envoy I'm sending to the Middle East, or what you boys will do on Lt. Commander Higgins's team?"

Tommy takes a deep breath and says, "Permission to speak freely, Mr. President?"

"By all means, Lieutenant."

"Well, sir, I know that diplomacy should always be a first consideration before military action, and since we're just tagging along to do some stealth recon, I think at this point both are of equal value. I think you and the Joint Chiefs know this, and you will use what both operations discover over there to determine how you will handle this crisis. Personally, sir, I hope you choose a military response. Some of us are really getting sick of the way these countries take advantage of us."

The president puts his hand on Tommy's shoulder. "Spoken like a true SEAL, Lieutenant. But your insight is spot on. We just don't know enough to make any kind of aggressive response, diplomatically or militarily. You have your father's gift for speaking your mind, Tommy. That will take you far, but just remember to know when and where it will best serve you."

"Thank you, Mr. President, uh, but I think I'm taking up a little too much of your time." Tommy looks over at Alysha, feeling the intensity of the laser-beam stare she is directing at him. He can also tell that most of the people in the room are taking an interest in their conversation as well.

The president scans the room then looks back at Tommy with a mischievous grin. "Let them squirm a little. Keeps them on their toes." He then holds out his hand to shake Tommy's and pulls him in close to whisper in his ear. "You watch yourself around Secretary Thompson's niece. That girl's ambitions have no ceiling, if you know what I mean? Would not surprise me a bit if she made a bid for my job someday."

Tommy mumbles a *thank you*, releases the president's hand and steps over to Alysha, who has already finished greeting the first lady and is awkwardly standing to the side, waiting for Tommy.

She grabs Tommy's arm as they make their way to their assigned table. "What were you and the president talking about?" she asks.

"He just wanted to talk about my dad a little. He told me he knew him and liked him a lot. That's all," Tommy says. He pulls back her chair for her and does his best not to make eye contact with her.

"Oh sure, and that's why the first lady pulled me away from you two so fast," she replies. She plops down in her chair with a little too much attitude. Fortunately for Tommy, they are seated at the same table as Secretary Thompson and his wife.

"Alysha, don't give Lieutenant Williams a hard time," the secretary says in a fatherly tone. "He's shown stellar behavior since coming to DC, and he doesn't deserve to be publicly humiliated by his date at a state dinner."

Mrs. Thompson, seated next to Tommy, puts her hand on his forearm. "Don't mind Alysha, Tommy. She's always been a little high-strung and really can't stand it when she's not in control of a situation." She looks at her niece. "Darling, when the president wishes to speak with someone, whatever the reason, we let him."

Alysha lets out a gasp of air and her shoulders sag slightly. "Yes, Aunt Marie, I'm sorry. It won't happen again."

Tommy does his best to fight the boredom as the table slowly settles down to small talk and gossip. Staff Sergeant Tsosie is seated across the room with some Marine Corps brass. The two subtly nod, acknowledging each other's presence. The president then stands up and thanks everyone who is leaving in the morning to help find a solution in the hostage crisis. He and the first lady then bid everyone good night and leave.

A short while later Tommy and Alysha find themselves in the parking garage, sitting in her car. They have talked little since Alysha's aunt and uncle reproved her at the dinner table, and Tommy feels uncomfortable with the silence. "Look, I'll just drive to the nearest metro stop and catch a train back to my apartment. There's a station three blocks away from it, and it's an easy walk."

Alysha puts on a very sultry smile and leans over to Tommy. "What about our date. Don't you want to go out and have some fun now?"

Tommy's eyes get gigantic and round as the tingles in his skin tell him that he really likes how fast and easy this girl can put her sexy on.

At 6:00 a.m. the next morning, Alysha is dropping Tommy off in front of his apartment. After coming up for air the third time from the heavy necking they are involved in, Tommy strokes the hair out of her eyes. "So, why did you become all nice and stuff? I thought that after the dinner at the White House it'd be the last time I'd ever see you outside of your uncle's office."

Alysha giggles as she sits up taller in her seat. "Let's just say you've got potential, Lieutenant Williams. Anyone who gets stopped in line at a state dinner to have a conversation with the president of the United States has a shot at going places in this town." She takes her palm and strokes the side of Tommy's face. "Do you want to go places, Tommy? I can help you get there if you do."

Tommy pulls her to him for one last kiss, then pulls back and gets out of the car. "The only place I want to go right now is to bed. I have to be at Dulles at 9:00 a.m. So, if I'm lucky, I'll get about ninety minutes of shut-eye."

Alysha gets out of the car and walks around to the driver's side and gets in as Tommy holds the door for her. "Tommy, be seen as much as you can with all those senators. Don't just do the photo ops and then go hang out in the bar with the rest of the military PR people. There'll be news crews there from every network. The more you're seen, the more pictures will be taken of you with them. Let Higgins and his camera boys get drunk and waste their time. We'll build your real image if the people see you as someone involved in the process and not just a pretty face."

Tommy stops for a moment and looks down at Alysha, momentarily dumbfounded. Then it dawns on him. *She knows nothing about what Higgins's team is really all about.* He leans in and kisses her one last time. "Thanks for the coaching, sweetie, I'll do my best. See you when I get back?"

She puts the car in reverse, looks up, and says, "Count on it, Lt. Tommy Williams. I have big plans for you!" Then she pops the clutch and peels out of the parking lot.

Chapter 9

First Mission

Two Days Later, Cairo, Egypt, Fairmont Niles City Hotel Near the US Embassy

"So, THE ENTIRE THING'S A sham. The Ayatollah Khomeini won't let anyone from Iran come here and talk," Higgins says as he walks into the hotel suite and slams the door. Tommy does not say a word as Higgins sits down on a bar stool and pours himself a shot of rum and quickly downs it.

Meanwhile, Tommy is looking at a local newspaper. He looks up at the lieutenant commander. "Sir, did you see this stuff about Hector Villalon and Christian Bouget meeting about the Iranians getting the Shah back? Apparently, it's happening today."

As he is speaking someone knocks on the door and Tommy gets up to answer. When the door opens, Chief Charley Swanson steps in and rushes over to Higgins. "Lt. Commander, the Russians are sending a lot of equipment and men to the Afghanistan border. All hell is breaking loose, and the president is thinking about recalling all of us."

Tommy's eyes squint as he walks over to the pair. "You know, Lt. Commander, there is a lot of shit going down at the same time. First, Iran stonewalls the US's diplomatic gestures here, then a secret meeting about the Shah, and now Russia threatening to invade Afghanistan."

"What's your point, Tommy?"

"My point, sir, is that I don't think it's time to turn tail and run back to the States. Why don't we use this move by the Russians to our advantage?"

"Oh, and just how can we do that, Lieutenant?"

"Well, sir, we have all this diplomatic clout with us right here in the middle of one of the biggest shitstorms this part of the world has seen in a while. I bet you that a lot of our folks stationed over here on the different military bases are getting nervous. How about we take all these champions of the people and go visit some of them just to reassure them that their country is one hundred and ten percent behind them, no matter what happens, and then ..."

"And then we use the opportunity to do some good old snooping around at all those different stops and try to find out what's really going on. Not bad, Lieutenant. I'm seeing why Captain Fargo liked you so much. I'll pass this up the ladder to Captain Smithers and see if we can get something rolling in that direction." Higgins stands and punches Tommy in the shoulder.

Tommy rolls his eyes and mumbles under his breath. "I don't think that Captain Fargo ever liked anyone in his entire life, and especially not me!"

Higgins and Chief Swanson both chuckle and head out to make the phone call back to the States.

Six hours later Tommy, Higgins, Tsosie, and the rest of the crew are taking a military transport copter from the US embassy to

NAMRU-3 US military base at the northern tip of Cairo, on the shore of the Mediterranean.

"So, Captain Smithers really liked my idea, and the president went for it, huh?" Tommy says with a hint of disbelief in his eyes.

"The hard sell was the senators. Out of the twelve who came for the talks, only four said they would do the tour. Since this is more about taking care of our men and women out here in the danger zone, and less about high-profile, career-advancing diplomacy, the liberals in the bunch do not want to be seen supporting a possible military solution. Which, I might add, this little idea of yours might imply."

Tommy stares at Higgins, trying to process the hypocrisy. Higgins just huffs. "That's Washington, kid. Learn how to swim these waters or you're going to drown." The copter touches down on the helipad, and Higgins taps Tommy on the shoulder and points out the side window. There are four politicians and their staffs waiting for them at the entrance to the base. "You and Tsosie will do some photos with them before we leave for our first stop."

Tommy and Tsosie disembark the craft first and walk up to a ranking Republican senator from Texas to shake his hand. The base commander, Admiral Bob Winston, is also there, and as soon as Tommy appears, he excuses himself from the group and walks up to meet them. Tommy and Tsosie come to attention and throw the admiral a salute. "Lt. Tommy Williams and Staff Sergeant Robert Tsosie, sir."

"At ease, gentlemen. I just got off the phone with Captain Smithers before the politicians showed up. He briefed me on your mission objectives. I am having my men stock your transport copter with everything Lt. Commander Higgins wants. It should be ready to go in the next two hours. In the meantime, you need to make these senators feel important. I'll go talk to Higgins, and you two can socialize with them and get them over to the photo op. My men will show you where that will be." He turns and makes his way to Higgins but stops and turns back. "Lieutenant?"

"Yes sir, Admiral?"

"I graduated from Annapolis two years after your father. He was my squad leader my second year. He was an honorable man and one hell of a fine officer. He didn't deserve to die like he did. Just so you know, you have one old-schooler who supports your career choice. Do me a favor—you take what the navy gave you at SGT and what Higgins will teach you, and find out who did it and why, and then you make them pay. You ever need some help, I'll be there for you, kid."

Admiral Winston holds out his hand and Tommy shakes it. "Thanks, Admiral. Finding those responsible for his death is the plan. It's nice to know others will help when I need it. Dad had a lot of friends and I just keep running into them everywhere I go."

Admiral Winston grasps Tommy's shoulder with his other hand and shakes it vigorously, then turns and walks toward Higgins and the others. "Carry on, Lieutenant."

Higgins and the rest of the crew wait for the helicopter rotor blades to stop so that they can unload the equipment and set up as Tommy and Tsosie do their best to make small talk with the politicians. They set up the photo equipment on the side of the base hangar where there are several US warplanes and helicopters staged. Tommy and Tsosie wait by an F-4 Phantom II attack aircraft favored by the US Navy and the Marine Corps. As the photo op progresses, each politician takes time to be staged with either Tommy or Tsosie at unique areas in and around the aircraft, while Higgins and the crew take pictures.

Tommy and Tsosie are standing on either side of the senator from Texas as Admiral Winston points to the 20 mm Vulcan cannon port for the internally mounted weapon under the nose of the aircraft. "The three of you should stand under that. It'll show those bastards we mean business!"

The senator looks up and smiles. "Grand idea, Admiral!"

December 7, 1979, Third Stop, Military Base at Port of Jabal, Dubai

Tommy stands on the civilian dock about a mile north of the base, looking at several armed men escorting a sizable group of African teenage girls onto a small ship. "Lt. Commander Higgins, check this out. What's going on there?"

Higgins looks up from the newspaper article he is reading. "Local slave trade. Probably resupplying some sheikh's harem. My guess is that they are going straight to Iran or Afghanistan." He looks back at Tommy, who has a disgusted, astonished look on his face. "Keep it in check, Lieutenant! I don't like it either. They didn't get the memo in this part of the world that it's wrong."

Tommy glares at Higgins for a few moments then blurts out, "Holy shit, Lt. Commander, are you freaking kidding me? I heard that slavery is still practiced in a number of Islamic countries over here, but doing it right out in the open and this close to a US military base? Who do they think they are?"

"They think that they're in their own country, and we're their guests! That's who they know they are, Lieutenant. They also know that we can't do a damn thing about it."

"So, we just let these assholes get away with this stuff because we need their oil? Is that it, Lt. Commander?"

"Yes, Lieutenant, that's it. We need their damn oil and right now no one wants to go to war with any of these guys over slave trading. Maybe someday, but not today. Do I need to remind you that we're here to figure out what's going on in Iran with the hostages at our embassy? That's our focus, not the slave trading in the Middle East that has somehow survived for fifteen centuries."

Tommy glares back at Higgins, endeavoring to control the volcano of rage threatening to erupt inside of him, when an outrageous thought crosses his mind. "Commander, don't you think it's funny that with a country as locked down tight as Iran is right now, that that group of African girls are being shipped there unhindered? None of our people can get anywhere in Iran, and especially not the capital. Wonder how many of these are headed there right now?"

Higgins looks at Tommy, then at the ship that the girls are being loaded onto, and then back at Tommy. "What are you saying, Lieutenant—that we need to get a spy in that crew and get our intel that way?"

"Yes, why not? One of us gets in there with them and takes a trip to Iran, then finds out what's up. We haven't learned squat while visiting all these bases yet. But if these guys' weak spot is their precious harem restock supply, let's use it!"

"Damn, Williams, Fargo was right about you. Outside-of-the-nine-dots-thinking really is your playground." He puts his newspaper down and puts his hand to his chin as he muses out loud, "Shouldn't be hard for the right guy to get on one of those crews."

"Great! We go back to the base, I get some local threads on, and hit the market until I connect with one outfit and sign up."

Higgins places a hand on Tommy's shoulder and shakes it. "Hold on there, Williams. It's an excellent plan, but they'll see right through you or me, or anybody on our crew. Except maybe ..."

"Tsosie! Yes, he told me he was stationed here for three years with a marine security detachment. He speaks the language and understands the culture. Said he was mistaken for a local all the time when he was out of uniform."

Higgins puts his newspaper under his arm and walks back toward the base. "Come on, Williams. First, we'll run this past Captain Smithers. He'll want to get the CIA involved in providing backup and a communication network between us and Tsosie. Then we get our favorite Navajo marine staff sergeant all set up as a slave hauler."

Two Days Later, Civilian Docks, Port of Jabal

The CIA contact for Tsosie walks past him and nods, showing him that contact was made with a slaver outfit and some representatives of that group will soon interview him. Tsosie leans against a wooden pole on the dock in front of a cargo ship that's getting ready to launch. He looks up to see a couple of men carrying Chinese-style SKS semiautomatic assault rifles, common in that part of the world, coming toward him.

Holding an Arabic unfiltered cigarette pressed between his fingers and his thumb the way the locals do, he takes it from his lips and blows out the puff of thick, dark smoke that he was holding inside his mouth for a minute to make sure his breath smells like everyone else's. He does not inhale because he has not smoked in five years, and even when he did, these Arabic cigarettes sometimes made him gag. But to look authentic, he sucks in a little smoke so he can exhale some out of his nose. He stifles his gag reflex and nods his head toward the men who are a few paces away.

One steps forward and speaks to him. "Are you the one looking for work?" asks the man in a northern Arabic dialect.

"I am," Tsosie answers in the southern dialect of the same language that he learned while stationed here.

"We were told you're an experienced smuggler of opium, guns, and contraband. Have you ever worked in a slaver's convoy?"

"No. You have to know the right people to get that good of a job."

The two men look at each other, laugh, and nod their heads affirmatively. "Your words are correct, my friend." He leans in close and presses the barrel of his rifle against Tsosie's stomach. "It pays much better than your previous employments, but you have to be trustworthy, especially when it comes to not damaging the merchandise—and that includes sampling it. Can you live with that, my friend?"

"I can live with any restrictions as long as the pay is good."

The man then leans in closer and sneers. "These sheikhs we deal with will pay handsomely. But they will not tolerate any disrespect to the teachings of the Prophet. We do not care what you do on your own time, but when we're around them, there will be no use of alcohol of any kind. Even the smell of it on us will ruin the deal." He then sticks his rifle barrel right into the bottom of Tsosie's chin. "Can you live with that restriction?"

Tsosie pushes the rifle from his face. "Peace, my friend. I will obey the Prophet's words at all times."

The two men in front of Tsosie look at one another and nod. "You'll do. What's your name again?"

Tsosie takes another drag from his cigarette and lightly inhales and exhales without coughing. "Abara."

"Well, Abara, come with us. We'll take you to your new job."

Tsosie takes the last drag of his diminished cigarette, then throws it on the ground and follows the men to the ramp of the ship. When he steps on the deck, his companions step on either side of him and the one on the right lightly elbows him. "Stand up straight and don't talk unless spoken to. The boss wants to have a look at you before we leave for Iran."

Pasto Niazai looks the new recruit over as he steps up to him. His contacts from the local crime syndicate gave him a high recommendation. Said he was one of the best smugglers in the area. "Abara, I'm Pasto. I run this entire outfit. My men tell me you're a faithful disciple of Islam. That is good. We will have need of you when dealing with our customers." He then steps in close enough to Tsosie that the man's fiery breath is felt on his face. "Know this then, Abara. My allegiance is to General Nuriah Turakine of The People's Liberation Army of Afghanistan. He has formed an alliance with Russia, and our business is to support his efforts. Do you have a problem with that?"

Tsosie lets out a deep breath. "Russia and the United States are enemies. The United States is my enemy as well. My father was a US soldier who used my mother as a whore until they transferred him back to his home. We never heard from him again. I have lived my entire life as an outcast of my mother's people and ignored by my father's. I do believe in the sacred teachings of the Prophet, but I have had to survive by being an outlaw. Working for you will be no different. I will follow your orders as long as you pay me what you promise."

Pasto throws his hands up and looks at both his men on either side of Tsosie and bursts out laughing as he wraps his arms around his shoulders and shakes him vigorously. "You are exactly what we are looking for! Come, let's get you settled in. We have a quick drop-off in Iran, then we're flying back to Afghanistan to get ready for our next trip to Africa to get more girls for our friends."

Chapter 10

Plans Within Plans

December 13, 1979, Northern Afghanistan, Military Camp of General Nuriah Turakine, People's Liberation Army

THE CHAMELEON SITS QUIETLY AS his superior, Lt. Col. Iban Wornski, discusses politics with the head of The People's Liberation Army of Afghanistan, General Turakine. He finds it amusing to take note of the difference in appearance between Colonel Wornski and General Turakine. The general is a heavily bearded, slightly overweight man who loves his ornately decorated uniform that has more ribbons and metals attached to his lapels than three soldiers could earn in a lifetime. Colonel Wornski, like himself, is clean-shaven, with a military-style short haircut. Unlike the general, one could barely distinguish him from any other officer in the Russian military. The standard-issue tan uniform shows only the rank insignia on each shoulder, with no other distinguishing paraphernalia.

He listens to their bantering about the necessity of Communism taking a permanently firm hold in the Mideast. He finds social and political idealism boring. Having been one of the most successful assassins in the world for over ten years now, he knows that genuine power will always lie in hands strong enough to take what they want and hold it.

Then the conversation shifts to something that interests the Chameleon. He hears General Turakine ask, "How do we go about killing such a man? He's too insulated by his followers. We can't openly assassinate him with any normal weapon. If he were to be shot or even stabbed, it would cause the wrong kind of chaos and the Americans would have their excuse to bring in their military might and take over the entire country, and everyone would suspect us to be at fault. How, pray tell, will Russia then be able to help me overthrow our own devil-spawned, capitalist regime when they would be at risk of a war with the United States? Something none of us wants to be in the middle of."

Lt. Col. Wornski looks over at the Chameleon. "Care to answer the good general's question, Comrade Major Rasmov?"

"Of course, Comrade Lt. Col. Wornski. General Turakine, it would be like when I assassinated his son, two years ago in Iraq. By all physical evidence, he died of natural causes. But that did not stop his father, the Ayatollah, from blaming the American CIA. That and other contributing factors caused the United States' president to fire eight hundred of that organization's top operatives, weakening their intelligence and covert might worldwide. When the man dies, his successors will act similarly and blame the Americans for another covert assassination. The embarrassment would cause their president to relinquish more of his hold on this region of the world, allowing us to move forward with our own plans, unhindered by the West."

General Turakine jumps out of his seat and gestures excitedly with his hands as he exclaims, "So, what you are saying is that if we can kill the Ayatollah similarly, as you did his son, then it would stall the efforts of the United States in this region and strengthen our chances of not only bringing Communism to Afghanistan but possibly to Iran as well?"

"That is exactly what my subordinate is telling you, General. All we need to do is get him to Tehran undetected, and he'll do the rest."

"I think I have the perfect way to get him into the city," General Turakine replies. "He will have to meet up with my men and go to South Africa and pick up some cargo, which includes a rather troublesome woman in Kenya, who's been causing us many setbacks in that country in recent months. Then take a ship around the Gulf of Aden to a port in Kuwait, then proceed on into Iran."

"You're referring to your human trafficking service to the sheikhs of Arabia and Iran, if I am not mistaken, General?" Wornski asks.

"Of course, Colonel. Before Mother Russia decided to aid us in our liberation of our beautiful country, I had to find other ways to finance our efforts." He grabs his radio, tunes it to a private frequency, and talks into the microphone. "Pasto, this is General Turakine. I have one more passenger for you. He'll be ready in …" He looks over at the Chameleon.

"Thirty minutes," the Chameleon responds.

The general waves his hand nonchalantly. "In one hour. He will brief you on what he needs when he has the opportunity. This man is very important to me. Obey his orders and treat him well."

"Of course, General. We will wait for him at the airstrip."

One hour later, Major Boris Rasmov, carrying only his sniper rifle case and a small duffel bag, climbs aboard the small Cessna jet. He climbs in as the pilot is prepping for takeoff. First, seeing that another man is seated in the copilot's seat, he looks over to the pilot then back to the man seated beside him. "You are Pasto Niazai, General Turakine's head man for this operation, correct?"

"Yes, and he told me to call you *Chameleon* and not ask you questions, and to obey your orders."

He nods his head and lets the slightest crease of a smile manifest across his face as he points at the man in the copilot's seat. "Well, I prefer to sit in that seat. I'm a trained pilot and should something happen while in the air I prefer to be in a position where I can control the outcome."

Pasto motions for the man to move, which he does immediately. As he stands, the Chameleon looks him in the eye with his chilly, hard stare. "What is your name?" he asks, in the Aramaic tongue.

"Abara. Peace, my friend."

"Strange, but I detect a slight American taint to your accent. Care to explain?"

An icy chill goes up and down Tsosie's spine as this Russian's question threatens to expose him. "It's not something I am proud to share, but my father was an American soldier stationed in Jabal. He was with my mother and me for the first five years of my life, but when he got transferred back to his country, he left us, and we never heard from him again. After that, I had to learn to survive as an outcast of my people. That is why I took work as a smuggler."

"The culture of the Mideast is famously intolerant of half-breeds. Your father must have had some American Indian in his blood. Your speech and cheekbones alerted me," the Chameleon says as he takes his seat next to the pilot.

"My father was a full-blooded Navajo."

The Chameleon turns around in his seat and smiles coldly. "Like the famous Wind Talkers of World War II. I understand that your father's people have an amazing ability to learn languages at a remarkable level of proficiency and speed."

"These are things he never shared with me or my mother. I do not mean any disrespect, but discussing my father and where he is from is very upsetting to me. He is the reason my life was so hard. I hate him and his people."

The Chameleon shakes his head and laughs. "This world is filled with individuals who are all responsible for their own decision. The key is to be wise enough to see opportunity or deception, no matter where it is coming from, my friend. A hard lesson to learn, but a valuable one." He then turns to Pasto. "What is our destination?"

"Pemba Island, off Swahili."

December 15, 1979, Ancestral Coastal Village of Tumaini Aalee, South of Gazi

Chineye and Adimu Kamau, fourteen-year-old twin daughters of Makena Aalee, walk along the beach in front of their grandmother's home, talking about their mother. "But why did she take back her father's name after our father died, Chineye? Ever since her speech to Parliament, we hardly see her. Grandmother is now more of a mother to us than she is."

"Our mother loved our father with all her heart, Adimu. She respected his wishes and never took up Tumaini Aalee's cause until after he died. And we know why Mother did that, don't we, Sister?"

"Yes, but Father was a simple fisherman, and he should never have confronted those men from Pemba Island that stole those girls from Gazi. If he had minded his own business, we would still have him today. Now our mother thinks it is her mission to confront all those in Kenya that do the same. What if the same thing happens to her?"

Chineye stops and puts her hands on her sister's shoulders and shakes her. "I know you are scared for our mother. I am too. But we must remember that she has Undersecretary Arachar as her protector, one of the most powerful men in Kenya. He sent his best soldiers to

Mombasa to protect her. We must be strong and not let fear grip our hearts. Remember, we too are the descendants of Tumaini Aalee."

Movement catches their attention and the girls look away from the ocean to the beach and see several men have surrounded them. Terror grips their hearts as a stern-looking Arab steps forward, sporting a devious smile. "So, you are the daughters of Makena Aalee. It took us some time to learn of your existence. Tricky woman, changing her name back to what it was before she married your father. Colonel Niazai was right. Now we have what we need to capture her and end her ridiculous and meddlesome campaign. Take them!"

Adimu and Chineye scream for their grandmother in the house not fifty yards up the beach, where her body lies dead on the kitchen floor. Chineye and Adimu's screams fall on deaf ears.

Chapter 11

Her Worst Nightmare

Monday, December 16, 1979, Mombasa Police Department

MAKENA AND UNDERSECRETARY ARACHAR SIT in her office discussing the latest news about the American embassy in Iran being overrun by dissident students. "First this, and then rumors about Russia wanting to invade Afghanistan. Madam Aalee, I truly do not know where this world is headed. I was counting on our campaign against the slave trade going on here capturing more worldwide attention. Now I fear all this will obscure it."

Before Makena can reply, the phone rings on her desk. "Makena Aalee, how may I help you?" Makena listens for a moment and then her face goes ashen and she drops the phone on her desk and screams. "They've taken Adimu and Chineye! How could this happen?"

Bosher swiftly steps around the desk and takes Makena into his arms, then picks up the phone and puts it to his ear. "This is Undersecretary Bosher Arachar. What is the meaning of this?"

An Arabic-accented male voice comes over the line. "If you and that whore Makena Aalee ever want to see her daughters alive again, you both will meet us at the port on Pemba Island at sundown in five days. Make sure you tell your attack dog, Colonel Eloi, and her men to stay away. Pemba is a sovereign country, and none of you have any authority there. If we see her or are attacked, the first to die will be Makena's daughters."

"Is that all? Why five days? Aren't there any ransom demands?" The line goes dead and Bosher hangs up the telephone and grabs his radio from Makena's desk. "Adessa, please join me in Madam Aalee's office at once!"

Fifteen minutes later, Colonel Eloi and Undersecretary Arachar are in a heated debate as Makena blankly stares at both of them. "Bosher, I cannot allow you or Madam Aalee to go there. They are right. We have no authority on that island, and they could easily take or kill you both with no fear of repercussion. Can't you see this is a trap?"

"Of course it is a trap, Adessa. But we must do something. General Tumba is behind this, and he knows you and your men. They will look for any of you, and when you're spotted, they will kill Makena's daughters. She and I must go there alone ..."

Adessa interrupts, exclaiming, "I forbid it. It's insanity!"

Bosher holds up his hand to stop her objections and continues. "But what if you are already there with your men? You could sneak onto Pemba tonight from the docks on the opposite side of the island and make your way through the jungle. I can only guess the reason they want us to wait so long before coming, but that could work to our advantage. Is this all part of a bigger plan? You have time to get there and get set up. That entire island is a cesspool of rival gangs. One more armed group trekking through the jungle could easily go unnoticed. But you must stay out of sight until we meet with the kidnappers and you have eyes on Makena's children. Then you can take them by surprise and rescue all of us from them."

Colonel Eloi, intrigued by his words, sits down next to Makena and places her hand on her shoulder. "What do you think, Makena? It is a perilous plan, but it could work."

With tears still streaming down her face, she clenches her fist and pounds her desk. "I will do whatever it takes to get Adimu and Chineye back. This is all my fault! They were so angry with me when I left them with their grandmother. I did not think that anyone could find them there. How do we even know that they are alive? I can't wait five days!"

Makena's phone rings again. She looks over to Bosher, who nods and picks up another extension and covers the mouthpiece as she answers. The same Arabic voice from before says, "My superiors have ordered me to let you talk to your daughters once a day until you and Undersecretary Arachar meet us at Pemba Island. We will call your office every day for the next four days. If you and the undersecretary are not there, one of your daughters will die. Am I understood?"

"Yes!"

Voices in the background come over the phone and her heart jumps inside her chest when someone says, "You can go first."

"Mama!"

"Chineye, are you okay? Where is your sister?"

"She is right here, Mama! What do they want with us? When are you coming to get us?"

"They want me because of what I have been doing in Mombasa. That is why they took you. We must wait five days and then I will come to get you. Have they hurt you or your sister?"

"No, only when they grabbed us on the beach, blindfolded us, and took us somewhere in a truck. But I don't like the way they look at us, Mama. It's awful!"

"That is enough, give me the phone." There is a shuffling sound and Makena can hear her other daughter cry out that she has not gotten to talk to her mother yet. The man tells her she can talk tomorrow. Then he gets on the phone. "Nothing will happen to them if you do exactly what I said. You and the undersecretary must be there in your office for the next four days at the same time."

Bosher hangs up the phone and looks at Colonel Eloi. "They are not even on the island yet. They said they went somewhere in a truck, not a boat or plane. They are definitely waiting for something."

December 17, Jungle of Pemba Island

Colonel Eloi scans the area and can see the early morning rays of the sun come through the deep jungle underbrush. She and her men were dropped off on the far end of the island late last night. The trek to the other side of the island and the docks where they are to meet Makena and Bosher to rescue the girls is about a day's journey on foot from where they are, but she knows that she has to get close enough to observe and still stay out of sight until the twentieth, when the exchange is to take place. She grabs her pack and hoists it on her back and then picks up her rifle and looks over to her second-in-command, Sergeant Niembo, coming her way.

"Colonel Eloi, what are we going to do here for the next three days? We can't just hike across the island and then hide by the docks. Someone will become suspicious. General Tumba's people will be looking for you and might recognize some of us."

She looks up at the trail as two men come through the bushes. She turns to her sergeant. "We do what any gang on this island would do. Find a job and make some money."

One of the men that just showed up comes up and introduces himself. "I am Maurice. My employer said that we are to meet up with a tall woman and four men in this clearing. Are you Adessa?"

"Yes, I am. This is Tibre. What do you have for us?"

He looks at Tibre then back at his associate. The man nods and says to Maurice, "Bring her. The others can wait here."

"Stay here, I will be right back." She shoulders her rifle. "Lead on, gentlemen."

She follows the two men back in the direction they came from. Tibre makes like he wants to go also, but she puts up her hand to block him and says in a hushed tone, "It's okay. They're just local smugglers. It's our cover for being here. They are no threat to me."

Colonel Eloi follows the men for about a quarter mile until they come to another section of beach south of where they landed. There are several more men with guns standing around big wooden crates that have been dragged up from the beach. When she gets closer, she sees the familiar Red Cross sign on the boxes. She surmises they are stolen relief packages of medical supplies intended for the needy. It is a common practice to steal these types of supplies when they enter an area and then turn around and sell them to the people they were supposed to be given to. "There is more here than my men can carry," she says, as she walks around the boxes and inspects the labels.

The man who told her to come alone with them laughs. "That is not my problem. Did you bring the payment?"

She sighs and takes her backpack off and opens it up to show him the cash she has on the inside, then points her finger at the man and barks, "If you think that you can come back and steal from us what we have to leave for another trip, think again. These villages had to pool all their money to afford this, and they are paying us well to deliver it. If you cheat us and them, you'll have two enemies—the villagers, who will ruin your reputation and make it impossible for you to sell anymore around here; and me, who will find you and kill you."

The leader stares at her for a moment, then a huge grin breaks out on his crinkled, leathery face. "Hold on there, girl. Don't get so excited. We have no intention of stealing this crap from you. We're in a big hurry. There are two dozen more shipments like this waiting for us on the mainland, and we have others waiting to pay us for them."

She returns the smile as she walks up to the man and hands him the bag full of money. He grabs it and signals his men to follow him.

As he leaves, he turns around and says, "My contacts in Mombasa assured me that you were a professional. We have a splendid thing going here. We don't need some hothead ruining it for everyone. If the United Nations peace-keeping forces ever catch us stealing Red Cross relief supplies, all our heads could roll."

She waves the man off and turns to make her way back to her men. When she comes into view, Sergeant Niembo walks up and gives a sigh of relief. "That was a little risky, Colonel. What is this all about?"

"Tibre, you need to learn to trust me. I did not get to where I am by being stupid. I could not tell you what we are doing until we got on the island. Those men were part of a network of Red Cross volunteers from different countries that steal medical supplies and relief packages to sell to the people they were supposed to be given to. Undersecretary Arachar has been trying to catch them for years. He had one of his undercover operatives in that organization set me up as a distribution source here. Now I know what one of their major smugglers looks like. When we rescue Madam Aalee and her daughters, we will use what we learn in the next two days while delivering this stuff to catch and prosecute those thieves once and for all."

Chapter 12

Allies Meet

December 18, 1979, Small Airport on Pemba Island

TSOSIE SITS IN THE FAR corner of the hangar, where he was told to guard a couple of teenage girls that they brought over from the mainland a few hours ago. He tries to listen as Pasto Niazai and the mysterious Russian known by the code name Chameleon are having a heated debate.

"Your slave trading enterprise in this part of the world is not my concern. There can be no delays. You know what is about to happen in your country, and I want to be in Tehran within twenty-four hours."

"Please, Major—" Pasto begins to say, but the Russian steps in very close to him, the threat of death in his hard, gray eyes. "Call me Chameleon, you fool!"

Pasto steps back. "Please, Chameleon, we only want to rid ourselves of their mother and that rat, Undersecretary Arachar. We will have you to your destination no later than the twenty-first, I promise."

The Chameleon stares at him. "I have never heard of this Madam Aalee you are so up in arms about here, but the undersecretary is another matter. He is a formidable figure in Kenya and has resisted Russia's efforts to influence that country. His capture could prove helpful. We'll proceed with your plan, but you must move your time schedule up by twelve hours, at least."

Pasto sighs with relief. "Thank you, Chameleon." Then he turns and yells, "Abara, find someone else to watch those girls, and tell the pilot we're moving our schedule up by twelve hours. He'll need to fly into Mombasa tonight and pick up Makena Aalee and the undersecretary!"

Tsosie raises his hand and waves to acknowledge the order. He spots a couple of men standing just outside the hangar and yells for one of them to come in and replace him. When the man comes in, he makes his way outside, where the pilot is doing something to one of the turboprops with a wrench. "Abara, hand me that screwdriver on the table over there. This hopping back and forth from desert to tropical climates is playing hell with my lubricants. This is the fourth time in a month I've had to pull this cover off and clean the wet sand and sea salt out."

Tsosie takes the tool from the nearby table and hands it to him. "The boss man says we're moving the schedule up by twelve hours. We'll have to fly into Mombasa tonight and pick up the girls' mother and the undersecretary."

The man stares at Tsosie incredulously for a moment, then huffs and grabs the screwdriver and pries off the cover to the turboprop and throws it on the ground. "If that's true, then I have to finish this entire job today. Do me a favor, Abara, and get inside and click the starter a couple of times so I can work around the propeller bearings."

"Sure." Tsosie steps around the plane to the door and pulls it open. The small stepladder drops, and he climbs inside. This is just the break he was hoping for when he came out here. On his way to the pilot's seat, he reaches under one seat next to the window and pulls out a CIA transponder box they had given him at the Port of Jabal, Dubai. As he sits in the pilot's seat, he opens the window and yells, "Tell me when!"

"Now. Push it once every twenty seconds until I tell you to stop," the pilot yells. Every time he pushes the button, the starter makes a loud grinding sound, causing the propeller to turn half a rotation. The next time he pushes it he quickly activates the transponder and says into the mic, "We're picking up Undersecretary Bosher Arachar and a woman named Makena Aalee tonight in Mombasa and flying them to Pemba Island. We have a high-ranking Russian military-type with us who goes by the code name 'Chameleon.' He's using the slavers as cover to get to Tehran by the twenty-first. Something big is happening in Afghanistan on the twentieth. He wants to use that as a setup to assassinate someone in Iran. We're meeting up with a boat on the docks at Pemba Island at 6:00 a.m. on the twentieth. That is the best place to catch him and bring him in for questioning."

He turns the transponder off and pushes the starter button one more time. The pilot holds his thumb up. He releases the switch and sticks his head out the window. "Is that it?"

"This thing has another engine," the pilot shouts back, "and then we have to work on the landing gear. If you help me, we might get it all done before we have to take off at midnight tonight."

Same Day, Makena Aalee's Office in Mombasa

Makena and Bosher sit nervously at her desk waiting for the phone call from the kidnappers. Both look like they have not slept in days. Bosher's mind is racing, trying to process the last report from Colonel Eloi on Pemba Island that he's holding in his hand.

Bosher. We have finished delivering all the medical supplies and relief packages to the villages. We met up with another gang that was transporting stolen military weapons to a local crime syndicate. We invited them to camp with us, and we shared our liquor and food. Once the alcohol softened them up, I asked them about any special goings-on with the island lately. The leader got silent and then told me that everyone is abuzz about how the human traffickers who stage their captives here are all afraid because their boss is bringing some big-time Russian KGB agent with him for his next pickup. He said that no one is supposed to know about it. But somehow the information got leaked and now everyone is afraid that they will be blamed for spreading the news. If this has anything to do with Madam Aalee's daughters, we will find it much more difficult to rescue them. Adessa.

He knows that Pasto Niazai, Tumba's contact, is a colonel in The People's Liberation Army and that the Russians back them. But that the Russians could be involved with the slave trade in West Africa and the Middle East has him terrified. The phone rings abruptly and both almost jump out of their seats as they reach for their phones. Makena is the first to speak. "Hello, this is Makena Aalee."

The familiar deep Arabic voice answers. "Is the undersecretary there as well?"

"This is him. Let us talk to the girls."

"Before we do that, there has been a change of plans. Both of you are to meet a small Cessna at the airport on the southern tip of Mombasa tonight at 3:00 a.m."

"I thought we were meeting you tomorrow on the docks at Pemba Island?"

"Your daughters will wait for you on Pemba Island, but we must move the rendezvous up by twelve hours."

"Let me talk to both of them this time," Makena demands as she nervously stares at Bosher.

They hear the man say, "Bring both of them over here." There is a shuffling noise as the man hands the phone to one girl, and Makena's heart goes in her throat when the sound of her daughters crying comes over the phone.

"Mama, they woke us up in the middle of the night, put bags over our heads, and put us on a plane. We don't even know where they took us. They are making us sit in the corner of an enormous airplane hangar while men talk and yell in languages we don't understand. When are you coming to get us? We are so scared!"

"Adimu, we will be there tonight. Please try to be brave," Makena says as the fear threatens to overwhelm her.

Bosher puts a hand on Makena's shoulder and says into the phone, "My dear, it is Bosher Arachar. They have taken you to Pemba Island. You know where that is, don't you?"

"Yes, we learned about it in school. It is a dangerous place, and they don't recommend travelers go there."

"We will be there soon. I do not believe the men you are with will let anything bad happen to you. Try to be brave, like your mother said. Let her talk to Chineye now."

There is some shuffling on the phone, then Makena hears, "Mama, are you coming soon?"

"Yes, we will be there late tonight. You and your sister must be brave and not give those men any reason to be angry with you."

Another man's voice in the background booms over the line. "That is enough! Give that to me." They hear the sound of slapping and Chineye screams.

Makena gasps and Bosher yells, "Stop that at once! You promised they would not be harmed!"

"You are in no position to make any demands, Undersecretary Bosher. Unlike my men, I have no limitations on what I can and cannot do with Madam Aalee's daughters."

Bosher pulls the phone partially away from his ear as he shockingly recognizes the voice. "Who is this?"

"I think you know. We've met a few times when I was in Nairobi, meeting with General Tumba."

"Pasto, or should I say, Colonel Niazai? Do you really think you can get away with all this now that I'm involved? All it would take is for me to reach out to the United Nations Security Council and report what you are doing to cause you more trouble and exposure than I think your superior, General Turakine, would want."

"True, Undersecretary, if you felt that Madam Aalee's daughters were a justifiable sacrifice to achieve that ideal. But we both know that you are not a true politician and will always let your pathetic sentimentality keep you from doing what would be most politically advantageous."

Bosher looks over at Makena and mouths *don't worry!* and then says into the phone, "We'll be on that plane tonight, and I'll alert no one in the United Nations about what you are up to. That I promise."

"Good, now that we understand each other I'll let you go. Oh, and Undersecretary?"

"Yes?"

"Don't think for a moment that we have forgotten about your attack dog, Colonel Eloi. We have not seen her here on the island, but my sources tell me that no one has seen her around you or Madam Aalee for days. Whatever foolhardy mission you have sent her on, know this—the first time she is sighted anywhere near us, we will kill the daughters and then both of you."

"I hear you, Pasto. We will be there."

The line goes dead and Bosher and Makena stare at one another for a moment, then she sobs. He holds her gently and strokes her hair. "Madam Aalee, didn't you hear? They have not spotted Colonel Eloi or her men on the island. I told you she was the best. There is still a chance we can pull this off. I will send her a message about the change in plans."

Makena stops sobbing and inhales deeply as she allows the positive insight to sink in. She looks up into his tender, brown eyes. "I trust you, Bosher. Please do what you must. I am going back to my apartment to prepare for the trip and try to get some sleep. Please come and get me when you're ready to go to the airport."

"I will. Now, getting some rest is the best thing. They'll challenge us beyond our limits in the next couple of days, so we must be ready."

She nods her head and leaves the office without another word.

Bosher walks around the desk, sits down, and picks up the phone to call a contact he has at the capital. A male voice answers. "Undersecretary Arachar, Colonel Eloi has not made contact since the note I sent you this morning."

"They have moved our timeline up twelve hours. We're not taking the ferry tomorrow. The kidnappers are picking us up tonight south of Mombasa and flying us out. I think it is time we ask for help. After you contact Colonel Eloi, reach out to our friend in the CIA and tell him what we are doing, and that there is a Russian KGB agent involved with the slavers. That should be the proper motivation for them to help us."

"I will do it, Undersecretary. You know my hands are tied to send you any of Tumba's people to help. Adessa is the only one in that organization you can trust. President Amoi has blocked any attempt by your office for contact. Whatever Tumba is up to, our president seems to have aligned himself with him."

Bosher takes a deep breath. "I think it is time, my friend. Prepare a speech for me to announce that I will run against President Amoi in the next election. Keep this quiet until we have Madam Aalee and her daughters safe and home."

"I will do it, Undersecretary. How will this affect Madam Aalee and her work in Mombasa and the coasts?"

A happy thought enters Bosher's mind. "If I win, I think that Madam Aalee will find herself to be overwhelmingly busier in many ways. Thank you."

December 20, 3:00 a.m., Small Airport South of Mombasa

Bosher and Makena drive into the parking lot of the small airport and immediately see the Cessna 414 twin turboprop airplane out on the field with its interior lights on and a man in the pilot's seat. As they stop the vehicle, another man carrying a rifle steps away from the compact building that has a watchtower attached to it and walks up to their car.

"Undersecretary Arachar and Madam Aalee, please get out of the car and follow me."

He looks over at the pilot and waves to let him know they are who they're waiting for, then steps back as Bosher gets out. In a hushed voice he says, "My name is Sergeant Robert Tsosie. I am an agent for the United States government. I'm on undercover assignment to infiltrate the organization that has kidnapped your daughters. I've contacted my CIA handler, and they know about your predicament. I believe that when we get to Pemba Island my people will try to attack and capture a Russian spy that we have in our group. I told them about the hostages, and I'll do everything in my power to protect them and you." He then looks straight at Bosher. "Undersecretary, I cannot force you to go into harm's way. If you order me to, I will get you out of here."

Bosher stares at the man for a moment. It almost seems too good to be true. But something tells him he can trust this man. He answers, "Sergeant, I am here for Madam Aalee and her daughters. I have also reached out to your CIA for help. Let's just proceed to Pemba Island and pray for the best." He walks around to the passenger side of the car and helps Makena out. As she is standing, he leans in and says, "This man says he is an American agent and will aid us when we need it. I believe him. Just stay close to me and be prepared for anything."

Makena nods nervously in Tsosie's direction and mouths the words, *Thank you!*

Tsosie gets behind them and points the rifle barrel at Bosher's back. "We need to make this look real. They know me as *Abara*. Just stay quiet and do as I say. The pilot is one of the more civilized in the bunch. Our flight should be uneventful."

Three hours later Bosher, Makena, the pilot, and Tsosie are in a car driving to the dock from the hangar. Pasto had already moved Adimu and Chineye to the docks and left instructions to meet him there with the undersecretary and Makena. The sun is just rising in the eastern sky as they pull up to the parking area of the docks.

Tsosie looks out to the end and sees a small tugboat tied off. He can see Makena Aalee's daughters standing on the deck with Pasto and the Russian. He and the pilot get out first and then open the rear doors of the sedan they arrived in and step back as Bosher and Makena get out. As soon as she sees her daughters, Makena lets out a gasp and hurries in their direction. Before Tsosie or the pilot can warn her, Bosher rushes to her side and restrains her from running. "Madam Aalee, we must remain calm. We have no idea what we are walking into here. If Colonel Eloi got my message, then she will be close."

December 20, 3:00 a.m., Port of Jabal

Tommy, Lt. Commander Higgins, and Chief Swanson stand on the airbase landing field, talking about what little intel they have gathered since being on the tour. Higgins says, "So, all the senators are flying home tomorrow, guys, and we know next to nothing about why those crazy Iranians took our people or how we can get them back. Captain Smithers is sending us back to Cairo until we hear more from Tsosie."

Tommy shakes his head. "Commander, there has to be something we're all missing here. The Russians will make their move on Afghanistan any day now. You can't tell me that the Iran crisis and that move have nothing to do with each other. The Iranians don't want the Russians sticking their noses in their business any more than they want us to. But if Afghanistan falls, next on the list is Iran."

"I don't disagree, Lieutenant, but what does that have to do with our mission?"

"It's just that this new leader in Iran is a real xenophobe, and I think the hostage crisis is a ploy to keep us close enough to back the Russians off, but far enough away that we don't usurp his hold on that country."

Commander Higgins and Chief Swanson burst out laughing as Higgins slaps Tommy on the back. "I thought you didn't want to be a diplomat, like your old man. Sounds like that was your calling. Shit, Lieutenant, we're just out here to be reconnaissance soldiers, not figure out world politics."

He shakes his head and looks over at Swanson, who says, "I'll go help the pilot, Parker, prep our helicopter for takeoff, sir."

"Okay, Chief. Williams and I will get the others and see you in a few."

Naval Warrant Officer Bob Parker got assigned to Admiral Winston's command in Cairo, Egypt, two years ago. The navy seemed like an excellent idea when he enlisted after high school. Being an average student from Wisconsin, growing up with a coal miner for a father and a nurse's aide for a mother, he did not have many college prospects. The navy offered to train him as a helicopter pilot after boot camp. It was like a dream come true. But then, immediately after graduating from flight school, they sent him to the Middle East. He owed the navy six years then. It now seemed like he would do the entire time in this armpit of the world. So far, he had been lucky and hadn't been asked to do anything too dangerous, and that's the way he preferred to serve.

At first, he liked this recent detail of carting around this naval public relations crew because he gets to get out and see some more bases in the area. He thought this was just a publicity stunt to boost the popularity of the US senators these guys were following around. But then Sergeant Tsosie suddenly is not with them anymore, and nobody around the base has seen him. Lt. Commander Higgins and Lieutenant Williams don't seem very concerned. They just told him that Tsosie got transferred to another unit. Then there is all the extra gear in the back that Admiral Winston told him to stow but not ask questions about.

He was glad when he got the orders this morning to return to Cairo. Something is a little off about this so-called public relations unit. The entire thing smelled like a black ops detail that Winston didn't feel it was necessary to tell him about. And now he is glad he can get away from these guys.

One hour later, Higgins has his crew board the navy transport helicopter to get ready to follow the senators' jet that already left for Cairo that morning. As the helicopter is powering up, the radio chirps and Higgins picks up the mic.

"Lt. Commander, this is Admiral Winston. I just got a communication from Captain Smithers in Washington. First, you should know that the Russians just invaded Afghanistan; and second, you and your men are to divert to Pemba Island immediately."

"Pemba Island! What's going on, Admiral?"

"You think I know, Lt. Commander? I've been stuck out in this sauna toilet for three years and nobody tells me shit. All they said is some spooks from the CIA got some fresh intel from your man, Tsosie, and that he will meet you. They will brief you on some shit they need help with in Kenya."

"What about the senators?"

"Don't worry about that, Lt. Commander. We'll get them home safe and sound. Looks like you guys are being sent to do something they trained you for. Make us proud, sailor!"

"Yes sir, Admiral."

Higgins leans forward. "Parker, we're going to Pemba Island off the coast of Tanzania below Kenya. Admiral Winston's orders. You know the way?"

Parker rolls his eyes. "Yeah, Commander, I know the way. So, you going to tell me what's really going on here, sir?"

Higgins puts his hand on the pilot's shoulder. "We're a special ops SEAL team working for Captain Smithers of Naval Intelligence. I don't know why we're going to Pemba Island, but some CIA people are meeting us at the airfield, and they'll brief us when we get there."

Parker gulps and puts his thumb up. "We'll be there in three hours. I hope they have someplace for me to refuel when we get there, sir. We'll be at a quarter capacity when we land."

Tommy gets up and sits next to Higgins and yells over the noise of the rotor blades, "What's up, Lt. Commander?"

Higgins smirks. "Looks like your idea to send Tsosie undercover is paying off. Some shit just hit the fan down in Kenya that they need us to fix." He smiles and looks around the cockpit area. "The Russians just invaded Afghanistan, boys, and we're headed in the opposite direction to Pemba Island, off the coast of Tanzania. Don't know if the two are connected, but we got a job to do, so let's go find out what it is and do it."

Three hours later, the navy helicopter lands at a small airport on Pemba Island. Higgins gets out first, followed by Tommy and Chief

Swanson. As Parker is powering down the helicopter, a small, two-seater jeep pulls up and a man whom Tommy recognizes right away gets out and heads toward them. "Rogers, is that you?!"

"Tommy Williams! Damn, dude. It's been a while. What the hell are you doing here? Last I heard you gave up being a SEAL and went to Washington to be a PR stuntman."

Tommy recoils from the jab. "Well, things are not always like they seem, Rogers."

"Lt. Commander Higgins, this is Lieutenant Bob Rogers. We were in SQT together."

Rogers holds up his hand to stave off Tommy from saying any more. "Commander, it's Agent Rogers. I'm with the CIA now, and I'm your contact here on Pemba Island."

Higgins sees the awkwardness between Tommy and Rogers. "What was it about you, Rogers? Some kind of injury that kept you from completing SQT with Williams?"

"As a matter of fact, Commander, it was hairline fractures in both ankles from all the web work in diving. It laid me up for six weeks. The CIA approached me in the hospital and said I got a good recommend from Captain Fargo and offered to transfer me over. Because of SQT and Fargo's good word, they skipped basic training and had me out on the field in three months."

Higgins laughs and nods his head. "Yeah, we've lost a lot of talented people to the CIA, FBI, and others because of stupid shit like hairline fractures and pulled tendons. If Fargo got you in with the CIA, then you're okay in my book. Just for the record, your buddy Williams here is still a SEAL, but like the rest of us in this unit, Naval Intelligence is making us lead a double life." Higgins shakes his head. "Enough of this bull, Rogers. Why are we here, and where's Tsosie?"

"He should be at the dock with Undersecretary Arachar and Makena Aalee very soon. If we hurry, we can be there in time." He then looks over at Tommy and grins. "So, you guys beat Fargo in War Games? I'd have paid good money to see his face when that happened."

Tommy grins back at him. "Best day of my life. But I paid for it. Ten solid days of extra KP, polishing shit in Fargo's office, and doing the obstacle course until I couldn't feel my arms or legs."

As the crew is getting out of the helicopter, a van pulls up. Two men who look like locals walk over to Rogers. The one who drove points at the van. "All the equipment is loaded. I spotted the plane landing here about an hour ago. We had them followed. Tsosie and the other guy just reached the dock where there's a tugboat, and we spotted the Russian we're looking for on it, waiting for them."

"Does Tsosie know he has help on the way?" Higgins interjects. "Who's this Russian?"

"Lt. Commander, my superiors ordered me to brief you privately on the Russian. Tsosie's the one who sent the message about what was going down today. Plus, some of the undersecretary's people just reached out to us yesterday for help. They told us that he has his own people already on the island, led by a Colonel Adessa Eloi of the Kenyan Security Force. I have a description of her and her men, so we will know they are friendlies when we spot them."

"Who's going to tell her that we're friendlies?" Tommy says.

Higgins smirks at Rogers, who just shrugs his shoulders then looks back at Tommy. "We'll cross that bridge when we come to it, Lieutenant. What's your concern?"

Tommy looks at Rogers and grins. "Well, sir, it's a woman from Kenya, no less, and she's in command of their security force commando unit. Kenya's not the most progressive culture in the world, and she's a colonel, which means she's a major player. She is also good enough for the number two guy in the country to send her in here beforehand to cover his ass and be there when he needs rescuing. Just seems to me we could be caught in a crossfire with someone who could do some actual damage if she doesn't know we're on her side."

Higgins, Rogers, and Chief Swanson, who is now with the group, stare at Tommy for a few minutes, bewildered at his insight. Tommy shakes his head. "What? I paid attention in my world sociology class at the academy. Kenya is part of the world, so we studied it." He looks at Swanson. "Come on, Chief. Let's get out of here so Rogers can brief the lieutenant commander about this Russian." He hoists his duffel bag over his shoulder and makes his way to the van.

Higgins walks up to Rogers and puts his arm around his shoulder. "Williams is the trainee who beat Fargo in War Games? We heard it really happened, but no one could ever get the name of the kid that did it!"

Rogers shakes his head and laughs. "A guy from our class named Boder visited me in the hospital after he graduated from SQT and told me the entire story. If it was anyone but Tommy Williams, I would not have believed it. Tommy's probably the smartest guy I've ever been around. Most dedicated too. That's why I couldn't believe it when I heard he bailed on being a SEAL."

"Williams has potential, no doubt about that. So, why don't you tell me about this Russian you guys are so worked up about? Then we'll work out some logistics on how we'll keep the undersecretary and his friend safe and still nab him." Higgins motions to the jeep with his chin.

"Fine by me, Lt. Commander. There is a parking lot in front of the dock. That's where we'll stop and regroup."

Higgins looks over to the van and whistles to get Tommy's attention, then yells, "Lieutenant Williams, you and Chief Swanson talk things over. I'm going with Rogers."

Tommy and Swanson wave back in acknowledgment. Tommy looks over at the helicopter where Parker is doing some checks on the outside. "Keep that bird ready to fly. They got a refuel truck coming. We might need you on site at the dock or here, ready to take off quick. I'll radio either way."

Parker waves back as Higgins and Rogers get in the jeep and leave. Immediately, the van pulls out and follows. Parker waves them off and mumbles to himself, "Yeah, sure. Leave me here all by myself." He then walks around the side of the chopper, grabs his sidearm from inside, and straps it to his hip.

Same Time, Underneath the Dock

Colonel Eloi and her men snorkeled into the dock area before sunup and have been waiting in silence ever since. She saw the tugboat dock about forty minutes earlier and instinctively knew that it was what they were waiting for. The message from Undersecretary Arachar barely got to her in time late last night, but she changed her schedule to be here for the rendezvous. Bosher's decision to reach out to the American CIA has her concerned. Mainly because she doesn't know who they are or what they look like.

The sound of a car pulling up and doors opening and closing captures her attention. She stealthily shimmies up a wooden pole that allows her to see just over the boardwalk. Her heart skips a beat as she recognizes Bosher and Makena walking onto the dock, being escorted by two men with rifles. She eyeballs them warily. At first, she doubts her instincts, but upon closer observation she can tell that Bosher and Makena's body language suggest that they trust the one closest to Makena. She concentrates on the man as he gets closer and, although he has a definite Arabic demeanor to him, she can also see that there is something not quite Middle Eastern in his posture and stride. She surmises that he is an American posing as an Arab slaver and decides to treat him as one of the CIA agents that Bosher reached out to. The party of four gets about halfway to the gangplank of the tugboat, and she hears a familiar voice:

"Abara, hold them there for a moment."

Pasto Niazai, Tumba's friend from Afghanistan, she thinks as she slinks down the pole. She makes her way over to her men. "The undersecretary and Madam Aalee are directly above us, guarded by two men. The one closest to her is a friendly, probably CIA. We need to get in place before they bring the daughters back out for her to see. This will be tricky, because she'll want to go onto the boat to be with them, but I don't think they will let them go when she gives herself over. Some of us need to get on that boat and take them from behind. The rest of us will cover the escape and protect the undersecretary and Madam Aalee."

She looks at Sergeant Tibre. "Take two others and swim under the tugboat and climb up the other side. Sneak up behind Pasto as he brings the two girls into view. If anyone gets in your way, kill them, but be quiet about it. Once I step onto the dock, overtake them and retrieve the girls and send them down. Do not let Madam Aalee or the undersecretary get on that boat."

Sergeant Tibre points at two men and motions for them to follow him as he quietly slips down into the water and makes his way to the end of the dock and the tugboat. The remaining two men go to the other side of the dock and get ready to shimmy up some poles on Colonel Eloi's orders.

Up on the dock, Undersecretary Arachar scans the scene before him and is anxious that Pasto has no intention of releasing Madam Aalee's daughters. The only thing he can see happening now is their being forced onto the boat and all four of them taken. His instincts tell him that Colonel Eloi is close, but he can't really see any opportunity for a positive outcome, even with her here and the help of their newfound ally from the CIA. While still looking forward at Pasto, he whispers to Makena. "We're very vulnerable here. Stay close and move only when I move." He then directs his attention to Pasto. "You and Colonel Tumba must be quite pleased with yourselves, having trapped the only two people in Kenya who stand against your business arrangement to sell our people into slavery."

Pasto takes a radio and puts it to his lips. "Bring them up." Then he looks down at them. "Undersecretary, please. This business is the oldest, most established dealing we have between our two cultures. Your leaders have always helped in the supply of fresh slaves for our use since before the days when the Persian Empire dominated the world."

As Pasto is responding to the undersecretary's statement, Sergeant Tibre and his men quietly make their way up and over the railing on the other side of the boat. They unbag their rifles quickly and scan the area. A door opens from the right and two men bring Makena's daughters to the side of the boat where Pasto is standing. As they lead the girls to him, two more men come up and stand by the door, armed with pistols.

Tibre gestures his men forward. They put their rifles on their shoulders, hanging from the straps, and pull out their knives. Then they stealthily approach the latter two and simultaneously wrap their hands around each man's mouth and then ram their knives into their backs. They lower the men silently to the ground.

The first two men bring Makena's daughters to Pasto, and he grabs Chineye around the throat and puts his pistol to her head. "Now, Undersecretary, you see that I have kept my end of the bargain. You and Makena Aalee come forward and join us on the boat."

Undersecretary Arachar can feel Makena tense as Pasto points the gun at her daughter's head. He squeezes her hand and holds her in place as she tries to make her way toward her children. He also sees the activity going on behind Pasto and his men, and he knows that if they are to be successful, they need to get to the other two armed guards with Pasto. He looks down at her and says between clenched teeth, "Adessa is making her move. Be ready!"

Tibre's men approach the three men who are holding the girls at the railing of the boat. Tibre points his rifle at Pasto as he steps forward. "Pasto Niazai, put the gun down and release the girls … argh!" Tibre drops his rifle to the deck and falls to his knees with blood gurgling out of his mouth. The Chameleon pulls his blade from the back of the sergeant's neck, then throws it at the man closest to Pasto. It hits him in the throat, and he drops his rifle and reaches for his throat while falling to the deck.

Like a Jaguar attacking an unsuspecting deer, the Chameleon nimbly jumps over the corpse of Sergeant Tibre and attacks Tibre's other man before he can respond with his rifle. He grabs the rifle by the stock and crams the butt end into the man's chest, then yanks it out of his grasp, spins the man around, places his right hand over his chin, and pulls his head to the side, snapping his neck.

Without a moment's hesitation, he picks up the fallen man's rifle and shoots Tsosie in the chest. The impact knocks Tsosie down. His head hits the dock with an audible crack. Makena screams and the Chameleon draws his sidearm, grabs Adimu, holds it to her head and orders Pasto to get the undersecretary and Makena on the boat.

A Few Moments Before

The jeep carrying Rogers and Higgins pulls into the parking lot next to the entrance of the dock, followed by the van with the rest of the men. Rogers had just informed Higgins that the CIA believes that the Russian they are looking for is none other than the Chameleon himself. He knows he has to handle Williams just right or this entire thing could go south in an instant. Higgins heads over to the van as Tommy is getting the men out and ready. He looks at the group. "All right, guys, Rogers gave me a complete brief on the way over. We got the number two man in Kenya's federal government on that dock, and he is with a very important woman who is fighting human trafficking in her country. The group that Tsosie has infiltrated kidnapped her daughters and killed their grandmother last week, and they're using the daughters to lure Undersecretary Bosher Arachar and Makena Aalee into a trap, where they can capture or kill them."

Tommy's eyes lock onto Higgins for a moment.

"Something on your mind, Williams?"

"No, sir. It's just that I've heard the name Aalee before. It belonged to a famous Kenyan war chief who used to fight off slave-raiding parties about ninety years ago."

"Well, thanks for the history lesson, Lieutenant. Anyway, our job is to secure the undersecretary and his companions, board the ship ..." He pauses for a moment and looks at Tommy again as he holds up a staying hand. "And endeavor to capture the KGB operative known as the Chameleon."

As Tommy is about to say something, they hear a shot ring out from the dock area. Higgins grabs his rifle. "Let's move out. No one shoots until I give the order. Fan out and watch each other's backs. Williams, you're with me."

Chief Swanson and his two men take up positions behind Higgins and Tommy. Rogers gets on his radio and calls in what is happening, then gets his men with Swanson. They arrive at the dock entrance, and Higgins creeps up the stairs and peers over. He sees a middle-aged African man leading an African woman up the gangplank of a tugboat. Then he sees Tsosie's collapsed form on the dock.

For a moment he does not see how he can get up onto the dock without being spotted and putting the undersecretary and his companion in danger. Then three individuals vault onto the dock boardwalk from the side. One of them is a tall, formidable-looking woman holding an assault rifle—Colonel Eloi of the Kenya Security Force, the one he was told to look out for as a friendly. It doesn't look like she or the people on the tugboat want to start a firefight for fear of hitting the undersecretary and his companions.

He turns around and in a hushed tone says, "We have three armed friendlies in front of us with their backs to us. They are facing two armed men on the boat and one escorting them up. They have the two girls and the undersecretary, and the woman called Makena. One gunman looks like he's the Russian."

Tommy tries to move forward, but Higgins pulls him back. "Stand down, Lieutenant. If that is who we think he is, you'll be dead before you can even line up your shot." He pulls him in close so that they are almost nose to nose. "Besides, we're here to capture him for interrogation, not assassinate him."

Tommy sucks air through his teeth and glares at Higgins for a moment. "If that is who you think he is, then he's the bastard who killed my father." He takes a deep breath and calms himself. "But that ain't gonna stop me from following orders and doing my job, sir. You're in command!"

Higgins reaches over and shakes Tommy's shoulder. "I will not lie. This doesn't look good, but I have one idea. Back me up and keep everyone ready."

Tommy nods and holds his hand up to order the men behind him to wait.

Commander Higgins then calmly walks up to Colonel Eloi and her men. He keeps his rifle pointing up to the sky as he looks to the deck of the tugboat, where the undersecretary and Makena Aalee are now being held at gunpoint by Pasto's men. He looks sideways at her with his peripheral vision and says, "Colonel Eloi?"

In broken but understandable English, she responds. "Yes. I am sorry about your man. He didn't stand a chance."

He looks down at Tsosie. "I know." Then he steps forward and directs his voice to the men on the tugboat. "Colonel Pasto Niazai of The People's Liberation Army of Afghanistan. My name is Lt. Commander Larry Higgins of the United States Navy SEALs. We have two dozen men surrounding the front perimeter of your boat, and three United States naval warships will be in this area within the next five minutes. You are trapped and have no options. Release your prisoners, lower your weapons, and surrender to me immediately."

Pasto nervously looks behind him to scan the sea and see if what this American is saying is true. An icy chill goes up his spine as he reasons that the man would not expose himself like this if he were lying. He looks over to Makena and the undersecretary and starts to speak. But before any words can come out of his mouth, the Chameleon pushes him to the side, raises his rifle, points it at Higgins and squeezes the trigger. As the bullet impacts his skull, Commander Higgins's hands fly up and his rifle drops to the boardwalk.

The Chameleon then turns to Pasto. "He lied. Get these people below and launch this boat."

Stunned, Pasto does exactly as he is ordered. Several armed men appear on the deck of the tugboat and open fire on Colonel Eloi and her men. They manage to get a few shots off as they dive into the water on either side. Colonel Eloi dashes to the side and wraps one arm around the pole she had shimmied up earlier and with her other arm holding her semiautomatic rifle, she points it at the men who are firing on them and returns fire, killing two and wounding one more. She then releases herself from the pole and falls down into the sea below.

An electric chill goes through Makena's chest. As she is being pushed through the door, she glimpses a tall, menacing-looking, dark-skinned American soldier move toward them with nothing but a pistol in his hand. For a moment their eyes meet, and she feels a whisper of hope in that intense stare.

Tommy saw Higgins fall as the firefight erupted before his eyes. "Cover the Kenyan security people, and don't shoot toward that boat until the undersecretary and his people are out of the way."

Because of Colonel Eloi's quick thinking in returning fire, Tommy can stand and move in closer. In the intensity of the moment everything slows down, and it's crystal clear to him what is happening on the deck of the tugboat. First, he sees Pasto move the prisoners to the door leading to the inside of the boat. For a moment, he makes eye contact with the one named Makena. He feels her intense call for help in the way she looks at him.

Then the man who just may be the person who killed his father makes his way to the same door. As he puts his hand up to hold the door open, Tommy raises the only weapon within reach—his 1911 .45 caliber duty pistol. He takes aim and fires.

As the Chameleon is stepping through the door, the bullet hits it just above his hand and right where his temple was exposed a millisecond before. He pulls back for an instant and looks in Tommy's direction. His sniper senses tell him that it was a shot taken from a pistol, about thirty yards away. He has only known one person that has ever come that close to killing him like this before. For a moment, their eyes lock and the Chameleon mouths *YOU!* Then he dives through the door.

Tommy curses at the top of his lungs as he unloads his clip at the space where his nemesis stood a moment before. The men on the ship return fire and Rogers tackles Tommy and pulls him off the dock before he gets hit. Rogers and Tommy fall to the rocky beach area beneath the dock. As they stand, they see Colonel Eloi and her two remaining men making their way to them from the beach. Before he can say something to them, a hand reaches out and tugs his shoulder. He whips around with his .45 and stares at Chief Swanson. Swanson and Tommy stare at each other for a moment as Tommy lowers his weapon. He shakes his head. "That bastard killed Lt. Commander Higgins so fast I barely had time to react. I'm sorry, Chief."

Swanson sighs and shakes his head. "Higgins was the best there is, Lieutenant, but he overplayed his hand up there. You kept your head and almost took that bastard KGB agent out. You're in command now, Lieutenant. What are your orders, sir?"

Tommy stands there for a moment, bewildered by what he has just heard. He knows the chief is right, but this is his first official mission and shit like this ain't supposed to happen. He looks over at Rogers. "What kind of help can we expect from your people?"

Rogers turns around and points to the two men who came with him. "Look, Williams, I'm on my first assignment too. Pemba Island was never considered a high-profile area for the CIA until yesterday. I'm the only one here, and these two are local assets that my superiors hired to help me. I called in to the CIA primary station in Nairobi, Kenya, before we hit the dock, but it'll take them at least six hours to send us any kind of help."

A woman's angry voice interrupts. "By that time, Undersecretary Arachar, Madam Aalee, and her girls will be long gone, or dead! We need to do something now!"

Everyone turns toward the water and sees Colonel Eloi walking up to them. She makes her way to Tommy and points at the boat pulling away from the dock. "I lost three of my best men on that boat." She then looks around at the others. "And you have lost your leader and one other."

From the surface, they hear a loud groan, and then they hear Tsosie's voice. "Where is everyone? Oh my God! Commander Higgins is dead! Lieutenant, where the hell are you?"

"Tsosie, stay down until that tug gets out of sight. We all thought you were dead too. How the hell did you survive that shot?"

"I had my vest and trauma plate on under my clothes. That Russian guy didn't know it, so he shot me in the chest. Higgins was in his gear, so he got it in the head."

Colonel Eloi makes like she is going up to help, but Tommy puts up his hand to stay her and shakes his head. "That is not a good idea, ma'am. If that Russian is who I think he is, then he's one of the best snipers in the world. We should wait until that tug is out of sight before any of us make a move."

The Chameleon is now on the deck of the tugboat as it pulls away from the Pemba Island dock, and he is scanning the area with his SV-98 Russian sniper rifle's high-powered scope. For an instant, he thinks he sees Abara, whom he thought he killed, move a little. But as he observes him closer, he decides the man is truly dead. He has been in the business of killing people long enough to know that a dead body makes movement and noise sometimes for hours after being killed.

It bothers him that so many got away by taking cover under the dock. He knows that now there are American soldiers involved, and he has killed two of them. It will get much more complicated from here on in. He knew the moment he met Abara on the plane in Afghanistan that the man was a spy. He only let him live as long as he did so that he might learn more about what he was after.

He takes his handheld radio off his side and puts it to his lips. "Colonel Pasto, when we rendezvous with the cargo ship, we'll have to alter our course. We cannot afford to get too close to any American military bases. You'll need to find the closest Saudi port and we'll have to make our way to Iran over land."

There is a few seconds' pause, and then Pasto answers. "What about your twenty-four-hour deadline? If we go by land, it'll take us at least three days, and we'll have to secure a convoy to transport all our cargo. That will cut deeply into our profit."

The Chameleon laughs at the man's sense of priorities. "You need not be too concerned about your losses on this load. Mother Russia is now financing your war in Afghanistan. As for my deadline, I do have a contingency plan. All you need to be concerned with is getting me to Tehran so that I may carry it out."

"What about the undersecretary and that woman and her two daughters. Should we kill them?"

"No, we may need them as a bargaining chip. We keep them alive for now."

Back at the Dock

Tommy and Colonel Eloi watch the tug disappear over the horizon and then quickly make their way to the dock. Once there, Tommy yells at Tsosie. "It's okay to get up now. If you can."

Tsosie slowly sits up and pulls off his outer garment to reveal a black Kevlar vest underneath. When Tommy gets to him, he grabs Tsosie's outstretched hand and pulls him to his feet. Tsosie rubs his chest area, then undoes the Velcro slit going across his chest and pulls out a 5x5-inch metal plate that has a dent in it where the bullet hit. The slug is still embedded in the metal. He looks at it for a second then puts it in his pocket. "Damn, when that bullet hit me, it felt like a truck. My head hit the ground so hard that I was out cold."

They both then walk over to Higgins's corpse, and Tommy cringes at the ghastly sight of the man's head having exploded from the bullet. He grits his teeth at the memory of the same thing happening to his father in Tokyo. He cringes as he kneels to get Higgins's radio to contact Parker at the helicopter. He grabs Higgins's shoulder and pulls it toward him to retrieve the radio from the utility belt. The corpse's head flips to the side and Tommy gets a close-up of the damage that was done. There is a fuzzy, static sound over the speaker when Tommy presses the button.

"Lt. Commander, is that you?"

"Chief Swanson, you and the others take care of Lt. Commander Higgins's body. I'm calling for transport."

"Lieutenant Williams here. Higgins is dead. Get here as fast as you can and radio Admiral Winston and get me a direct line to Captain Smithers at Naval Intel. Oh, and Parker, we have one CIA operative and three Kenyan Security Force personnel here. Plus, the five of us who were with Higgins. Make sure you have enough room for everyone."

Rogers and Colonel Eloi, who have been hanging back to let the SEAL team deal with their dead CO, step up.

"Tommy," Roger says. "You're in charge now, so what do you want to do?"

Colonel Eloi's face is unreadable as she stares at the Americans and then out to sea, where they just watched Pasto and his men abduct two people she cares for very much. She heard the American lieutenant tell his pilot to make sure there was enough room for her and her men, but she has to know if they intend to pursue and rescue her friends. She steps up to Tommy and puts a finger on his chest and pushes him back. "Yes, Lieutenant, what do you intend to do? My men and I have no way to pursue those men and rescue Arachar, Madam Aalee, and her children, but you do."

In the depth of his heart, he knows what he wants to do, and looking at the others in the team, he can see that they want the same. But he knows it is not his call.

"Look, Colonel, my CO just took a bullet in the head from probably the same guy that killed my dad. So ..."

He pushes her hand away. "There is nothing more that I want than to chase after those bastards and kill every damn one of them. But it will take my transport about fifteen minutes to get here, and besides, we have no idea where that tug is going. I have a call being patched into my superiors. When I get on with them, I'll find out what I can do."

Tsosie walks over to the pair. "Lieutenant, that tug is rendezvousing with a cargo ship anchored thirty miles southeast of Pemba Island. They loaded it with girls destined for some sheikhs in Iran. The Russian is with them because he wants to use it as cover to get into Tehran, where he is supposed to assassinate someone. They were to sail through the Gulf of Aden and then the Gulf of Oman on up to Kuwait, where they'll transport their cargo overland to Tehran. But we have way too many military bases on all those coasts. They have to know that since they just killed an American military officer, they can't go that way. I think they'll have to divert west and seek a port along the Saudi coastline."

"If that's true then we might intercept them before they hit one of those Saudi ports." As he is speaking, they hear the military transport helicopter coming toward them. "Swanson, when he lands, get Higgins in a body bag and then get everyone situated. Sergeant Tsosie, you're with me. When we get Captain Smithers on the line, he'll want to talk to you too," Tommy says as he makes his way to the parking lot.

"Yes sir, Lieutenant."

Parker finishes powering down and steps out of the chopper. "I have Admiral Winston on the line. He says his people are patching Captain Smithers in as we speak, but he wants to talk to you first."

Tommy nods, steps up into the cockpit area, and puts the pilot's headset on. "Admiral Winston, Williams here, sir."

175

"Williams, damn sorry about Higgins. He struck me as a straight shooter."

"I haven't known him for long, Admiral, but I agree, and thanks."

"Listen, kid, I will patch your boss through in a minute. Smithers is an agreeable man, but he doesn't know what it's like out there. He's a desk jockey, and he's got a lot of pull in Washington right now. When you talk to him you have to present things to him in terms of what will be the best for the administration, not how you feel. I did some checking, and for the brief time you've been in Washington you've turned some important heads, and that includes the president. Looks like you've got your daddy's flair for that stuff. I know what you want. I want it too. Somebody has got to go after those bastards and put them down. Keep your head and play every card you have. You just might get what you're after." There is a slight pause and Tommy hears someone else's voice in the background. Winston gets back on the line. "Okay, Williams, we got him for you. Now, remember what I said. And kid …"

"Yes, sir?"

"I meant what I said earlier when you were on my base. I have your back. If you need me, just call."

Before Tommy can respond, another familiar voice gets on the line. "Lieutenant Williams, Captain Smithers here. What the hell is going on over there?"

Tommy leans back in the copilot's seat and takes a calming breath as he tries to arrange his thoughts. "For starters, sir, Lt. Commander Higgins is dead, and it looks like it was the Russian operative known as the Chameleon who killed him. He's working with a Colonel Pasto Niazai from Afghanistan, helping him with his human trafficking business in Kenya."

There is a brief pause on the line, then Smithers answers. "Higgins was the best we had, Lieutenant. I'm sorry you're in the middle of all this on your first assignment. We knew that Pasto was helping fund his boss's army with the profits they made from human trafficking. Now that the Russians have invaded their country and Pasto's people are in bed with them, it makes little sense that the Russians would even care about that business."

"Sir, Tsosie said that he's using Pasto and his cargo as cover, so that he could sneak into Iran and assassinate someone."

There is an even longer pause on the line. Tommy hears Smithers discussing something with someone else in the room. When he gets back on, there is desperation in his voice. "Williams, I have some CIA people with me. They say we must stop the Chameleon before he gets to Iran. We cannot under any circumstances allow him to accomplish his mission. If he does, that entire region could fall under Soviet control. I will send a request for Secretary Thompson to allow a strike force of warships to intercept that transport as it passes the Port of Jabal on its way to Kuwait. You and Higgins's crew are to proceed back to Cairo and report to Admiral Swanson."

A chill goes through Tommy's spine as he contemplates the orders. He knows that Smithers doesn't think he is anywhere near ready to take command of Higgins's crew, but he also knows he has to speak up. "Sir, we don't believe that the cargo ship will take that route. They know they just killed an American navy Lt. Commander and will expect retaliation."

"Where do you think they are headed, then?"

"Tsosie got to know a little about their operation while he was undercover. He thinks that they will try for a Saudi port somewhere along the Red Sea." Several voices come in over Tommy's receiver as Smithers and his companions discuss the intel Tommy just gave.

"Williams!"

"Yes sir?"

"We can't get anyone there before they would make the closest port. Besides you, Swanson, and the rest of the team, who else do you have there for an operation?"

Tommy smiles, remembering Winston's words earlier. "There's Rogers, our CIA contact. I know him very well. We were in SQT together. He's a good man. Then there is someone here who might make this entire thing work, even if we have to pursue on land."

Tommy hears a low guttural growl over the phone as Smithers responds. "No way, Williams, have you lost your mind? We can't send our people into Saudi territory without permission. That would be a diplomatic disaster."

Tommy smiles as his daddy's flair for imaginative diplomatic solutions germinates in his mind. "Sir, I have Colonel Adessa Eloi with me here. She's already lost three of her men trying to rescue her boss, Undersecretary Bosher Arachar, and a very prominent woman, along with her daughters. The Chameleon is on a ship carrying dozens of kidnapped girls from Kenya destined for slave markets in Iran. What is interesting is that the woman who was taken with the undersecretary is the great-granddaughter of a historic Kenyan hero, Tumaini Aalee. He patrolled the Kenyan coast a century ago and pursued slavers into Saudi Arabia to rescue his people. Back then, because of political pressure put on him by Great Britain, the Saudi king granted Aalee permission to come into his lands and take back his kidnapped people. As far as I know, that permission has never been rescinded. If we must pursue the Chameleon into Saudi territory, we can use Colonel Eloi's position in the Kenyan security force to justify being there to rescue the undersecretary and the woman with him. While we do that, we can stop the Chameleon from killing whomever they are sending him in for."

A bunch of voices start talking at once on the other end, and Smithers gets on and says, "Hold on for a moment, Williams. I'll get back to you. Don't go anywhere."

The line is dead for a solid five minutes. Then he hears a chirp and Captain Smithers's voice comes through again. "Williams?

"Well, the CIA people here think you're on to something. Anyway, we called our people in Nairobi and from what they said it sounds like this Colonel Eloi has about as much combat experience as Captain Fargo. They want you to enlist her help. Now, I want you to do a sea capture of that cargo ship before it hits a Saudi port."

Tommy's mind goes back to his advanced combat training after SQT. They did do maneuvers at sea where they had to rappel down from a hovering helicopter under cover of night onto a moving vessel. "Sir, we would have to helicopter drop right on the deck. Not impossible, but it's definitely a do-or-die scenario. If we blow that, there won't be a second chance. What about my idea of pursuing them after they make port?"

"These CIA guys are saying the same thing here, Williams. I just don't like it. If you go into Saudi territory, technically this Colonel Eloi will have operational control. They're telling me I can trust her, but I don't like handing control of an operation off to a foreign country. This is a US naval operation, and I have the final say. Boarding that ship at sea and getting control away from the hostiles is the best-case scenario. Work out your plan with this Colonel Eloi and make it happen before they can get to a port. That is an order, Lieutenant!"

Tommy sits there for a moment trying to slow his heart rate down and keep from exploding on his commanding officer.

"Keep us up to date, Williams! We'll keep this line open through Winston up in Cairo."

"Yes sir, Captain Smithers. Williams out!"

The line goes dead and Tommy sits there in the copilot's seat and tries to think through how they will accomplish this without getting everyone killed. He knows that trying to do it during the day would be a disaster. Pasto and the Chameleon would see them coming a mile off. He stands up, opens the door, and sticks his head out.

"Swanson, Rogers, come here." He then looks over at Colonel Eloi. "Colonel, could you join us, please?"

All make their way over to the helicopter. The pilot Parker decides he's invited and walks over with them. Tommy looks at all four, decides Parker needs to hear this too, and says, "All right, people, Captain Smithers wants us to try to take that cargo ship at sea before it hits a Saudi port. Colonel Eloi, what port do you believe they will go for? Their objective is Iran, so they'll want to go to the port that will give them the fastest overland route available."

Colonel Eloi thinks about it for a moment, then responds. "These men want to keep you out of their hair. That would mean they would try for the Port of Jiddah. It's the closest to Mecca, their holy city. They know that Americans will not want to cause any kind of incident around that place. Plus, it has the most roads leading to it from all over the country. Millions of Muslims make pilgrimages there every year. From there they can make the straightest route to Kuwait and then into Iran."

Tommy stares into her eyes for a moment and a slight crease of a smile manifests on her face. He smiles back. *She knows that our best bet is a land assault on these guys and is already planning it out.*

He nods and then looks over at Rogers. "Get me a detailed weather report for the next twelve hours on the area between us and that port." Rogers nods and walks off to his jeep, where he can contact his people. Tommy then looks over at Chief Swanson. "Chief, I've only done this kind of maneuver in training exercises. You've done it for real. I want you to oversee setting it up and getting us on that ship."

He then looks over at Parker. "So, Parker, you ever done anything like this before?"

Parker looks back and forth nervously between Tommy and Swanson. "Hell no! At NAS in Florida, we did a couple of rappel maneuvers on land and one at sea to an anchored cutter in the harbor. I've only done a couple of sea landings on a moving boat and it still scares the hell out of me."

Before Tommy can reply, Chief Swanson walks up and wraps his arm around Parker's shoulders and ruffles his hat with the other hand. "Well, today is your lucky day, pilot, because the lieutenant is right. I've done over twenty combat rappels onto a moving boat and it ain't no big thing. All you got to do is allow for wind and visibility, match the speed of the vessel that you're boarding, and make sure your guys don't get blown overboard before they cut loose from their ropes."

Parker gasps, "Oh, is that all? You forgot to mention that we can only do three people at a time, and there are nine of you."

Swanson looks over at Tommy and winks, then pulls Parker to the side. "Come on, let the officers here figure the other stuff out. We'll go over every detail of the maneuver until you know it backwards."

As Swanson and Parker move up into the helicopter, Tommy turns to Colonel Eloi. "You don't like doing a helicopter drop on the boat at sea, do you, Colonel?"

"I'm guessing your superiors probably don't want you going into Saudi Arabia uninvited. But how does one sneak onto a ship by being dropped out of a noisy helicopter? If they see or hear us coming, they could just pick us off from their deck as we rappel."

"Believe me, Colonel, I voiced the same concerns to my CO. I even told him that because we have you with us, we could legally enter that country and endeavor to retrieve your undersecretary and the great-granddaughter of Tumaini Aalee because of the access the Saudi king granted him back then."

Colonel Eloi's eyes go wide with astonishment. "You know about Tumaini Aalee and his agreement with the Saudis?"

Tommy huffs and rolls his eyes. "Yeah, well, my dad was a United States ambassador and before that a navy JAG lawyer. That was the direction I was headed before sniper fire killed him in Tokyo. We studied Tumaini Aalee's history in one of my sociology classes at the academy. Funny, people remember him as an outstanding warrior and liberator, which is true. But my instructor showed us he was a cunning diplomat. He reached out to Great Britain and the United States for help back then, and that's where he got most of his weapons and supplies. He even talked Sir Andrew Bryan Bullard, the British ambassador to Saudi Arabia, into pressuring the Saudi king to allow Aalee to go into his lands and attack any slave caravan that was carrying people from his country. He also almost won the Kenyan presidential election of 1918. Quite a guy."

"So, what did your superior say about us doing a land rescue?"

"He said that it's not off the table, but he wants us to try the sea capture first."

"That makes little sense. If we fail—"

"We probably won't get a second chance. I know, but he's worried about a bunch of things, mainly because once we step onto Saudi lands you'd have command of the mission."

Colonel Eloi raises an eyebrow and nods. "I understand, Lieutenant Williams. We will try it your superior's way first. But if we fail and somehow get another chance, we must try again on land."

"Agreed!"

Chapter 13

Air Assault

ONE HOUR LATER, TOMMY IS sitting in the copilot's seat next to Parker as they endeavor to trace the cargo ship's most likely course to Jiddah's port. The nine people in the transport copter are pretty cramped, and it's making it a little cumbersome for Chief Swanson and his crew to prepare for the rappelling exercise. Rogers is helping, but Colonel Eloi's men are just sitting scrunched together, trying to stay out of the way.

"How soon before the storm system hits the cargo ship's path?" Tommy asks.

"About another hour, Lieutenant. It should provide us with a little cover."

The radio chirps and Tommy picks up the mic. "Williams here, go ahead."

"Admiral Winston here. How are you guys doing?"

"So far so good, sir. We're about ninety minutes from the ship. Swanson and our men are prepping for the rappel and boarding. We do have some weather moving in that might provide us with some cover. It'll be tricky and tight, but Chief Swanson has done this several times, and he thinks we've got a good shot, sir."

There is a brief pause before Winston replies. "Smithers should have listened to you, Lieutenant. A ground assault and rescue make much more sense, especially with that intel about that Kenyan hero's deal with the Saudis a hundred years ago. Just so you know, I've dispatched a Spruance-class destroyer your way. Should be there in four hours. If you guys get in trouble at sea, we can help. But once that cargo ship makes port at Jiddah, they can't do anything."

"Whew, that's some heavy metal response and backup, sir. Was Smithers okay with that?"

"Humph! Last time I checked, he was a captain and I'm an admiral. This is my command down here, and if I want to send a ship on a routine maneuver, then that's none of his business."

Tommy grins and looks over at Parker, who is listening to the conversation on his headset. "We appreciate the backup, Admiral," Tommy responds. "Please forward our status to Captain Smithers. We'll contact you before we start our sea assault. Williams out."

"Stay frosty, Lieutenant. Do your job and get everyone home safe. Winston out."

Cargo Hold of the Ship Heading for the Jiddah Port

Makena Aalee and her two daughters sit huddled together in the corner of the cargo ship's inner hold. She is doing her best to console Chineye and Adimu as they have their heads buried in their mother's chest, sobbing and shivering for fear. The hold has about twenty girls from Kenya, Somalia, and Tanzania all crammed together, and most are the same age as Makena's daughters. She looks up as the door opens and two guards shove Undersecretary Bosher Arachar through.

Bosher has both hands tied together in front of him and he raises them to remove his glasses and rub his bloodshot and swollen eyes. There is a gash along his left eyebrow where someone struck him earlier, and he endeavors to stanch the flow of blood with his sleeve. When Makena sees what he is doing, she grabs the left sleeve of her blouse at the shoulder, rips the material off and takes and wraps it over the cut and around his forehead. Then she reaches inside her skirt pocket and pulls out a small scarf and wipes the blood and sweat from his face. "What did those animals do to you, Bosher?"

"That Russian wants to take me back to his home country where he believes his superiors can use me to force President Amoi to sign an allegiance treaty with the Soviet Union. I told him that Amoi will probably thank him for getting me out of his way. That is when they started interrogating me. They want something they can use to force him to do what they want. I've resisted their attempts to influence Kenya for some time, and they know I have secrets that will help them control many key figures in our government."

Makena finishes wiping the blood off his face as best she can. "Who were those men behind Colonel Eloi? After the Russian killed their leader, another one started shooting at him. I thought I saw fear in the Russian's eyes. He seemed to recognize the shooter."

"We reached out to the United States CIA, as you know. I believe they were the men who were working with Tsosie. As for the shooter, your guess is as good as mine."

Makena struggles to hold back her tears. "I saw Colonel Eloi shoot at least two of their men before she jumped into the ocean and we were forced down the stairs. Do you think enough of the Americans survived to help us, Bosher?"

"You saw more than I did, Makena, but the Americans don't take kindly to anyone killing their own. The man on the dock who was shot was a US Navy SEAL. They will not want to let something like that go unpunished."

"Let's hope they're successful and that Colonel Eloi is with them," Makena says.

Up on the Bridge of the Cargo Ship

Pasto Niazai and a few of his men are gathered around the radio phone while he is in a heated debate with Colonel Tumba about what just transpired on the dock at Pemba Island. "Tumba, that was out of my control. My superiors instructed me to follow the KGB agent's orders to the letter. When he killed the American, I had nothing to do with it. But that doesn't matter anyway, because his government's involvement is the only thing that'll keep you alive at this point. Now that we've taken Undersecretary Arachar off the board, I suggest you talk to President Amoi and persuade him to reopen negotiations with the USSR."

Pasto listens for a few moments then replies. "You and Amoi have no other place to turn than to our Russian friends. Oh, and I expect that within the next few months I can move my people back into Mombasa so that we can continue our business arrangements." Pasto places the microphone back on the table and looks at his men. "Has the Chameleon decided what to do with the undersecretary?"

Before any of them can answer, a voice from behind answers. "After you get me into Tehran, you'll bring him back to Afghanistan. My people will have him transported to Moscow. There we will see what other uses we can squeeze out of the man. Now, I have a question for you."

"Yes, Chameleon?"

"Why is there only one armed man stationed on the deck this evening?"

Pasto nervously glances at his men then back at the Chameleon. "We're only three hours away from our Saudi port, and there's a nasty storm coming our way. I sent the others down to get the cargo ready to move once we arrive."

The Chameleon shakes his head and sneers at Pasto. He walks over to retrieve his sniper rifle from the corner of the room. He inserts a round in the chamber and picks up some extra ammo and his sidearm. As he makes his way to the door, he looks back at Pasto. "With high-ranking fools like you in The People's Liberation Army of Afghanistan, I am challenged to believe that even with our help your General Turakine will accomplish his goals. All of you grab whatever armaments you have and follow me. Those men we dealt with on Pemba Island were part of an elite US force. Very elite. Underestimating them would prove disastrous. Follow me!"

The wind from the storm is just starting to pick up as they make their way to the deck. Though it is only 5:00 p.m., the skies are turning dark. The ocean, churning with whitecapped and building waves, is rocking the ship, making it difficult to remain upright. The Chameleon fights his way to the bow and sits down on the deck. He wraps an arm around some railing and pulls his sniper rifle to his shoulder, so that he can use its scope to scan the sea. He makes a couple of sweeps from left to right, scanning the horizon for anything in the air or on the sea that might be pursuing them.

He is about to stop when the slightest reflection of glass arrests his attention. He focuses his scope on the phenomenon and waits. In a few moments the barely discernable silhouette of a transport helicopter against the dark gray sky comes into his view. As it grows closer, he sees the white USN (United States Navy) insignia on the side. Some movement catches his eye, and he sees the door to the helicopter open and three men jump out and rappel down. He contemplates killing the men on the ropes. His rifle is a bolt action and only takes one round at a time. He could do it, but by the time he got to the third one, the helicopter would already be close enough for them to retaliate. He raises the rifle slightly and scopes the base of the large rotor blades. Better to kill them all at once and be done with it, he decides. He lines up the shot, calculates the exact spot that will do the most damage, and squeezes the trigger.

A heartbeat later, the Chameleon smiles. A spark from the impact of the slug severs a fuel line and causes a fire to erupt at the base of the rotor blades.

Back at the helicopter, Chief Swanson and two of his men are the first to deploy on the rappelling lines. Parker spotted the cargo ship about five minutes ago on his radar and Tommy agreed with Swanson that he should go first, having done this before. The next two groups follow.

"About two more minutes, Lieutenant, and we can lower them on the deck. I must do a circle around the ship to reposition for the second group. The wind is too heavy to do more than one drop at a time," Parker says to Tommy.

Suddenly lights and warning sounds erupt all over the console. Panic erupts on Parker's face. He looks over and flips a switch and checks the fuel gauge. "*Lieutenant!* The chopper is on fire and we're losing fuel fast. We're going to *crash!!*"

Tommy stands up and tries to look at the top outside of the chopper. He sees thick black smoke and flames dancing over the front. He looks back at Tsosie, Eloi, and her men, and points to the back cargo area of the chopper. "Get the inflatable life rafts back there and any other equipment you can grab." He looks back at Parker. "Hold her as long as you can. Get Swanson and our guys closer to the water so they can safely cut free." He grabs the mic. "Chief, we're going down. The engine is on fire. We're going to get you as close to the water as we can so you can release and jump in, then we'll throw you a raft." He looks back and sees that Eloi has both rafts and some equipment up by the door. He nods and tells her to open the side doors and wait.

A few seconds later, Swanson's voice comes over the radio. "We're dropping in now, Lieutenant."

Tommy jumps up with the mic in his hand and he and Eloi grab the first raft and push it partway out the door into the open air, then he pulls the *inflate* cord and kicks it over at the same time. "The raft is right behind you, Swanson. Make your way to the coast as fast as you can. If we stay within a two-mile radius, we can communicate on our handhelds. Good luck!"

"I can't hold it any longer, Lieutenant!" Parker screams.

"Okay, shut the engines down and get over here. We're bailing."

Parker pushes a couple of switches and jumps up and runs over to the rest of the group. Tommy, Tsosie, Rogers, and Eloi's men already have their life preservers on and he takes one from Tommy's outstretched hand. As soon as Tommy hands it to him he pushes the other raft halfway out, pulls the cord, and kicks it into the sea. Tommy sticks his head out and looks to the east where the sun is setting and marks where some light is still seeping through the clouds, then he looks over to his right and marks the coastline. "Okay, guys, let's go!"

Tommy pushes Parker out first, then lets Colonel Eloi and her men go, and then Tsosie and Rogers. Just before the flame-engulfed chopper hits the ocean, Tommy jumps out as well. When he hits the water, it feels like jumping into a bathtub full of ice. He shakes off the sensation by immediately swimming in the raft's direction and toward the shore. The wind and the waves make it impossible to see anything farther away than six feet. He is a SEAL though, and they have trained him to swim in almost anything, and swim he does. He almost collides with the raft before he sees it, but instinct and training take over and he is up and over the edge before he realizes it.

Much to Tommy's relief, he sees Parker, Tsosie, and Rogers already there. Parker says, "Geez, Lieutenant, when you threw me out, I practically landed in the raft. My shoulder hurts like hell." Before he can answer he sees several hands reach over the side and moves over to help them in. Once Colonel Eloi and her men are safely in the raft, he reaches for his radio inside his jacket and yells, "Chief, are you guys in your raft yet?"

"Affirmative, Lieutenant. We were waiting to see if you needed our help. Did everyone make it on your end?"

"Yes. Parker may have a dislocated shoulder, but we're all here."

Before Swanson can respond, a loud boom catches everyone's attention. They watch the helicopter explode and sink into the sea.

Tommy looks around and finds the point in the horizon where the sun is setting and grabs an oar. "We need to get to the shore as soon as possible," he yells. "If this blows us out to sea too far, we're done."

With only three oars available, Tsosie and one of Eloi's men take the other two and Tommy takes the rear to steer with his oar, as the other two paddle. "Chief, we're headed for shore. Once there, we'll regroup and figure out what to do next."

"Roger that, Lieutenant. See you there."

Tommy takes one more look at the cargo ship and mutters, "You haven't seen the last of me, not by a long shot!" He sees that Colonel Eloi has an anxious look on her face. "We're not giving up, Colonel. We'll get your people back, and we'll make the bastards who took them pay!"

Colonel Eloi stares at Tommy for a moment, then slowly smiles and nods her head. They end up being less than half a mile from the coast and make it to the beach within thirty minutes. As they hit the shore and pull the raft in, Tommy reaches for his radio. "Chief, you there?"

"Look to your left, Lieutenant."

Tommy looks up and over to his left and sees Swanson and the other two about thirty yards up the beach, coming in their direction while hoisting their raft over their heads. The storm is gaining in intensity, so he hurries everyone to get the raft up and make ready to get off the beach. He scans the immediate perimeter and looks for easy access off the beach, then waves at Chief Swanson to follow them. He reaches down and checks to see that he still has his .45 caliber 1911 sidearm, and makes a mental note to take it apart to clean and dry it as soon as they find shelter. Then he checks his belt for the extra clips and sees that one got lost when he bailed and one is left. He asks Colonel Eloi and Tsosie, "Were you able to salvage any weapons when we bailed?"

"I have my 9mm sidearm and two extra clips. My men could not get to their rifles in time," Colonel Eloi answers.

He looks over at Tsosie, who just shakes his head no.

They make their way to a path that runs between some large sand dunes. Swanson and his men catch up and Tommy is relieved to see that the three of them kept their rifles and sidearms. He orders Tsosie to help them carry their raft, making the teams even. Thunder and lightning crack in the sky above.

A gigantic bolt of lightning strikes a piece of rock protruding out of the sand at the top of the hill where the beach ends. The entire area shakes from the blast and the sand starts to avalanche down onto the trail they are following. Tommy and Swanson see the danger and order their groups to run up that hill as fast as they can. Both parties start tearing into the ever-increasing loose sand as it flows into their path. Tommy's team is in front, and he looks up to see that they are only about ten yards away from the top and the promise of more solid ground. Another blast of wind and rain mixed with sand slams into both groups, and Swanson's men lose control of their raft. It quickly rises into the air and blows back out toward the ocean.

Swanson is about to go after it but Tommy yells, "Leave it, Chief. We need to get out of here."

As they get closer to the top where the lightning had struck, they see that the small piece of rock that was protruding through the sand has now been uncovered as the surrounding sands are falling away. As they get within a few feet of the area, it becomes apparent that the reason the massive outcropping of rock—that now looks more like the side of a cliff—is visible is not only because of sand flowing toward the beach but also because sand is falling into a crack that has opened up in the side of the rock's face. Tommy makes his way to the area. He inspects the crack and sees that it's not a break but an opening, like a door. He reaches in and grabs the stone from the inside with both hands and tries to pull it farther open, but it's too heavy and won't budge.

The rest of the party catches up and sees what he is trying to do, and they join him in trying to pull it open. It budges a little, but not enough to get into the now-obvious cave that would provide them with protection from the storm. As they continue to tug, Tsosie suddenly loses his footing and falls flat, with his face in the now exposed hole. When he lifts up his head and lets a little light into the hole, he sees some type of cranking bar, like on a car jack, about a foot down in the hole.

Chapter 14

Help from the Past

Saudi Arabia, 1911, Red Sea Coastline, South of Jiddah and East of Mecca

Tumaini Aalee peers at the horizon, endeavoring to spot the area of cliff he must get to before a band of angry slavers can catch up to him. The faint scent of the sea touches his nostrils and he knows his destination is at least a half day's journey. The slightest of vibrations manifests itself in his feet, and he stops and holds a hand up to stay the advance of his fleeing caravan. His warriors see to it that the girls they freed a day ago stop and remain calm as their leader thinks. He's worried that the cavern hideout where he keeps supplies and weapons will not be big enough for this group that numbers almost two hundred.

One day ago, he and seventy-five of his best warriors pursued a slave caravan to the jungles of Medina, where under cover of darkness they ambushed the flank of that party and freed most of the hostages, consisting of girls taken in a raid of a coastal village at the northern tip of Somalia two weeks earlier.

He feels another vibration and turns to his flank to see if his pursuers are closer than he thought. His senses tell him that they are still too far away to cause any vibrations of the ground. His mind races to explain the phenomenon they are experiencing. The earth beneath his feet moves again, but this time it is no mere vibration but an actual shaking of the ground. He quickly scans his area and finds a low mountain range to his right only a few miles away. He puts his fingers to his mouth and blows out an ear-splitting whistle, then points and yells, "To the mountains. *Run!*"

Two hours later, Tumaini and his party stand at the crest of the mountain that now gives them a panoramic view of what has just transpired. The earthquake took place deep in the Saudi desert to their west and unleashed millions of tons of sand that traveled for miles until it met the sea. There was so much sand that it completely engulfed and buried the cliffs that he and his party were making their way toward. His son comes up and stands beside him, looks in the direction of the cliffs, and sighs. "All is lost, Father. Not just our weapons and supplies, but those ancient treasures we found, so long hidden there. How can we replace any of this? No one in these lands will sell us arms or supplies. The Saudi king only allows us to use what we bring and forbids us to take anything out with us except those we have rescued."

Tumaini takes one last look toward the new sandy beach and the slight hill that replaces the cliffs, now buried under them, and shakes his head. "That place was there for thousands of years before we discovered it. I do not believe it is lost, only buried. As for your other concerns, I think this is the last time we will have to pursue raiders in this country. That whole raiding party was surely killed in the earthquake and buried under the tons of sand we now look upon. Their deaths will be seen as an omen of evil and will cause them to avoid these lands for a while. We have not seen raids on our coast for years because they concentrate their efforts further south in Somalia. Soon they will be forced to take the sea routes to the Persian Gulf, and that is how we will have to pursue them from here on." He turns to his son and grabs both his shoulders and lightly shakes him as he continues. "Do not despair. That treasure is merely buried. and who knows, someday others may need and find our lost treasure and hopefully use it for a worthy cause."

Back to Present-day Saudi Arabia, Red Sea Coastline

The whole time the others have been trying to get the cave door open, Colonel Eloi has been staring at it in wonder. She looks over at Tsosie and yells, "What do you see?"

"Some type of cranking bar!"

She motions her men over, runs up to the hole, kneels down, looks at it, then looks back at Tsosie and her men. "We need to push this bar back and forth several times and the cave door will open."

Tsosie looks up to Tommy for confirmation.

"Do it!" he says as another bolt of lightning strikes the ground nearby. Four sets of hands reach in and push the bar forward. At first it feels tight, like rusted metal, but at a certain point something gives and the bar begins to move. When it does, the door budges open a few more inches. Tommy sees that and runs over and sticks his hands down in the hole and helps crank. The door slides open and the entire party scrambles in through the opening.

Colonel Eloi seems to understand where she is. She walks over to the wall, reaches up into the darkness, and grabs a metal pole with a domelike open canister on the end. She twists a knob at its base, then turns the pole over, shakes it vigorously then turns it back upright. She then takes a piece of metal attached to the pole with a small chain and strikes it at the base of the canister. It immediately bursts into a flame that provides light.

She walks over and grabs a similar cranking bar like the one outside and moves it back and forth. This one is not so stiff, and the door immediately closes. She turns around and faces her seven companions. The light from her torch now shows that they are standing inside a huge cavern filled with wooden crates, shelves stacked with all sorts of provisions, and even some old cots and a fire pit with chopped wood next to it.

"Gentlemen," she exclaims, "welcome to the long-lost supply and weapons cache of Tumaini Aalee, The Legend!"

Astonished, Tommy stares at the sight for a few moments, then sees another pole like Colonel Eloi's torch on a rock shelf close to him. He reaches over, takes it, and mimics Eloi's earlier maneuvers in igniting it. When it is lit, he looks back at Colonel Eloi and points to the entrance. "That doorway is thousands of years old. Look at the symbols—they are ancient Aramaic. Tumaini Aalee did not construct this cavern. What's the story here, Colonel?"

Colonel Eloi's eyes twinkle as she considers this man who continues to astonish her with his understanding for this part of the world. She raises her torch to illuminate the ceiling. As they all look up, much more can be seen of the same symbols and some ornately drawn pictures depicting a burial procession of some ancient royalty in the same spot just inside the door where they are all standing.

She looks at Tommy. "One hundred years ago this area was not a sandy beach that gently led up to the land. It was a sheer cliff wall that rose two hundred yards up from the sea. In it was this cavern. An ancient Persian prince who had been exiled to this land by his elder brother, who had just ascended to the throne, did not want any challenges to his rule. The prince had his tomb built inside this cavern, thinking that the cliff would conceal its location, for he had much wealth entombed in here with him.

"Millenniums later, Tumaini and his warriors were being pursued by a large army of slavers and they came upon this cliff. They were climbing down it when he quite miraculously came upon the same stone that covered the entrance lever outside and accidentally uncovered it. He and his men took refuge in this place for several days and discovered the many treasures that he later used to buy weapons from Great Britain and the United States. That is when he gained enough favor with the British ambassador to force the Saudi king at the time to grant him and his men safe passage into this country from the Port of Jiddah. From there, it allowed him and his warriors to pursue and take back any of our people who were being transported through these lands by the slave caravans. I am told that many of the artifacts from this cavern are still displayed in the Persian Empire section of the British Museum."

Before Tommy can ask the next obvious question, she stays him with her hand and continues. "Sixty years ago, there was a great earthquake in this region and an avalanche of sand a million times more powerful than the one we just experienced completely engulfed the cliff section of this beach that spanned for miles in both directions. That is why Tumaini's cache has been lost until we found it today."

Fascinated by her words, Tommy raises his torch and examines more of the symbols on the ceiling, then he walks deeper into the cavern to inspect the supplies. Tsosie, Swanson, Rogers, and their men eagerly follow behind. The first set of crates has the old Colt gun manufacturing logo on it, along with "Made in the U.S.A." stamped below the logo. Other boxes have English and French flags on them.

He uses the end of his torch to pry open one crate. When he gets the cover off, he reaches down to pull off some tanned yellow cloth on the top. As his fingers wrap around the cloth, he feels that it is saturated with some very thick grease. Once he gets that off, he sees ten little pouches made of the same cloth. He picks one up and opens it. When the contents are revealed to him, his heart goes to his throat. There in the palm of his hand is a perfectly preserved 1889 Colt .45. Tommy quickly inspects the pistol by opening the revolver and exposing the cylinder, which allows him to look down the inside of the barrel. He then snaps it back together and cocks the hammer and pulls the trigger. The sound from the single action is smooth, and the click tells him that the firing pen is still viable. He then pulls the trigger several more times and tests the double action of the gun and decides that next to a live-fire test, it seems to be in perfect condition.

Colonel Eloi walks over and grabs one pouch and retrieves another of the Colts and says, "It would appear that you are familiar with this weapon."

The right side of Tommy's mouth twists into a half grin. "My dad gave me one of these as a present when I graduated from Annapolis. In high school I was on a revolver competition team. We were the East Coast champions for two years. My scores were always the highest."

"Tumaini Aalee's skill with that gun is legendary among my people. While at a full run he could get twenty-four shots off in twenty seconds using a speed loader."

"That's damn good shooting. My senior year in high school I did the twenty-yard course getting thirty rounds off in twenty-nine seconds with a ninety-seven percent accuracy. That is still the East Coast record as far as I know." He looks around at all the crates, then back at her. "Smart of him to store all these Colts in oil cloth bags. Do you think the ammo is good?"

Colonel Eloi scans the area and sees some metal boxes stacked together close to the rear, where the pistols are. She grabs one and uses her foot to brace it against the ground as she pulls on the flat release lever on top that unlocks the compression hinge. When she opens it up, she finds similar oiled cloth lying on top. She removes the cloth, reaches in and grabs a handful of .45 caliber slugs, and hands them to Tommy. "You tell me, Lieutenant."

Tommy holds one bullet up with his right hand and looks at it closely. He does not see any green or rust color around the seals and can feel the grease on the casing. He picks up the Colt .45, releases the cylinder, and inserts three rounds at once, using the old hand speed load technique he learned in competition. He then snaps the cylinder back, aims at the woodpile in the center of the room, and rapid-fires all three rounds into the same piece of wood, splitting it in half. He looks over at Colonel Eloi, spins the pistol around in his hand a few times, like the old western cowboys used to do in the movies, and sets it down with a broad grin on his face.

"Works just fine, Colonel. Looks like we've just been resupplied with some weapons."

"You got that right, Lieutenant. Look at this."

Everyone turns around and sees Tsosie and Chief Swanson at the other end of the room, inspecting some other crates and shelves. Tommy and Colonel Eloi walk over and Chief Swanson hands him an old-style lever-action rifle. Tommy eagerly receives it, turns it around in his hands a couple of times, then places the butt end to his shoulder. He cocks the lever and squeezes the trigger. He reaches in his pocket and pulls out some more .45 rounds and inserts them into the rifle, cocks it again, then aims and fires twice at the woodpile across the room. He then hands the rifle to Tsosie. "You recognize this weapon, Sergeant?"

Tsosie takes the rifle and grins from ear to ear. "Sure do, Lieutenant. This is an original Winchester 1873 Colt .45. Uses the same ammo as the revolver you were shooting. And it appears to be in perfect working order."

Tommy looks over at Swanson. "How many of these are there, Chief?"

"Two crates of four, Lieutenant. But look at this." He raises the torch that he and Tsosie found, and it illuminates the back part of the cave. There, against the wall and ornately laid out, is what looks like something one would see in the African section of a museum—several leopard and panther skins, skirts, headdresses, spears, bows and arrows, and other paraphernalia.

Colonel Eloi and her men rush up to the display and start talking to one another in their ancestral tongues. As they pick up the items and discuss them, Tommy hurries over to her. "Colonel, what's this all about?"

She looks at Tommy with a mystical glee in her eyes. "This is how Tumaini Aalee did it, Lieutenant. He and his men were fierce warriors, and he was a cunning leader. But they were always outnumbered and usually outgunned as well. But he was wise, like the panther, and only hunted at night. His men would track the slave caravans taking our people across the desert. They dressed in our traditional warrior fashion, armed themselves with modern weapons, and swooped down to take the caravans by surprise, breathing fear into their very souls. They almost completely halted the slave trade out of our country."

Tommy picks up a panther skin skirt and a headdress, and holds them up to Colonel Eloi. "Is this the one he wore?" She nods and smiles. "So, tell me, Colonel. Is Tumaini Aalee still remembered by these slavers today?"

She laughs. "Oh, Lieutenant Williams, they will never forget *Shaytan al-Layl, The devil who comes in the night!*"

Port of Jiddah, Saudi Arabia

Pasto Niazai walks up to the transport truck carrying Undersecretary Arachar and Makena and her two daughters. The driver is just getting ready to pull out from the dock loading area to join the convoy of five other vehicles ready to transport them and the rest of the cargo across the desert to Kuwait and then Iran.

He motions for the man to roll down his window. As he does, Pasto climbs up to the door. "We can't afford for any officials in this port to find out that we have a man like the undersecretary in our custody. Our agreement with these people is that no one of any importance will be part of our cargo. You must keep them quiet. Have your men bind and gag them if they must, but do not damage any of them, especially the undersecretary. Those are the Chameleon's orders."

The man nods and Pasto looks inside the cab. He sees that the door between the cab and the back area is open and that there are two armed guards in there with the prisoners. "When you go through the checkpoint, be sure to close that door. They won't look in any of our vehicles, but if someone causes a disturbance, they are supposed to check it out."

The guard in the passenger seat reaches back and slides the door closed. Pasto grabs the driver's shoulder and shakes it. "Soon we will be home and this promises to be a very lucrative haul!" The driver smiles and nods his head again. Pasto jumps down and walks back up to the first transport vehicle where the Chameleon is sitting in the passenger seat. He opens the door and climbs into the rear seat. "We're ready to go."

"How soon will you have me in Tehran?"

"If we drive in shifts and don't stop, we'll be in Kuwait in two days. We must take some time there to bribe the border officials, but after that it should only take another two days, and you'll be there."

The Chameleon folds his hands across his lap, leans back, and pulls his hat down so that the bill shades his eyes. "That is acceptable. I prefer to travel in quiet, so let's keep it that way."

The driver looks back at Pasto through the rearview mirror to see his reaction to the Russian's rude request. Pasto puts his hand up under his chin and slides it across his throat, silently telling the man to comply. "As you wish, Chameleon. We are here to follow your orders."

Back in the Transport Carrying Makena and her Companions

Adimu and Chineye desperately cling to their mother as the transport truck moves away from the guard station on the dock. The guard sitting closest to them takes his gun away from Makena's head and sits back down on the wooden plank seat across from her.

Undersecretary Arachar sneers at the man. "You are a fool. Didn't you hear your boss? What if she screamed or one of her daughters cried out? He will have you shot if anything happens to us."

Before the man can reply, the door between the cab and the cargo area slides open and the driver looks in the rearview mirror and yells, "He's right, you idiot. Pull that weapon again on any of the cargo and I'll put a bullet in your head and dump you on the side of the road."

The man next to him then slams the door shut and the five people in the back sit there for a few moments, all dealing with their own fears. Chineye weeps again and buries her head into Makena's chest. "Mama, what will happen to us? Are we really to be slaves in some pig's harem?"

The undersecretary reaches out and grabs Chineye's hand and squeezes it gently. "I believe Colonel Eloi survived the encounter on the dock. If I know anything, it is that my wife will never give up. Adessa will come for us."

Makena catches his eye and nods. "There was another one on that dock who will not give up either. Colonel Eloi has found a formidable ally."

Chapter 15

History Repeats

Back at the Cave

TOMMY AND CHIEF SWANSON INVENTORY the weapons and ammo while Colonel Eloi and her men examine the other supplies. Parker has been hanging back, resting on a cot as Swanson's men are endeavoring to help him with his shoulder. Richards, a field medic for the team, eases Parker's arm up and down and palpates his shoulder. "The good news, Parker, is that it's not dislocated, but you're going to have a nasty bruise. I'll make up a sling for you—and you'll need to take it easy for a while."

Tommy stops what he is doing and walks over and looks at Parker for a moment. "Richards, can this man function in combat?"

"I don't know, Lieutenant. His left arm isn't useless, but it's close."

Before Richards can answer, Parker blurts out, "Lieutenant, I'm not a combat soldier. I'm a helicopter pilot."

Tommy stares at the man. "Look, flyboy, we got shot down in your aircraft. You have a duty as its captain to ensure that all of us get to safety as soon as possible. If that means fighting off an enemy combatant, then you're a combat soldier." He stops and takes a calming breath. "Can you drive a stick shift vehicle with that arm, Parker?"

Parker endeavors to straighten out his left arm in front of his face as he makes a fist. "Yeah, I could probably drive a truck or something, but we don't have a vehicle and—"

"Lieutenant, will you get a load of this!" Tsosie shouts, cutting Parker off in midsentence. Everyone turns to look at the rear of the cavern, where Tsosie is looking into a chest.

Tommy and the others walk over. Tommy peers into the chest, and his eyes go wide with astonishment. The chest is about two feet long, a foot high and a foot wide.

And it's filled with gold coins.

"Whoa! What kind of money is that?" he says to no one in particular.

Colonel Eloi and her men come around Tommy and kneel to survey the contents. Eloi holds one coin up to the light, then hands it to Tommy. A huge grin creases her face. "This is a Saudi guinea. It's solid gold, and today it's probably worth about six hundred of your American dollars. Tumaini Aalee procured a lot of wealth raiding slave caravans over the years. He knew he could never get this money out of the country when he was bringing his freed hostages back, so he would hide it here and use it to finance his missions when he needed to buy something or bribe an official."

Colonel Eloi digs further into the chest and finds a round leather tube with a cap on it. She opens it and pulls out a document stamped with two seals. The first is an official ambassadorial seal of England, and the second is a royal seal from the Saudi Royal Family. She holds the document up and translates it into English for everyone.

This proclamation gives the bearer the right of safe passage in and out of all Saudi territories with the purpose of finding and retrieving any citizens of the bearer's country who were stolen from their lands with the purpose of being sold into slavery. I give the bearer permission by his royal eminence, King Aleukia Mohammed Abdul, to pursue and take by force those aforementioned individuals. No Saudi forces under His Eminence's domain will either aid or hinder the bearer's endeavors. The bearer will not act aggressively against any of His Eminence's forces unless they are directly involved in the slave caravan that the bearer is pursuing. This proclamation is permanent and sealed unchangeable.

She looks up from the document. "This is what you were talking about earlier, Lieutenant. All I need to do is get to the Port of Jiddah and present this to the customs officials. When I identify myself as a representative from Kenya here to retrieve our people, they will have to comply. They might even tell us where to find the ones that took the undersecretary and Madam Aalee."

Tommy looks at the gold again. "Well, we must get transportation to that port. But there is no way in hell we can take that much loot with us. If anybody catches wind that we have that kind of treasure with us, then our human trafficking slavers will be the least of our worries." He looks up at everyone. "Okay, folks. We're moving out. Our destination is Jiddah. Tsosie, you know the language here, so stick a couple of those coins in your pocket. With any luck, we can find someone close that would sell us a truck or something. Colonel Eloi, you pocket whatever you think we'll need for bribes and necessities. Swanson, you and Rogers and Colonel Eloi's men see how much of these supplies, weapons, and ammo you think we can carry out of here and take with us. Your men are still armed, but I want each of you to get one of those Winchesters for backup."

"What about the costumes, spears, and bows and arrows, Lieutenant?"

Tommy looks over at Colonel Eloi and her men and says back to Tsosie, "Grab the black panther one and spear for me, and let the good colonel and her men pick out whatever ones they want. Oh, and make sure we get enough of those holsters, speed loaders, and .45 slugs for all of us."

Tsosie and the others immediately jump on Tommy's orders and get the supplies and arms ready.

"We can't take all this stuff with us, ma'am, but it would be a shame for it to fall into Saudi hands. It really belongs to the Kenyan people. Do you have any idea how to keep it safe?"

Colonel Eloi walks over to the corner of the room, pulls out another crate, opens it up, picks up the contents, and shows them to Tommy. "I believe the English term for this is dynamite."

Fifteen minutes later, Tommy and the rest are outside the entrance to the cavern. They could barely get the door open with the inside lever because the sand that was flowing had already re-covered part of it. He looks around and spots some trees and foliage about fifty yards straight up from where they are standing. "Swanson, Tsosie, let's get our people and supplies up to that point. Once there, Colonel Eloi and I will use the dynamite to bury this entrance and then we'll join you."

Tsosie, Rogers, and Swanson grab a couple of crates and direct the others to get some more stuff, and they make their way up the dune. The storm has dissipated and the morning rays of the sun are just piercing the eastern horizon. Tommy suspects that it will be a scorching day.

Colonel Eloi takes the pouch that she filled with dynamite earlier, and makes her way over to him. "Lieutenant Williams, we should get the rest of our supplies above the sand before we set off the dynamite. This sand is very loose. Another avalanche could happen at any moment, with no help from us."

Tommy and Adessa set the dynamite in two sections above the cave entrance in the sand, light the fuses and run up to the others at the trees. In fifteen seconds, there is a huge explosion and the sand from above once again covers the entrance to the cave.

Once there, Adessa stops, catches her breath then looks around. "We need to get some transportation. Your man Tsosie looks the most like any of the locals, and I believe you said he can speak Arabic. He and I should go now to see if we can buy some transportation."

Tommy nods to Tsosie. "We're close to one of the major roads to Mecca. There will be a lot of Muslims making their pilgrimage on that road. I've seen video documentaries of it. There are many people who offer rides in old buses for a fee. See if you can flag down an empty one that is on its way back, and see if they'll sell it to you. Most people in that business have never even seen gold pieces like these."

He then thinks of something and looks at Colonel Eloi. "You got some of these coins for when we need them in Jiddah?"

She nods and smiles, turns in Tsosie's direction, and walks with him to the road that is about a half mile inland. Once out of earshot of the others, she quizzically stares at Tsosie for a moment then asks, "Is there anything Lieutenant Williams does not know something about? I swear, sometimes he irritates the hell out of me."

"Join the club, Colonel. I don't know him that well, but Lt. Commander Higgins said that he graduated second in his class from Annapolis Naval Academy. His father was also a grad from that place and later became the United States ambassador to Japan. Williams was supposed to follow in his old man's footsteps and go to some Ivy League grad school to get his law degree. A real intellectual, that one. But then his dad got assassinated, and he dropped all those plans and became a navy SEAL. From what the Lt. Commander said, he went through the program with a vengeance. He even beat the CO of his training base in War Games. Something no one has ever done. I guess you could say our Lieutenant Tommy Williams is a bit of an enigma."

"Then Lieutenant Tommy Williams is exactly what we need right now. Come, Sergeant. Let's go find that bus our enigma sent us after."

As the pair make it to the road, it becomes apparent that they are somewhere between the Port of Jiddah and Mecca. The road is fairly busy with buses, cars, and even some donkey-pulled carts filled with people making their pilgrimage to the holy city. At first, they both get a little frustrated about how they will flag one down and persuade the owner to sell his vehicle while he's transporting passengers.

They both hear it before they see it, coming up the road from Mecca. The old gasoline engine coughs and sputters as black smoke spews out of the tailpipe. A twenty-year-old black and white bus appears out of the haze of the desert sun on the highway. It sputters by the pair and then makes a sharp right onto an old dirt road that leads down into a small oasis. Tsosie looks over at Colonel Eloi. "Did you see anyone but the driver in that one?"

She shakes her head no.

"I think we found our ride. Let's go introduce ourselves."

They cross the road and walk about a mile to an old hut built in the oasis of trees near a pond. The bus is out in front of the hut with the hood open and an older Caucasian man is using a wrench to work on the vehicle's engine. They get within earshot of the man and Tsosie yells out in Aramaic, "Is your bus for sale?"

The man steps out from under the hood and walks over to get a closer look. As he is sizing up the two, he sees that they are dressed in military uniforms, so he puts his hands on his hips and responds in English with a deep British accent. "Neither one of you blokes is from around here, and from the looks of you, I don't think you're supposed to be here either."

Tsosie steps forward with his palms open to calm the man. He decides he will lay some of his cards on the table and tell this man at least part of the truth. "My name is Sergeant Robert Tsosie of the United States Marine Corps, and this is Colonel Adessa Eloi of the Kenyan Security Force. We were on our way to Jiddah last night in a military transport helicopter when we crash-landed in the sea during the storm. Colonel Eloi is here to search for and rescue a high-level Kenyan government official who was kidnapped by some human traffickers when he tried to stop them. She has diplomatic papers stating her clearance to pursue the perpetrators, but we need transportation to Jiddah so she can show her papers to the proper officials and get some help in locating those responsible."

The man stares at the two for a moment, trying to decide if he believes what he's hearing. He finally just shakes his head and walks up to Tsosie with his hand extended. "Name's Clifford Nezzle, formerly First Sergeant of the 105th Airborne of the British Army. Been stuck in this hellhole for ten years now. They caught me trying to smuggle out some Arabic artifacts when I first got here. Ended up spending six years in the prison near Tabuk. After they let me out, I scraped together enough to buy that heap back there, and I've been using it to transport Muslims and tourists to Mecca since. When I get enough saved up, I'll head for the first port, bribe my way out of here, and make my way back to merry old England. If I can keep it running. It needs a new carburetor, and the one I'm putting in took all my profits for this season right out of me pockets."

Tsosie looks over at Colonel Eloi with a sly expression. She nods her head yes. He then reaches in his pocket and pulls out three of the gold coins they took from the cavern. He holds them out to Clifford. "Would this be enough for you to finish installing that carburetor and then sell us your bus?"

Clifford's eyes go wide with astonishment as he stares at the coins in Tsosie's hand. He reaches out. "May I?"

"Go ahead!"

He takes one coin and holds it up and looks at it in the sunlight, gives a whistle, and looks back at them. "Mate, you know this is over a hundred years old! That would make it worth over two thousand of your American dollars. I am not for turning down a fortune, but you could easily buy four buses like mine with just one of these coins."

Colonel Eloi steps up. "We were not aware their value was that great, but the offer still stands. It sounds like you're the type of man who could get these coins exchanged for regular currency without gaining attention. We just need transportation."

Clifford grins from ear to ear. "You got yourself a deal, Colonel. This bit of luck will get me home the fast way. I'll be done with the carburetor in about an hour."

Four Hours Later, Port of Jiddah Public Administrator's Office

Tommy, Colonel Eloi, Rogers, and Tsosie stand in front of the desk of a Saudi mid-level government administrator named Bar Tamal of the Office of Customs and Port Authority. He is a pudgy, middle-aged man with bushy, black eyebrows and a full but thinning black beard and mustache. His beady, brown eyes are wide with astonishment as he scrutinizes the document Colonel Eloi just handed him. He looks up at the colonel for a moment then reaches for the desk phone, picks up the receiver, and dials a number. He starts a conversation with someone on the line and Tommy and Colonel Eloi both look to Tsosie to tell them what is being said.

"Whoever he is talking to, he's telling them that the document is legitimate and has both the Saudi Royal Family seal and the British diplomatic seal. He knows who Tumaini Aalee was and ..."

The administrator holds up a hand to silence Tsosie and listens as he finishes his conversation on the phone then hangs up.

Bar Tamal looks up and responds in heavily accented broken English. "I did not know you could speak English. Mine is not that good, but I get by. That was the regional representative of the Royal Family here in Jiddah. I am to give you every cooperation that this document entitles you to. If what you say is true and Undersecretary Bosher Arachar of Kenya has been kidnapped and is being smuggled through our lands and hidden among those headed for slave markets, then this is something we want to take care of as quickly as possible."

He reaches over and picks up a document on his desk and runs down the page with his finger. "There was a cargo ship that docked last night during the storm. It says here that Pasto Niazai of Afghanistan requested that we allow him to transport his cargo to the Saudi-Kuwait border. They left in a caravan of six trucks about two hours ago and bribed an official to gain access to a military road that bypasses Mecca. Normally, no one of the Muslim faith would forego visiting the holy city when they are this close, but Pasto said that because of the recent invasion of Russia into his homeland he could not do that this time around. Taking that road will shave off an agreeable day of their journey."

Tommy walks over to the wall behind the desk of the Saudi official and traces his finger along the road that leads to Mecca from Jiddah and then from Mecca to the Kuwait border. He sees the road he is referring to running above it, then he sees a broken line going straight up further along that intersects the road to Mecca and dead-ends straight into the road that Pasto is taking. "Is this a road here and is it accessible to us?"

Bar Tamal gets up from his desk and looks at the map, and an astonished look crosses his face. "That's an old military access road that has fallen into disrepair. Funny that you should ask about it. It's the road that Tumaini Aalee used when he pursued those who stole his people from his country and brought them to this port. We have it gated off because we're still waiting for funds to be allocated for its repair before we can reopen it."

"Is it passable?"

"Well, yes, but it'll be slow going most of the way. It has many potholes and half of it is not paved. But the road Pasto and his caravan have taken is a rough, mountainous road that goes through a canyon. One might head them off right there."

He points to where the broken road dead-ends into the one Pasto is taking. "Where the canyon ends and the road dead-ends into it. That was Tumaini Aalee's strategy as well. He came to find that those bringing slaves through our lands preferred not to travel the road to Mecca because of how crowded it was. So he and his men would be granted access to that same road by an official of this office in order to catch those who were taking his people. Eventually, that strategy became known to the slave traders, and they stopped using our port here for access to the inland. But it's been seventy years since Tumaini Aalee or any other representative from Kenya has pursued anyone here using the diplomatic privilege granted him. Until now."

Tommy studies the map for a few more moments, then looks back at the others. "He's right, you know. After a while the slavers stopped using any port along the Red Sea to offload and transport their cargo. They chose to sail around the coast and up the Persian Gulf instead. There they would have easier access to Kuwait, Iraq, Iran, and Afghanistan."

Colonel Eloi steps up to the map and studies it some more, and points at the intersection. "This is perfect. We can head them off here, rescue our people, and retreat down the same road we came up. If any survive our attack, they dare not follow us because of our proximity to Mecca."

Bar Tamal cautiously wags his finger at both. "Remember, you will receive no help from any Saudi forces. If you do bring chaos to any place near the holy city, the consequences will be dire. Oh, and my report shows that Pasto has over thirty armed men with him. How are you going to overtake and defeat such a force?"

Colonel Eloi and Tommy grin at one another. "We will reintroduce them to *Shaytan al-Layl*—the devil who comes in the night. He's been on sabbatical for seventy years."

Colonel Eloi remembers Bar Tamal's earlier comment about their gaining access to the road from an official of his office. She then reaches in her pocket and pulls out one of the coins they found in the cavern and hands it to Bar Tamal. "We want to have access to that road when we come to it. Can you see that we do?"

He receives the coin and holds it in the light, admiring its tingly golden sparkle. "My great-grandfather had some of these in a chest. We found them when he left this world to go to paradise and be with Allah. My father used two of them to pay for my entire education." He puts the coin in his pocket and pats it adoringly with his hand. "You understand Tumaini Aalee's ways well. I will open the gate for you. When you have retrieved your people, come back the same way and we will give you safe passage to this port."

Later that Day, Military Access Road

As Parker drives the bus, Tommy and Colonel Eloi sit sideways in the two front seats facing each other and talking over their plan to overtake the caravan. Tommy holds up a detailed map of the area where the military access road meets the end of the canyon and the road that Pasto and his crew are now on. "It'll be pitch dark in the canyon once the sun goes down. They should be at this point by 10:00

p.m." He points to where the canyon ends. "We should be able to use the rest of the dynamite to block the road and make them stop."

Chief Swanson gets up from his seat in the back and makes his way to Tommy to get a better look at the map. "May I?" Tommy hands him the map. He holds it up and studies it for a moment, then looks at Tommy and smiles. "Not bad, Lieutenant. If we can catch them far enough in, it'll be difficult for them to turn around, and the only way to escape is back. I do have one concern, though."

"What's that, Chief?"

"They number over thirty armed men with about twenty prisoners, including the high-level Kenyan official. There are only nine of us." He motions with his chin at Parker in the driver's seat. "And only eight of us are trained combat soldiers. This Pasto Niazai is a colonel in The People's Liberation Army of Afghanistan, and he has his own men, plus the Chameleon to boot. My guess is that in a frontal assault, even after stopping them we might get about half of them and lose ten prisoners before they overwhelm us. What if they try to use this undersecretary or the Kenyan hero's great-granddaughter as a human shield?"

Tommy looks over at Colonel Eloi, then gets up and makes his way to the back of the bus and rummages through the gear. He pulls out Tumaini Aalee's black panther headdress and holds it up. "Good questions, Chief. Number one, they will not see more than two or three of us at a time, and the ones they do see will be their worst nightmare. Number two, you three SEALs will be in the background on sniper duty, using your night vision scopes and glasses. Rogers will be with you. We'll arm him with a Winchester rifle, and a bow and arrow. All of us will make them think they've just driven into hell."

Chapter 16

Shaytan al-Layl

10:16 p.m., Canyon Road, Toward the End

NAZEEM HAS ALWAYS HATED TAKING this road through the canyon.
Pasto insisted that he drive point because he was one of the few of the
crew that grew up in this part of Saudi Arabia. He also remembers the
legend of Shaytan al-Layl and all the people that got butchered coming
through here doing exactly what he is doing now—transporting slaves
for the market. But Pasto insisted. "You know this road better than
any of us and the Chameleon wants to make the best time possible."
He grudgingly obeyed the order and mumbled under his breath that
only a fool who knows this canyon would ever drive it at night, and
not because the roads were rough either. He looks ahead and sees
that the sky is opening up above and the stars are coming into view.
Relief spreads across his face at the thought of being out of this cursed
canyon and to the road that leads north from Mecca, which is just a
few more miles ahead.

He pushes in the clutch and shifts down to take a sharp corner
when a thunderous explosion erupts from his left, causing rocks and

dirt from the canyon wall to cascade down onto the road. He barely stops in time to avoid the avalanche. As the dust settles and the beam from his headlights cuts through the cloud of dust, what he sees standing on the top of the rubble that is blocking the road is something that he has only envisioned in the nightmares he had as a child. Two figures stand on the mound of dirt—a dark-skinned man and woman clad in skins and headdresses formed from the bodies of a black panther and a leopard. Their faces are painted in the traditional Swahili warrior fashion. They are holding long spears in one hand and a revolver pistol in the other.

Terror paralyzes him as they both raise their spears over their heads and scream their strange African war cry and hurl the spears into the windshield, impaling him and the man next to him through the chest. Within seconds, six men with rifles in hand hop out of the back of the truck and make their way forward. But gunfire from the sides of the canyon wall takes them down.

Tommy looks up to where Chief Swanson hides behind some rocks on the left face of the canyon, holds up eight fingers and nods his head. Swanson sees the cue, and he and Rogers stealthily make their way back to the next hiding spot. The other two on the opposite side of the canyon do the same. Tommy and Colonel Eloi vault onto the hood of the first truck and retrieve their spears, while Tsosie and Parker go to the side doors and yank the corpses from the truck and open the door between the cab and the back. They help five prisoners, young Kenyan girls, get out and take them to the bus that's hidden just past the mouth of the canyon. Tommy and Adessa cover their retreat, then make their way back to their next target.

Colonel Eloi's two men appear in front of the next truck, dressed in jungle cat skins and armed with spears and revolvers. They, unlike Tommy and Adessa, are too close to get any power in hurling their spears, so they pull their revolvers and fire into the windshield several times. The glass shatters and two corpses fall forward against the dashboard. Five armed men jump out of the back of the truck. They crouch down low and look for a way forward to engage the attackers They move slowly around both sides of the rear, looking for the enemy.

Swanson smiles as he sees them come into his sights. He raises his hand to give the signal to his men across from him on the canyon wall. He, Rogers, and the other two fire. The slavers fall without being able to fire back.

As Tommy and Adessa crawl into the front of the cab after taking the corpses out, they hear some screaming from the cargo area. Before they can open the cargo area door, someone fires a shot through it, barely missing Tommy. He rolls to the side and throws himself to the ground outside the truck. While holding his revolver up, he gets on all fours and crawls toward the back under the truck. Adessa stays in the cab to cover the door that was just shot through.

When Tommy gets to the back, he sees a man holding a woman from behind, using her as a human shield. She is almost as tall as the man is, and there is no clean shot. Strangely, two younger girls get out with him, using their bodies to cover him as well. As Adessa makes her way back through the interior of the cargo area of the truck, she sees the woman and girls and yells out, "That is Madam Aalee and her daughters. Hold your fire!"

Meanwhile, in the truck at the rear of the convoy, the Chameleon had already ordered his driver to stop as soon as he heard the explosion. They are about fifty yards behind—the fifth truck in the line. Three of the other four trucks are all bunched together. He quickly surveys the area in front of him. After the explosion he heard some small weapons fire come from the front, but he could also tell by how Pasto's men were being attacked that there are men on both sides, hiding in the canyon walls.

He looks over at the driver. "Get the prisoners and the men out of the back and bring them around front and get behind them. Bring the undersecretary up here, then radio Pasto and tell him the attackers have sniper fire covering them from the canyon walls. Our only chance is to use the undersecretary as a hostage and the rest for human shields. Get the Aalee woman and her daughters back here with us."

The man nods and grabs his radio as he is climbing into the back. The Chameleon climbs over into the driver's seat as they shove Undersecretary Arachar into the cab from the cargo area. As his men are moving the five prisoners out in front of the truck, they hear another scream, and a firefight erupts in front of the third truck in the line.

Pasto, just having received the message from the Chameleon, frantically looks for the safest way to get back to them. Then another war cry erupts in front of the third truck, and he turns to see the same two who had attacked his truck hurling their spears through that truck's windshield then firing on his men behind. Seeing his way blocked to the rear, he fires at the strange African woman dressed like a jungle warrior to his side, and grabs Makena by the hair and pulls her and her daughters around front. Tommy sees what is happening and jumps out from under the truck and points his pistol at Pasto but he can't see a clear shot. Colonel Eloi yells from the side, where she just ducked to avoid being shot.

"Tommy, we cannot let him take them!"

Makena recognizes Colonel Eloi's voice off to the side, but can barely believe what she sees standing before her. Never in her wildest fantasy did she think that she would see the spectacle that faces her now. Exasperation and joy are mixed with terror and panic as Pasto's gun presses against her head and Adimu and Chineye cling tightly to her sides. The only thing that comes out of her mouth are the Swahili words, *Hadithi inosishi—The Legend lives!*

Confused by the woman's words, Tommy ignores them and says to Pasto, "Colonel Niazai, we have already taken out half of your forces. You have nowhere to go. My men are trained snipers and will kill you if you do not surrender. Now, *where is the Chameleon?*"

Before he can answer, a shot rings out from behind, and one of Colonel Eloi's men grabs his shoulder and drops to the ground. As Tommy dives to the ground, Chief Swanson yells from the canyon wall, "Lieutenant Williams, that was the Chameleon. He's in the last truck about fifty yards back, behind the rest of the prisoners. They're being used as human shields. He has five men with him and there are at least another ten behind the fourth truck. He wounded Johnson and has us pinned down."

Tommy looks up at Colonel Eloi, then over at Pasto. "You are surrounded. I have four men behind you and more scattered around. You have nowhere to go. If one of those girls gets hurt, you die. Plain and simple." Then he looks back at Colonel Eloi. "Keep him covered, I'll be right back!"

He gets to his feet while crouching down low. His leg muscles tense as he reaches down with his left hand and checks for the three speed loaders he has on his belt, then holds his pistol out and explodes up onto the truck's hood in front of him and then to the roof. He sees one slaver and quickly fires a shot into the man's temple, then jumps down to the side of the truck, just missing being shot by the Chameleon.

When he gets to the back of the truck, he confronts a group of men struck with terror as he explodes into them, zigzagging at a full sprint and emptying his revolver of the five remaining rounds and killing an equal number. He reaches down while still sprinting and grabs a speed loader, pops open the cylinder on the .45, ejects the spent cartridges and reloads in a matter of seconds.

While still running to the truck he yells, "Swanson, take care of the prisoners and try to keep the Chameleon pinned down until I can get to him!"

When he gets around to the fifth truck, he sees what Swanson is talking about. There, silhouetted in the headlights, are five more girls being held at gunpoint by an equal number of Pasto's men. He sees that Swanson is firing at the driver's side of the truck, but carefully enough not to allow any rounds to penetrate the interior. The Chameleon can't get out to shoot from the side of the truck, but the men are still holding the prisoners in front, and that's a problem.

"*Argh!*"

Tommy looks toward the noise and sees that one of the slavers on the opposite side of the canyon road has been hit in the throat by an arrow. The slaver drops his weapon and falls to the ground, gurgling and choking in his own blood. Tommy looks up onto the canyon wall and can barely make out Tsosie with a bow in his hand and a quiver full of arrows on his back. He looks back at the terrorized four remaining slavers huddled around the girls. They are too close for him to risk using his pistol. He looks for something else he can use for a weapon when he hears a sharp whistle and then sees a spear stick in the ground just in front of him. With no hesitation, he holsters his revolver, seizes the spear, lets out an ear-piercing war scream and launches himself into the party.

The four men holding the girls are so focused on returning fire in Tsosie's direction that they don't see or hear Tommy launch into them until it is too late. Tommy takes the girl away from the closest man and spears him through the gut, then kicks him to the ground. The second tries to bring his rifle up to shoot, but an arrow pierces his chest and he falls. Tommy uses his spear to vault over that man and while flying in the air sidekicks the third in the head, knocking him to the ground.

Swanson then brings the fourth and fifth men down with sniper fire. Tsosie and the other SEAL quickly rush in and secure the girls and get them out of harm's way. With his spear still in his hand, Tommy stands upright and retrieves his pistol with his right hand and stares into the windshield of the truck where he knows the Chameleon is sitting. Though he can only see silhouettes inside the truck, he is positive that the Chameleon can see him in the beam from the headlights. He's pretty sure that the undersecretary is in there with him, so he does not dare take a shot. He glares at the man and slowly mouths the words, *I BEAT YOU!!*

A rage that he has never felt before possesses every fiber of the Chameleon's being as he glares at the boy he should have killed four years ago in Japan.

"WILLIAMS!!" he screams. He shoves the truck in reverse and backs it away from the scene at full throttle.

Bosher has been sitting silently this whole time, watching the mind-boggling events transpire before his eyes. He looks over at the Russian and sees that the man does not have a weapon trained on him and is in a crazed rampage to get out of the area. They have tied his hands together, but he swiftly swings both fists into the man's face, then swings back to his right, opens the door and throws himself to the ground.

Tommy sees the move by the Kenyan official and takes his revolver and unloads six shots at the fleeing truck. One shot misses the Chameleon's head by mere inches as he quickly cuts hard to the left while still backing at full throttle and maneuvers the truck around so that he can go forward at a much faster pace. Tommy sees the move and takes off after the truck at a full sprint. He reloads and expends six more rounds at the truck before he hears gunshots from behind and Colonel Eloi screaming, "He's taking Makena and the girls! Don't let him get away! Tommy, we need your help!!"

Tommy stands there for a second, his heart pounding with frustration. How does he let the man go who killed his father? He looks over at the undersecretary and can see that he is unharmed. He looks back at the truck ahead and muses that if he took it, he could chase him down and kill him once and for all. Then a thought comes to his head, the last words his father ever said to him. *Here's to the son that has made his father the proudest man alive. May he exceed every expectation and become the man I've always seen him to be.* He bows his head and sighs. "You wouldn't approve, Pop, would you?" He looks up at the fleeing truck and yells, "Another day, Chameleon, another day! But we stopped you from going to Iran, didn't we, you bastard!?"

He looks over at the undersecretary. "I got to go. Make your way forward but be careful. One of my men will help you."

As the Chameleon drives away, he plays back in his mind the events that have just transpired. He thinks how Tommy Williams so perfectly capitalized on the fears of his enemies and used the persona of the one-hundred-year-old legend of that Kenyan liberator. "Magnificent!" he utters out loud as he goes over Tommy's strategy of stopping his caravan while still in the canyon, then placing his men so that their lesser numbers were not a hindrance. Half of the men in the caravan were so terrified that they could not respond like proper soldiers, and the others were so taken by surprise that they did not have a chance. "I should have killed you with your father, Tommy Williams. We'll meet again, my friend, I promise."

Tommy checks his pistol, sees six rounds are left, holds his spear up, and takes off toward the first truck. When he gets there, he sees Pasto with his hand at Makena's throat, holding his gun to her head and making his way inside the front truck. He looks down and sees that Parker is supine on the dirt road with a bullet hole in his forehead. Behind him is Colonel Eloi with Makena's daughters next to her as she holds one of the Winchester .45 rifles aimed at Pasto. She sees Tommy. "Pasto tried to take all of them, but Parker grabbed the girls away and was rewarded with a bullet to the head."

Tommy grinds his teeth and looks at the truck, then at the mountain of dirt and stone in front of it. He realizes that the man is half crazed with desperation, and that worries him. He takes his spear and hurls it at the front driver's side tire and punctures it, then fires a round from his revolver into the rear tire. He points his gun at Pasto, sitting in the driver's seat, as he walks around to the front of the truck. Pasto's eyes dart from side to side as he nervously twitches and holds Makena tightly against his pistol barrel.

Tommy looks at the man for a moment then holsters his revolver and smiles. "You can't go anywhere, Colonel. If you hurt her, we'll fill your body with enough lead to poison an elephant. Tell you what. You let her get out of that truck and you and I will settle this. You take me out in a fair fight and you're free to go. Deal?"

Pasto stares incredulously at Tommy for a moment. "You're insane. You want me to step out and have some kind of American western gunfighting contest with you?"

Tommy opens his hands wide at his side. "Sure, why not?"

"Okay." Pasto shoves the door open and as he is stepping one foot to the ground raises his gun to fire. Tommy sees the move and reaches down and draws his revolver at incredible speed and puts three slugs in Pasto's chest. As Pasto falls forward to the ground, he drops his pistol and grabs his chest with both hands. Tommy comes up to him and aims his pistol at Pasto's temple and puts another slug between his eyes. "That's for Parker, you son of a bitch slaver bastard!"

Tommy stands there staring at the man when out of nowhere five more of the slaver crew jump from the shadows and rush him all at once. The first man gets within a few feet of him and is about to shoot when Colonel Eloi vaults in front of Tommy and impales the man with her spear. She pulls it free and before the man hits the ground, she thrusts the second in line the same way. Tommy dives for the first man, retrieves the rifle he was carrying and rolls over and shoots the third man.

Colonel Eloi sees that Swanson and the rest have rushed in to aid her and Tommy and sees that the remaining two attackers have noticed it too. They drop their weapons and hold their hands in the air. Tommy stands and walks over to her. "Can I borrow a couple of your speed loaders?"

A savage grin spreads across her face as she reaches down to her belt, retrieves them, and hands them to him.

He then looks back at Tsosie. "Sergeant, translate for me if you will."

Tsosie runs up to him and smiles. "With pleasure, Lieutenant."

Tommy steps up to the men who are now shaking so badly that it looks like they will lose control of their bladders. He takes his pistol, ejects the spent shells, and reloads and points his weapon at them. "I will let you miserable slavers go so you can tell your friends that wherever there are people like you who think it is okay to buy and sell other human beings, there will be people like us who will stop you and make you pay for your crimes."

When Tsosie finishes translating, he then lets out a savage guttural scream and unloads his cartridges into the ground at their feet. Colonel Eloi mimics his actions and they both laugh with glee as the two slavers scramble over the mountain of dirt piled up in front of their caravan and head down the road.

Bosher comes up with Chief Swanson, the two wounded, and the others. He sees Colonel Eloi and makes his way to her and stops to marvel at her leopard skin warrior outfit. "I think I like this look, my wife!"

She holsters her pistol and reaches out to embrace her husband. After they kiss, Bosher pulls back and looks over at Tommy. "Who are you?"

Before he can answer, Chineye yells, *"Hadithi inosishi."* Adimu steps up and says the same thing. They both run to their mother, who is making her way around the truck. She nods and looks over at Tommy and repeats, *"Hadithi inosishi."* The same phrase erupts all around them as the girls who were just liberated come out from the cover where they were hiding and surround Tommy and all exclaim, *"Hadithi inosishi."*

Tommy looks around the area until his eyes finally fall on Tsosie and he yells, "You're the language guy, Sergeant! What are they saying?"

"My Swahili is not that good, Lieutenant, but it sounds like they are calling you *'The Living Legend'* or something."

Tommy's jaw drops and he holds up his hands and yanks off his black panther headdress. "No, no, I'm not him. I just used his persona and reputation to complete this mission. My name is Lieutenant Tommy Williams of the United States Navy SEALs!"

Tommy glances over at Swanson and the men as they are pointing and laughing at him as he frantically tries to get the girls to stop. He can hear Rogers the medic say, "Now he's a living legend. That's rich."

Some of the girls in front giggle with glee and nod their heads vigorously, "Tumaini *'Hadithi inosishi'.*"

Tommy looks pleadingly over at Colonel Eloi. "Please explain to them who I am. If this ever gets out, I'll never live it down. You don't know the guys I work with. They'll never stop!!"

One Week Later, Mombasa Airport

Tommy, Tsosie, Chief Swanson, Rogers, and the crew are standing by the access ramp to the military jet that Admiral Winston sent down from Cairo to take them back to the States. Four days ago, it was Winston's warship that he sent out on patrol that picked them up at the port in Jabal to take them back to Mombasa. Seeing them off is Undersecretary Bosher Arachar; his wife, Colonel Eloi, and Makena Aalee and her daughters, Chineye and Adimu. Colonel Eloi has recently been put in charge of Kenyan's security forces, and Bosher has announced his candidacy for president. Colonel Tumba was arrested for treason and President Amoi had recently gone into hiding until after the elections.

Tommy is now in his United States Navy dress blues, as are his men. Both Chineye and Adimu are fawning over how handsome he looks. "So, you all understand some English," Tommy says with a slight tone of reproof in his voice. "You all had me going with that *Living Legend*, or *The Legend Lives* stuff earlier. You know I just used his reputation to scare those guys so we could rescue you. No one deserves that title in your country but Tumaini Aalee." He raises his finger and shakes it at the girls. "So, no more calling me that."

Chineye looks at Adimu for a moment and both girls giggle and then say, *"Hadithi inosishi!"*

Tommy blows out a big breath of exasperation, but before he can say something Makena steps between her daughters and puts calming hands on their shoulders. She smiles at Tommy. "I only met my great-grandfather once, and he asked me to make our legend live before he died. I did not believe it possible. But on that road in Saudi Arabia, you showed us all that his legend, the commitment to stand against those who think that they can buy and sell people like cattle, lives and is possible. Our cause is still only waking up again in our country, Tommy Williams. We need a warrior to help us fight for its right to prevail."

Makena's words are moving, and Tommy has to admit they tempt him, but he sighs, then points to Colonel Eloi, locks eyes with her as

226

an unspoken understanding is acknowledged by the two warriors, and replies, "Believe me, Madam Aalee, you already have one, and she will be everything you will ever need!"

Chapter 17

One Hell of a SEAL

Two Days Later, Office of The Secretary of the Navy, William Thompson

"INCREDIBLE, TOMMY. AFTER LOSING ONE'S CO on their first mission, most guys would have cracked. Higgins was one of our best. You must have felt overwhelmed."

"You know, Uncle Bill, it was tough. but we're talking about the Chameleon, and I just couldn't let it go."

"But that's just it, Tommy. You had a choice to catch and kill the Chameleon or save Madam Aalee, and you chose the latter. What persuaded you?"

Tommy leans back in his seat, shakes his head and sighs. "It was thinking about Pops, Uncle Bill. I knew he would not approve of my going after vengeance when innocent lives were at stake. When I thought about that, I didn't have a choice. I had to go back and do what I could to save them."

William Thompson nods his head. "And save them you did, son. Maybe you really do deserve that title the Kenyan Parliament gave you, 'The Living Legend.'"

Tommy sits straight up in his chair and throws his hands up. "Uncle Bill, you promised!"

"Sorry, Tommy. I couldn't resist. Besides, the new CO of Naval Intelligence thinks we can use that title to keep your and Higgins's old team undercover and still operating."

Tommy settles back into his chair and calms down a little. "So, Uncle Bill, how come no one will tell me who this new guy is? All I know is that he just got promoted to admiral."

Secretary Thompson looks down at his desk clock and then up at Tommy. "Time for you to go find out. You're expected in his office in fifteen minutes, so you better get cracking."

Tommy jumps up and holds out his hand. "Thanks, Uncle Bill. We'll see you tonight at 7:00. Alysha told me to pick her up at 6:30. You know how she gets if I'm late."

As Tommy reaches the door, he hears William say, "Funny you should say that, Tommy. They tell me your new CO is the same way, only worse!"

Tommy feels a slight chill go up his spine hearing that and rushes out the door and into the outer office. Alysha is waiting for him at the end of the hall. She has a demure smile on her face as she steps up and kisses him lightly on the cheek. "So, Senator Williams, you off to see the new boss?"

Tommy pulls back a little dumfounded and asks, "Senator? What are you talking about, Alysha?"

"Oh, just trying it on for size, after what you pulled off in Saudi Arabia, and with your popularity in Kenya. Five years from now, when you're old enough and with my help of course, you could run for a senate seat and easily win. Now, you better get going. I hear your new boss can be a real tyrant. We don't want my boyfriend, *The Living Legend,* to get on his unpleasant side so soon."

Tommy starts to rebuke her for the use of that title but ignores it, kisses her back on the cheek, and hurries out the door and toward the Naval Intelligence wing of the Pentagon.

Twelve and a half minutes later, he is standing at the receptionist desk for the head of Naval Intelligence. A navy chief by the name of Rodriguez sees Tommy's Pentagon ID before he can introduce himself and says, "You're almost late, Lieutenant. The admiral said to send you back as soon as you got here. You know the way."

Tommy rushes back to the door, hoping to see the nameplate that will tell him who it is, but instead he sees that Captain Smithers's name is still on it. He tentatively knocks and immediately hears a gruff, familiar voice bellow, "About time, Williams. Now get in here!"

Cold panic erupts in Tommy's stomach as he eases the door open, steps in, and comes to attention with a very stiff salute. "Lieutenant Tommy Williams reporting as ordered, Captain … uh … Admiral Fargo!"

"Have a seat, Lieutenant."

Tommy comes forward and tentatively sits down in front of the admiral but remains very stiff as he contemplates whether he should wipe off the drop of sweat that is running down the side of his face.

Admiral Fargo lets Tommy sweat it out for a few more moments, then with a broad grin across his face he bellows, "For God's sake, Williams, at ease. We're two old friends here, aren't we?"

Tommy nods his head. "Congratulations on your promotion, sir. May I ask where Captain Smithers is now?"

Fargo lets out a sigh. "That pencil-pushing bureaucratic politician wannabe was asked to retire after the secretary of the navy found out he ordered you and your team to take the Chameleon and his crew at sea. Humph, all cloak and dagger, that guy. Never saw a day of combat in his life. You and your crew being out there with an inexperienced combat pilot, and just having lost Lt. Commander Higgins, could have gotten you boys killed. You and Swanson held it together, though, and pulled off a miracle—because you're SEALs, first and foremost. That's why they offered me this post. Naval Intelligence was never supposed to be another CIA."

Tommy relaxes a little as he ponders the admiral's words. "You know, Admiral, it would be nice if we all knew how to work together a little better. The military, intelligence, and law enforcement are all on the same team. Too bad we can't act like it."

Fargo slaps his desk with the palm of his hand. "From your mouth to God's ears, Williams. Now, let me introduce you to your new team leader. Captain, come in here, please."

From a side door steps in another familiar face that has Tommy on his feet and throwing another salute. "Captain Thorpe, good to see you, sir. Congratulations on your promotion."

"Thanks, Tommy. Have a seat. The admiral and I have some ideas on how we can capitalize on this new title the Kenyans gave you. Since you're fluent in Spanish, we're going to start by concentrating on the team's activities in South America. Having 'The Living Legend,' who rescued those Kenyan girls from human trafficking, will give us a lot of entrée in getting you and the team down there under the guise of military PR for the United States."

Tommy squirms in his seat at the mention of the title. "You know, sirs, that title belongs to a very important Kenyan historical figure who gave his entire life doing what I just barely pulled off once. I am not very comfortable having people call me that."

Fargo lets out a big humph! "Williams, since when the hell did I or Thorpe here ever give a spit in the wind about how you feel or what makes you comfortable?"

Tommy leans back in his chair, puts his elbow on the arm, rests his chin in his palm, and shows Fargo a big grin. "Never, sir. Not even when I kicked your ass in War Games back at SQT."

Captain Thorpe throws his head back, lets out an enormous laugh, and smacks Tommy on the back. "He got you with that one, Admiral!"

Fargo stares blankly at Tommy for a moment and then slowly a smile surfaces. He lifts both his hands and rubs them together. "Gentlemen, this is going to be fun!"

Epilogue

TOMMY EVENTUALLY MAKES CAPTAIN AND becomes one of the most successful SEAL team leaders to date. He also develops an intra-military/law enforcement task force that under his leadership goes a long way in defending and protecting his country from enemies both foreign and domestic. He becomes the confidant and special security advisor to four presidents and is more often than not their go-to man in emergencies that no one else can handle. During his long and illustrious career, Tommy Williams never gets rid of the label, *The Living Legend*. After a while they forget why people started calling him that. But anyone who knows him well or works with him is quickly convinced that he deserves it.

One year after Tommy Williams helped Adessa Eloi rescue Makena Aalee, her two daughters, and her husband, Bosher Arachar, she stands with them on the parliamentary floor in Nairobi, Kenya. They are all at the podium as Bosher is finishing his first presidential address to Parliament.

"I have two exciting announcements that I would like to share with you. First, few have known that Adessa Eloi of the Kenyan security force is in fact my wife. Her diligence and unparalleled service in that branch of our government is something everyone in this room can testify to. And because hardly anyone, including her former superior, General Tumba, knew that she is my wife, she has earned all your respect with no help from me. Today, it is my pleasure to inform you all that General Adessa Eloi is now the official commander of all the Kenyan security forces."

Everyone in the room comes to their feet as Adessa steps forward and smiles and waves. When the clapping settles down, Bosher looks over at Makena and winks, then turns back to the crowd and continues. "I have long served in this chamber as undersecretary and have been responsible to set the agenda of discussion for our Parliament daily. It has been a responsibility I have deeply cherished, and I am pleased to announce that the great-granddaughter of our beloved national hero, Tumaini Aalee, will continue in my stead. Ladies and gentlemen of Parliament, I present to you Madam Undersecretary, Makena Aalee!"

The End

Made in the USA
Middletown, DE
02 February 2022

59219592R00146